MW00628434

DEADHEAT

BIBA PEARCE

LIQUID MIND PUBLISHING

Copyright © 2021 by Biba Pearce. All rights reserved. No part of this publication may be copied, reproduced in any format, by any means, electronic or otherwise, without prior consent from the copyright owner and publisher of this book.

Liquid Mind Publishing
This is a work of fiction. All characters, names, places and events are the product of the author's imagination or used fictitiously.

ALSO BY BIBA PEARCE

Want to stay up to date and to read the latest news from Biba Pearce? Sign up here:

https://links.withoutwarrant.ink/Pearce1

1

She was at the Christmas market with her friend Bethany. It was a perfect Miami evening—warm, balmy, not a breath of wind. The holiday village sparkled with Christmas cheer. Fairy lights hung from the storefronts; the sound of music filled the air along with chatter and laughter, and Kenzie could smell roasting chestnuts and the sweet aroma of cotton candy.

An enormous Christmas tree stood in the middle of the square, reaching for the sky. Green elves with pink cheeks sang carols around it, while Santa overlooked everything from his grotto.

Bethany nudged Kenzie. "Look, there's Tom and Christian."

Kenzie glanced over to where Bethany pointed and spotted the two boys from school. They were both cute, with long, tousled hair, torn jeans, and loose-fitting T-shirts.

"Hey, Mom. Can we go over to Santa's grotto?" she asked.

Angie, Kenzie's mom, didn't hear her. Angie had linked her arm with her husband's, and Uncle Larry was leading them into the mulled wine tent. There was nothing of interest to Kenzie in there, and the tent was filled with adults.

She patted her mother on the shoulder. "Bethany and I are going over to Santa's grotto, okay?"

Angie smiled. "Sure, honey. Actually, I'll come with you. I want to look at the other booths. I haven't finished my Christmas shopping yet."

"I'll meet you back here." Angie gave Kenzie's father a peck on the cheek. Then the three of them walked out of the tent together. "Be good, girls."

Kenzie gave her a half-wave and ran off with Bethany towards the grotto. That was the last time she ever saw her mother.

The girls flirted with Tom and Christian until the boys left to go to a friend's house. Then Kenzie saw her father standing in the middle of the square, looking around. "Have you seen your mother?" he asked as she and Bethany walked up.

"No, she was looking at the booths."

"I can't find her."

Uncle Larry emerged from the mulled wine tent, his cheeks flushed. "She's not in there."

They walked around the market, still busy with festive shoppers, but her mother was nowhere to be seen.

"Could she have gone home?" Larry asked.

"I don't think so. Not without telling me." Bud, Kenzie's father, scratched his head.

"Maybe she felt sick," offered Bethany.

"It's possible." Her father pulled out his cell phone. "I'll call her."

The call went straight to voicemail. He shook his head and hung up. "Her phone's not on."

Kenzie's voice trembled. "Where could she be?"

Her father shrugged. "She must have wandered off. I'm sure there's no reason to worry."

"I'll call Nora," Larry said. "She can check at the house."

"Thanks, Larry."

Her uncle pulled out his phone and spoke to his wife. They lived a few doors down from Kenzie and her parents. Nora had brought them a flower arrangement to welcome them to the neighborhood when they'd first moved in. That's how they'd become friends.

Bethany's phone beeped, and she glanced at it. "That's my mom. She wants me home."

Bud hesitated. He had to get Bethany home, but Kenzie could tell he didn't want to leave the square without his wife.

"I'll walk her back," Larry offered. "I'll let you know when I hear from Nora. Keep your phone on."

"I will. Thanks Larry. We'll wait here in case she comes back."

"No problem."

Larry left with Bethany, while Kenzie stood beside her father under the giant tree's flashing lights, wondering what had happened to her mother. A strange pressure was building inside her chest, which she later recognized as panic.

"I'm going to look again." She took off before her father could stop her. She ran from booth to booth, peering inside, expecting to see her mother's blonde hair as she inspected ornaments or jars of spiced jam. The market was large, and Kenzie was exhausted and overwrought when she got back to her father.

"She's not anywhere." She burst into tears and clung to her father. "Where is she?"

"I don't know. She's not at home. Nora checked." He glanced around helplessly. "I think I'll have to call Vic."

Vic was his partner at the Miami Police Department. A bear of a man, or that's how he seemed to Kenzie. Vic and her father were as close as brothers. Her father always said he'd trust Vic with his life. Bud turned his back on Kenzie and spoke rapidly into the phone for a few minutes. She caught the tension in his voice. It made her worry even more.

Mom, where are you?

A short time later, Vic arrived, followed by two police vehicles. Their blue lights drowned out those from the Christmas tree. People stopped to stare.

"She disappeared." Bud threw his hands up in the air. "Vanished into thin air."

That's when the nightmare really began.

Kenzie woke up covered in perspiration. She hadn't revisited that awful night for years. It wasn't a nightmare, rather a reliving of the events leading to her mother's disappearance. A lucid dream. And it was always the same. The market, the smells, the grotto, then the overwhelming fear.

She propped herself up in bed and reached for her glass of water. The police file was still open on the bed beside her. She'd fallen asleep reading it. She took a glug and then fell back onto the pillows. Reading the case file was getting to her.

Reid.

She needed to speak to Reid. He'd know where to start.

Kenzie showered and dressed, then left the house. The ex-police detective would be at home, in his isolated cabin in the Everglades. She'd once asked him why he lived all the way out there. He'd said he liked the solitude.

After his last job consulting for the Miami PD, he'd decided not to go back to the police force full time. A pity, since he was so good at it. As someone who would give anything to work for the Miami PD, she didn't understand it, but she wasn't him. She hadn't lost a colleague and lover in the line of duty. She didn't carry the burden of that death on her shoulders, though it wasn't his fault.

But that was Reid. He took his responsibilities seriously. He had integrity, and that was a rare trait. It was one of the reasons she trusted him.

Trust. That was huge for her.

Kenzie Gilmore trusted no one. Not until she'd met Reid earlier that year and they'd worked the Swamp Strangler case. Now he was helping her figure out what had happened to her mother almost twenty years ago.

She got into her car and drove out of her condo complex, the manilla folder on the passenger seat. After a forty-minute drive, she turned off the busy US-27 highway and onto a narrow road leading to the Everglades Holiday Park. The signpost specified airboat rentals, alligator tours, boat hire, and a general store.

It was a muggy, overcast day and the clouds above signified rain— and lots of it. It had been humid as hell for a week now, and they were due a thunderstorm.

Reid's cabin was five miles down this road. Previously an airboat tour company right on the water's edge, he'd converted it into a livable home. It was very rustic, no AC and annoyingly temperamental Wi-Fi, but the view was spectacular, and he enjoyed being away from the chaos of the city.

Kenzie pulled off the road and parked beside his Ford Ranger pickup. Good, he was home. She knocked on the door, but as usual, there was no answer. Not waiting, she edged around the house and squeezed through the gap in the foliage, her feet squelching in the soggy ground.

He was cleaning his airboat, the water gushing from the hose onto the deck. She climbed onto the wooden deck in front of the house. "You really should get a buzzer. You can't hear a thing from out here."

"That's the point." He grinned up at her.

She shook her head. "Can we talk?"

"Sure, just give me a moment." He didn't need to ask what she wanted to discuss. She'd had the case file for a week now. He finished hosing down the boat, then climbed onto the small walkway leading out into the water from the deck. He curled the length of the hose around his hand and elbow, then looped it over a low wooden pole.

"Help yourself to a drink." He strode past her into the house, leaving a trail of wet footprints. "I won't be long."

"Sure."

She took a jug of iced tea out of the fridge and poured each of them a glass. When he got back, she was sitting in the living room, the folder on the coffee table in front of her.

"Thanks." He picked up the glass and downed it in one gulp. She watched his Adam's apple bob up and down as he drank it. He hadn't shaved, but it suited him. The stubble made him look gritty and a little dangerous.

"I dreamt about her last night," she said, fiddling with her earring.

He sat down opposite her, the wicker chair creaking under his weight. "Your mom?"

"Yeah. We were in the market square on the night she disappeared. I remembered everything like it was yesterday."

He watched her, waiting for her to continue.

"I haven't had that dream in years, yet it felt so real. I could smell the mulled wine and pinecones." Her earring fell out onto the floor. "Oh, shoot." Bending to pick it up, she said, "My mother gave me these for my twelfth birthday, a couple of months before she disappeared. They're faded now, but I still wear them. They remind me of her."

"Reopening the investigation will bring back those memories," he said softly. "Are you sure you want to do this?"

She didn't hesitate. "Of course I'm sure. I need to find out what happened."

"Okay." He leaned back. "I said I'd help you, and I will. You have to realize, though, we might not find anything. It's been a long time and—"

"I know." She cut him off with a wave of her hand. "But we have to try."

He nodded.

She took a shaky breath. "Should we start with Uncle Larry and his wife Nora? Larry was there. He's not really my uncle, more like a family friend. I just used to call him that."

"What about Captain Reynolds?" Reid asked. "He was your father's partner, the detective in charge of the case. We should probably speak to him first."

She liked the way he said 'we.' It helped her recognize she wasn't doing this alone. As a reporter, she was used to investigations, but this was personal. It felt good having Reid there to bounce ideas off.

"We should speak to him, but it might be a good idea to get some background first. He's a busy man, and I don't want to waste his time."

Captain Reynolds headed the Miami PD. He'd come a long way since being Bud Gilmore's partner twenty years ago.

"Sure," agreed Reid. "I'm happy to tackle this however you want. Where is Larry now?"

"We lost touch after my mother's disappearance," Kenzie admitted. "I never saw him or his wife again. They're in Orlando now. I found an address for them in Winter Springs."

"Then, that's where we'll start."

2

"Maybe I should have called ahead." Kenzie gnawed on her lip as they drove into Winter Springs. It was an attractive suburban area nestled against the blue waters of Lake Jesup. They passed several lush, green parks, a quaint town center, and neatly lined streets with spacious houses set back from the road.

"It's a bit late now," Reid retorted. "Anyway, the element of surprise is always good."

Larry and his wife lived in an attractive, new-looking house similar to others in the neighborhood. The garden was well taken care of, and the driveway was swept clean despite the leaves turning a burnished orange above it.

Kenzie remembered Nora had been a florist back in Miami. That's why she hadn't been at the Christmas market. She'd been preparing for a function the following day.

"Nice place." Reid turned off the engine.

The front door opened and a slender woman with gray hair walked out. She'd aged, but Kenzie recognized her straight away and was jolted back to afternoon barbecues at their house, helping her mom and Nora in the kitchen.

"You okay?" Reid glanced at her.

"Yeah." She got out of the car and walked toward the woman. "Nora, it's Kenzie Gilmore. Do you remember me?"

Nora stared at her, stunned. "Why Kenzie, yes, of course I remember you. This is such a surprise. What are you doing here?"

Kenzie gave her a brief hug. It seemed fitting after all these years. Their families had been close, after all.

"I'm sorry to drop by unannounced. I was hoping you'd be able to talk to me about my mother. About the night she disappeared."

Nora sighed, then gave a little nod. "I suspected this day might come." She turned to Reid and held out her hand. "And you are?"

"Oh, I'm sorry." Kenzie flushed. "This is Reid Garrett. He's helping me with her case."

Nora gave a sad little smile, then beckoned them inside. "I'll put some coffee on."

They gathered in the spacious living room. Wide windows overlooked the front driveway and garden, which was how Nora must have seen them arrive. The floor was tiled, but a large rug covered most of it. A well-used leather sofa and matching armchair were positioned around a deep wooden chest. It was stylish and functional, but Kenzie recalled Nora always had good taste. On a side table stood an arrangement of photographs in silver frames.

Kenzie walked over to inspect them. Nora and Larry in their younger days. Larry fishing. A wedding picture of a young couple Kenzie didn't recognize. The Eiffel Tower.

"Have a seat," Nora called from the kitchen. "I'll be right in."

Reid came over to look at the photographs. Always observing.

Nora came back with a tray. "I must say, I am surprised to see you after all this time. I was sorry to hear about your father's passing. He was a good man."

"Thank you." Kenzie sat down on the sofa next to Reid. Nora poured the coffee into three mugs and handed them around.

"Now tell me, how *are* you, Kenzie? What are you doing with yourself these days?"

"I'm a reporter." Kenzie smiled as Nora settled into the armchair. "For the Miami Herald."

"That is impressive." She glanced at Reid. "And your boyfriend? Reid, was it?"

Reid spluttered his coffee.

"Oh, he's not my boyfriend. Reid's a—a friend." She hoped he wouldn't notice her pink cheeks. "As I said, he's helping me find out what happened to my mother."

Nora glanced between them, then smiled. "Well, it's lovely to meet you, Reid."

"Likewise, ma'am."

Kenzie kept her gaze fixed on the elderly woman. "Nora, is Larry around?"

Her shoulders slumped. "No, my dear. I'm afraid Larry died several years back. He had a heart attack, like your father. It was very sudden."

"Oh, I'm sorry to hear that."

Damn.

She'd been hoping to get a first-hand account from him. Nora must have sensed her disappointment, because she said, "But I remember that evening as clear as day."

"You do?"

"Yes. I wasn't there when Angie disappeared, but Larry was in such a state, we talked about nothing else for weeks afterwards."

Kenzie stared at her. "Would you mind refreshing my memory?"

"Of course, dear. I'll tell you what I know." She settled back in her chair, still holding her coffee mug. "I was at home arranging flowers for the Christmas dinner at the Community Center. It was about eight-thirty when Larry called. He asked me to go to your house and see if Angie was there."

Kenzie nodded. She remembered Larry making the call.

"The house was dark. I rang the buzzer and tried the front door, but it was locked. Nobody was home."

"Did you look inside?" Reid inquired.

She shifted her gaze to him and nodded. "Yes, I peered through the windows but couldn't see any movement. I even tried the kitchen door around the back." She shook her head. "Your mother wasn't there."

Kenzie swallowed. "What happened then?"

"Well, I drove into town to help your father and Larry look for her."

Kenzie vaguely remembered a policewoman taking her home and sitting with her until her father got back late that night.

"Didn't Larry take Bethany home?" Bethany. She wondered what had happened to her. After her mother had disappeared, Kenzie had taken time off school, except when she went back, it was a different place. The people were distant. Those she thought were her friends suddenly didn't want to talk to her anymore. Perhaps their parents had warned them off. A mysterious disappearance. A father under suspicion. It didn't make for comfortable friendships.

"Yes, he did. But he came back again. We had quite a search party. That detective Vic Reynolds was there, along with a few of his officers. There was also a group of locals, mostly stall owners. We looked everywhere." She shrugged. What more could she say? Angie had vanished.

"What about the residents?" Reid asked. "I didn't read anything in the report about door-to-door inquiries."

"We did that ourselves," Nora confirmed. "I remember taking several streets and walking up and down, asking if anyone had seen Angie. The others helped. We even had a photo of her, but no one had seen a thing. It was as if she was never there."

"How can that be?" Kenzie muttered. "How can she disappear like that?"

"It's a mystery. And after all these years, no one ever found her body?"

Kenzie gripped her mug. "No. Not that we know of."

"It's most bizarre. It's almost as if...as if..." She paused, her gaze faltering.

"As if what?" prompted Reid.

"Well, as if she left on her own accord."

Kenzie opened her mouth to refute that claim when Nora held up a hand. "I'm sorry, Kenzie, Angie would never have left on her own volition. It's just that there was no trace of her. There were no reports of a kidnapping, no struggles or screams, nothing. It was like she walked out of that market square, climbed into a car, and drove away."

"Did they put out an alert at the airport?" Reid asked.

"I believe so, but that was some time after she disappeared. If someone had picked her up and driven her straight to the airport, she could have gotten away before anyone noticed."

"Her name didn't appear on any passenger lists," Kenzie insisted.

"That doesn't mean anything," Reid muttered.

It was true. False passports were possible to get hold of. If she'd left by boat, she may not even have needed one.

Kenzie shook her head. "I can't see her running away. Why would she do that? Why would she leave me? Leave her husband?" She looked at Nora. "She was happy, wasn't she?" Was there something she wasn't aware of, something her father hadn't told her?

"Yes, dear. Your parents were thrilled. In fact, they were celebrating because they'd just found out about the baby."

"The baby?" Kenzie went cold. "What baby?"

"Oh, I assumed you knew." Nora's hand fluttered to her mouth. "Oh, gosh. I'm so sorry to be the one to tell you, Kenzie. Your mother was expecting."

3

"She was pregnant!" Kenzie exploded once they got back to Reid's car. "How did I not know this?"

"I'm surprised Captain Reynolds didn't tell you." Reid could understand her father not wanting to mention it, not after her mother had gone missing. It would have been too raw, too painful.

If Kenzie's father hadn't told her, he'd wanted to leave it that way. As the years passed, he probably thought it best if she didn't know. It would lessen the heartache from losing a little sister or brother, along with her mother.

"He didn't say a word. How could he keep this from me?" Her chest rose and fell as she ranted. Heat emanated off her.

"They probably didn't want to upset you," he said reasonably, but that was no excuse. She'd deserved to know.

"Maybe he didn't know," she blurted. "Captain Reynolds, I mean. Perhaps my father didn't tell him."

"It's possible, although unlikely. They were partners, right?" Partners usually knew everything about each other's lives.

Her face fell. "If Larry and Nora knew, Vic must have known. He was like a brother to my father."

"On the other hand, none of the police reports mentioned it," Reid pointed out.

"Hmm." She paused as he backed out of the driveway. "Don't you think that's strange?"

He frowned as he drove down the street. "Yeah. If your father had told the police she was pregnant, the report would have shown she had no reason to run away. Wasn't that the theory they eventually came to?"

Kenzie bit her lip. "It was a ridiculous theory. They were happy. You heard Nora say as much. They were expecting a baby. Why on earth would she run away?"

He shook his head. "I don't know, Kenzie, but we need to speak to Captain Reynolds."

She gave an eager nod. "Agreed."

The sun was a thin, orange slit on the horizon when they got back to Miami. The dense cloud cover prevented it from putting on a show, but the sea below shimmered with a peachy glow. It still hadn't rained, but it would. Soon.

Reid dropped Kenzie off, then drove back to the Glades. He was almost home when his phone rang.

He glanced at the screen. Lieutenant Pérez. Now what did he want?

"LT, how's it going?"

Pérez worked for the Miami PD and used to be Reid's boss. They'd always had a mutual respect, and Reid might say they were becoming friends.

"I'm in the neighborhood. Wanna meet at Smiley's for a drink?"

"Sure." He was only going home to an empty cabin.

"See you in ten."

Reid passed his house and drove on to a small village deeper in the swamp. If you could even call it a village. It had a bar, a motel, and a convenience store, along with a couple of fishing companies and a gator farm. The locals were not the friendliest types, and it had taken Reid six months for them to accept him. He wasn't sure if they knew he had been a cop, but no one had said anything about it.

He drank at Smiley's, minded his own business, and bought a few supplies at the store from time to time. That was about it.

He'd just sat down at the bar when Pérez walked in. A few locals glanced up, then went back to their beers. Rock n roll music played in the background, and four rowdy men were competing at darts in the corner. They'd probably be beating each other up by the end of the night. It was that kind of place.

"Hey, how you doing?" Pérez shook his hand.

"Good to see you," Reid said. "What can I get you?"

"Bud Light. I'm watching my weight."

Reid chuckled. "Fair enough." He ordered, then turned to Pérez. "What brings you out this way?"

"I had an errand to run. Nothing important. Thought I'd check in and find out what you're doing with yourself."

"You mean am I bored yet?"

Pérez shrugged, but his eyes twinkled. "There's a job at Miami PD if you want it."

"I told you, I'm not coming back."

"I know, but I had this feeling you were going to change your mind."

Reid shrugged. "Hasn't happened yet."

The barman put their drinks down and Reid paid.

"Fine, have it your way." Pérez glanced around. "This place gets worse every time I come here."

"Yep. There are fights every night. The cops don't even venture out here anymore."

A leggy blonde stalked past and gave Reid the once over. He didn't respond, and she kept walking.

"Why do you come here?"

"It's close. I can walk home if I have to."

"Quite a walk."

"It sobers me up."

Pérez laughed. "So, what are you going to do now? Give airboat tours?"

"Maybe. I haven't decided yet. I'm working a case for Kenzie Gilmore at the *Herald*."

"Investigation work?"

"Yeah." He didn't say what. It was best that Pérez didn't know he had that file. Maria, manager of archives at the station, wouldn't tell. He'd gotten her husband off a DUI charge a couple of years back. She owed him.

"I see how this is going. Private dick, eh?"

He shrugged. "What do you want, LT? I know you didn't come all this way to see how I was doing."

Pérez reached for his beer. "We're having trouble finding qualified detectives to work cases," he admitted. "Jonny's good, but he's young and now that Ortega's on suspension, we're a man down. We need someone with experience to run the department. We need you, Reid."

"How's his nose?" Reid asked. The last time he'd been at the Miami PD, he'd punched his fellow detective, Xavier Ortega in the face, and broken the lying shit's nose.

Pérez rolled his eyes. "Fine, thankfully. You're lucky he didn't sue you."

"It was his fault," began Reid, getting riled.

Pérez lifted a hand. "Yeah, I know. Let's not go there. He's off for six months. Lesson learned."

Except it wouldn't bring Bianca back. Ortega blew her cover, and the cartel man had executed her before they could get to her. Before *he* could get to her.

He took an angry pull on his bottle.

"I take that as a no?"

Reid almost felt sorry for Pérez. He was doing his best under difficult circumstances. Crime rates were skyrocketing. The drug gangs were regrouping after last month's bust, but they'd be back. Domestic violence was out of control. And as Lieutenant, Pérez had the public to answer to, quotas to live up to. No matter how you tried, you couldn't make those stats look pretty.

"Look, I wish I could help you out, but—" He broke off as a bottle smashed behind them. They spun around to find a man clutching his head. Blood dripped through his fingers onto the floor.

"Here we go," muttered Reid.

"Bastard," growled the injured man, launching himself at his attacker. The two men went sprawling backwards into a table. The occupants scrambled out of the way, but not before their drinks went flying.

"Hey!" The barman leaped over the bar.

The overweight bouncer lumbered over. He tried to wrestle one of the men off, but they flung him aside like he was nothing more than an irritating mosquito.

Reid glanced at Pérez, who nodded.

They got up to break up the fight. Reid took the guy with the head wound, still bleeding profusely, and tried to pull him off the other guy. He got an elbow in the eye for his efforts. He grunted, then got the guy in a headlock.

"Easy," he growled, wrestling him into submission.

Pérez helped the guy on the floor to his feet. Both were panting.

"Okay, calm down, you two," Pérez snapped. The brawling men stood down, catching their breath.

Reid released his guy. Freaking hell, his eye stung. He blinked several times to clear it. The injured guy was bleeding all over the floor.

"Here, hold this against your head." Reid reached over and grabbed his drink napkin from the bar.

The man did as instructed. The blood had left a dirty, red smudge down his cheek. He was a mess.

"You need a doctor?" Reid asked.

The man shook his head.

"Okay, then. You'd better get out of here. Go home and get washed up."

"Yeah." The man stumbled out of the bar, shooting a last penetrating look at his adversary.

"What the hell you do that for?" Pérez asked the guy who'd smashed the bottle on the other guy's head. "He could have pressed charges."

"Bastard deserved it," was all he said before he too stormed out of the bar.

"I'm going to call it a night." Reid grimaced at his shirt. It was smeared with the injured man's blood, sweat, and God knows what else. Plus, he wanted to ice his eye.

Pérez went back to the bar and drained his beer. "Yeah, good idea. We'll pick this up another time."

Reid hoped not. He didn't know how much longer he could keep saying no.

4

"WHAT HAPPENED TO YOU?" Kenzie exclaimed when he picked her up the next morning.

"Bar fight," he muttered.

"Seriously? You?"

"I broke it up. I wasn't in it."

"Ah." She studied his black eye. "Quite the shiner you've got there."

He grunted.

She tried not to laugh. "I swear. I can't leave you alone for a minute."

That made him chuckle. She was glad. He was in a foul mood and needed lightening up. "What happened?"

"Nothing. I went for a drink with the lieutenant and these two guys got into a brawl. We tried to separate them and wham, I got elbowed in the eye."

"Ouch."

"Yeah."

They drove along the coast to the Miami PD building. "You sure you want to come in with me?" she asked. "I know you don't like going back there." He'd made his feelings pretty clear on that front.

"No, I'm fine." She was secretly glad. Even though she'd known Vic most of her life, he was still the most intimidating man she'd ever met. He must be close to retirement age now, but he was broad and brawny with a shock of white hair and a lined, rugged face that spoke of his years in the force. He also had a loud voice and a tendency to talk over you if he didn't agree with what you were saying. Having Reid there would make it more difficult for him to do that.

"Kenzie, this is a surprise!" He stood up as she walked into his office. "When my secretary told me you'd made an appointment I couldn't believe it. You could have just called. I'd have taken you out for dinner."

Reid followed her in. Vic's gaze shifted to the ex-detective. "Garrett, what are you doing here?"

"I'm with Kenzie." He sat down on one of the chairs opposite the captain's desk.

"He's helping me with something." She also took a seat. "Do you mind if we talk?"

"Uh, sure." He was thrown, she could tell. He squinted as he lowered himself into his chair. "What's this about?"

"My mother's disappearance."

He sighed. "Kenzie, we've been over this. I can't help you. The case was shelved a long time ago."

"I'm reopening it," she said.

He frowned. "I'm sorry, I don't understand."

"I've decided to look into it. I want to know what happened to her."

His jaw tensed and she saw his blue eyes sharpen ever so slightly. He wasn't happy, but she hadn't expected him to be. This was an inconvenience to him. He had more important things to focus on than a twenty-year-old cold case.

"I'm not sure how much help I can be."

"You could talk us through the investigation," Reid suggested.

Vic's eyes narrowed. "I'm a bit fuzzy on the details. It was twenty years ago."

"Please, Vic. It's important to me," Kenzie implored him.

He softened. "Okay, do you want to do this now? Why don't we schedule a dinner date, and we'll talk over steaks and beer at Marty's?"

Marty's was a steakhouse near South Beach. It had the best rib eye in town, as far as Kenzie was concerned.

"Tempting, but no. I think it's best if we talk now." She forced a smile.

"Okay. I'll tell you what I know."

"Please."

He leaned back in his chair. "I got a frantic call from Bud at about eight-thirty on the night your mother disappeared." His voice was hollow, as if he'd been through it so many times, he'd completely disassociated from it. "He said Angie was missing. She'd disappeared at the Christmas market."

"That's right."

"I alerted a unit in the area and raced over. We searched for most of the night but couldn't find her anywhere." He waved a hand in the air. "But you know all this."

"Yes, but I don't know what happened afterwards. Please, Vic."

He sighed. "I set up roadblocks, we checked with the port and airport control, we questioned local stall and shop owners, residents, anyone we could find. Nobody had seen her."

A mystery, Nora had said.

"Then what?"

"Well, we thought maybe she'd disappeared on her own accord. You know, left him."

Kenzie frowned. "What made you think that?"

"Well, the nature of her disappearance. It was so thorough. Usually, when someone is taken, they leave behind a trail. A broken cell phone, a discarded purse, a ripped jacket. Signs of an abduction. Blood. There was none of that. It was seamless."

"Vic, you knew my father better than anyone. Was he happy?"

The captain hesitated, but only for a split second. "Yeah, I think so. I mean he didn't tell me everything."

"Did you know about the baby?" Her voice was barely audible.

Vic blinked at her. "What baby?"

"My mother was pregnant. Nora told me. I think it was very early on in the pregnancy, though, because no one else knew. They hadn't even told me."

His eyes grew wide. "Jesus Christ. I didn't know, I swear. I had no idea."

Kenzie believed him.

"That's terrible." He raked a hand through his hair.

"I believe Bud Gilmore was questioned by your detectives in connection with her disappearance." Reid filled the silence that ensued after her revelation.

"Yeah, we took a statement from everybody who was there that night."

"So, he wasn't singled out?" asked Reid.

"No, of course not. He was my partner."

"Yet you got a search warrant for his house."

"How do you know that?" Vic gave a terse nod. "Ah, you've read the file."

Reid nodded. He'd been working as a homicide detective for the Miami PD at the time. It wasn't illegal.

The captain turned to Kenzie. "I suppose you've seen it too?"

She gave a rueful grin. "You know me, Vic."

"I'm afraid I do, Kenzie. To answer your question, Garret, yes, we searched the house. We had to. It was standard operating procedure."

"Even though he had an alibi for the time of her disappearance?" Reid asked.

"Yeah, he may have been working with an accomplice. He could have paid someone to take her. These were questions we had to ask, no matter how unpleasant." Vic glanced at Kenzie. "Your father understood that. He went along with it."

"Because he had nothing to hide," Kenzie insisted.

"Look, Kenzie, I didn't for a moment think Bud had anything to do with your mother's disappearance. I was just doing my job."

Beside her, Reid nodded.

She calmed down. "Okay, fair enough." She knew from her training, and from her experience as an investigative reporter, that in most murders where the victim was a female, the spouse or partner was responsible. Except they didn't know for certain her mother had been murdered.

In a way, she hoped she had run off on her own accord. Then at least there was a chance she was still alive. Even if it meant she had deserted her husband and daughter.

"What happened next?" Kenzie asked.

"The search turned up nothing, as you'd expect. One thing that was odd, however, was that your mother left her cell phone at home. She usually took it everywhere with her, at least according to Bud. It was as if she didn't want to be traced."

That was concerning. "What about her clothes? Her belongings?"

"Everything was there, right where it belonged. She hadn't returned home. She hadn't packed a bag. She hadn't taken anything other than what she was wearing at the time and her purse."

"You didn't find the purse anywhere?" Reid asked.

"No. We assumed she'd taken it with her, or the kidnapper had."

Kenzie cringed. She'd spent years wondering what had happened to her mother in those minutes after she'd walked out of the tent. If only she'd turned around and taken note of where she'd gone. If only she hadn't been so intent on talking to the two boys with Bethany. Boys she'd never spoken to again after that night.

She let out a shaky breath. "Was there anything else that struck you as odd?"

Vic shook his head. "No, that was it. It was the strangest bloody case I've ever worked. It still irks me that I never found her. My own partner's wife. A friend. I felt helpless."

"Yet you shut the case down after a few weeks." She gazed at him.

He shuffled in his chair. "Kenzie, there was nothing more I could do. We had no leads."

"What about the appeal?" asked Reid, frowning.

Kenzie sat up. She'd read about that in the file. "Yes, didn't you put out an appeal for information?"

"We did. Two people came forward. One was a guy on his way home from the market. He was inebriated, but he thought he'd seen a blonde woman. It wasn't very definitive. It could have been her, but then again, it might not have. We questioned everybody who lived and worked on that street, and nobody else had seen her."

Kenzie bit her lip. The name of the man would be in the report.

"What about the other person?" Reid asked.

"A female store owner. A woman fitting Angie's description had come into her shop."

"Did you follow up on it?" Kenzie leaned forward.

"Yeah, but it couldn't have been her. The woman in the shop was chatty, friendly. A woman about to run out on her family wouldn't have been so calm."

"That's if she was about to leave," Reid pointed out.

Kenzie scratched her head. "No one else came forward?"

"Nobody. We canvassed for a while. Put up Missing posters, sent out alerts, but there was no response. Eventually, we shut it down. Our resources were needed elsewhere."

Less than a month. That's all the time they'd dedicated to finding her mother.

"I'm sorry, Kenzie." The captain stood up, his message clear. The meeting was over. "I know it's not what you want to hear, but it did look like she planned her disappearance. It's the only thing that makes any sense."

5

"Does it?" she asked.

Reid studied Kenzie across the table. The wind caught her hair and lifted it off her shoulders. Her blue eyes were subdued, anxious, and she hadn't even looked at the menu in front of her. "Does it what?"

"Does it make sense? His theory."

Reid knew she was talking about Captain Reynolds.

"It does," he admitted, anticipating her frown. "But that's not to say it's what happened."

"Vic said there was no sign of a kidnapping. No scuffle. No screams."

"She could have been taken by surprise," he pointed out. "Or maybe she knew her attacker."

"That's right." Kenzie perked up. "If she knew her attacker, it would explain why there was no trace. Maybe she went willingly, not knowing he was going to kidnap her?"

"It's a possibility."

Kenzie continued her train of thought. "It could have been a friend, someone she trusted." Her hand flew to her mouth.

"I'm sure your father investigated all the possibilities," Reid said. "He was a detective too, don't forget."

"Yes, he was." She cleared her throat. "It nearly killed him, her disappearance. He didn't return to the force for almost a year. I thought that was it. Then one day, he got up, got dressed and said he was going back to work. We never spoke about her again."

Reid pursed his lips. That couldn't have been easy for a kid who'd lost her mom.

"Do you think he came to the same conclusion as the others?" Reid asked.

She shrugged. "That's the problem. I don't know. I wish we'd spoken about it more, but every time I tried to bring her up, he shut me down. It was a no-go area."

Sounds like Bud Gilmore had also thought his wife had run away. Maybe he'd even found something that had led him to believe that. He glanced at Kenzie's stiff shoulders, her anxious expression, and worried they might never know the answer.

"We've still got those two witnesses to speak to," she said, her brain ticking over.

Reid nodded. "We'll go and see them tomorrow. Do you have their current addresses?"

"No. I'll see what I can find out this afternoon when I get back to the office."

He knew she'd taken a few days off for "personal reasons," but now she needed the newspaper's network of contacts and access to various databases to track down the two people who'd responded to the alert.

"Okay, I'll pick you up at ten tomorrow morning. Does that work?"

"Yes, and Reid—"

"Yeah?"

"Thanks for doing this. I know you don't have to."

He gave her a tight grin. "That's okay. I'd like to help you get some closure on this. Besides, I'm intrigued."

She gave a little snort. "Careful. This case has the potential to drive you mad. Trust me. I know."

Reid had just gotten home when he heard a cacophony of sirens wail past and disappear into the Glades.

What the hell was going on?

He went outside. More police cars followed, along with an ambulance. That wasn't good. He watched until they rounded the bend and disappeared. He could see the night sky pulsing with orange and blue lights and knew exactly where they were.

Smiley's Bar.

A white CSI van flew past, and that's when curiosity got the better of him. Grabbing his keys, he jumped into his pickup and followed them. The narrow road was pitch black. The crescent moon was suffocated by heavy clouds, so he flicked his high beams on to alert any vehicles coming in the opposite direction to his presence. Swerving at the last minute on this road meant landing in the swamp.

A couple of minutes later he pulled up outside the bar. He was wrong. The drama wasn't at Smiley's; it was at the seedy motel next door.

The Gator Inn was flooded with light. Not only the strobe effect from the emergency vehicles, but also a spotlight that had been set up to illuminate a crime scene.

Onlookers were gathering. Swampers, guests from the motel, patrons from the bar, and several provocatively dressed working girls. They did a lot of business here. This motel was happy to rent rooms by the hour.

A group of police officers stood together gawking at a man lying on the ground. He wasn't moving. A forensic team was processing the scene, but there was no cordon, nobody was taking witness statements and there didn't appear to be any attempt to interview the public.

"Who's in charge here?" Reid walked up to them, making them jump.

A middle-aged man with a mop of thick black hair and sweat patches under his arms turned around. "I am. Lieutenant Roberto Casillas. Who are you?"

"Reid Garrett. Ex-Miami PD. Do you need some help here?"

"No, why would you ask that?"

"No reason. I just thought you might like to put up a police cordon and start interviewing witnesses. Someone might have seen something."

"Uh, yeah. We were just getting to that." He issued the command to his team who sauntered off, unhurried.

Jesus.

"Which department are you from?" Reid asked.

"Sweetwater. Why?"

"No reason," he said again, and took a few steps back.

The CSI guys hovering around the victim meant that he could only see his feet. One shoe on, one off. The exposed sock had a hole in it and his big toe was poking through.

Reid walked around the body, hoping for a better look. The police were taking their time with that cordon. If he could get this close, others could too.

Out of habit, he surveyed the onlookers, looking for anything out of the ordinary. The killer often came back to the scene of the crime. Sometimes they even involved themselves in the investigation. He looked for furtive glances, undue interest, glee. He'd seen it all during his ten plus years at Miami PD.

No one jumped out at him.

A couple of hookers were talking in hushed voices a few feet away from the main group of onlookers.

Reid approached them. "Hey girls." They stiffened and eyed him up and down.

"I'm not a cop," he said hurriedly.

They relaxed.

"Did you know this guy?" He still hadn't got a good look at him. The medical examiner was bending over the body, obscuring his head.

"Nah, not really," said a fiery redhead. Her lipstick matched her hair and her shoes. "He's been hanging around the bar for a few days now. He's from out of town."

"Oh yeah. Got a name?"

A shrug. She didn't care what his name was.

"I think he was called Barry," the brunette said. "That's what he told me in the bar."

"Did he try to solicit you?"

She frowned at his words. He sounded way too much like a police officer. He cleared his throat. "Did he proposition you?"

Better, but not by much.

"You're sure you're not a cop?" the blonde asked. She was the oldest and had a face that said she'd been around the block a time or two.

"Yeah, I'm sure. Look, no badge. No gun." He held up his T-shirt and spun slowly around. They appeared pacified.

"He tried, yeah." She sniggered. "But then he got into a fight with another guy, so I left them to it."

"He got into a fight?" Reid frowned. "When was this?"

"Last night." She cocked her head at him. "Hey, weren't you the guy that stopped it? You and that other dude."

Reid spun around, his eyes on the body. He moved around the medical examiner so he had a clear view of the guy's head.

He froze.

It was him. The guy with the head wound. It had partially healed, but the dried blood was still visible. In fact, Reid was sure he was wearing the same soiled jeans as before, just with a different T-shirt. Yeah, there were faded blood stains on the denim.

He took a deep breath. There was no mistaking it, this was the guy from the bar.

6

KENZIE GLANCED AT HER PHONE. It was half past ten and still no sign of Reid. It wasn't like him to be late—or at least not without a reason. She frowned. Then dialed his number. It diverted to voice-mail. Strange.

She left a message. "Hey, Reid. It's Kenzie. I was expecting you to pick me up at ten. I hope everything's okay. Call me when you get this."

Now what?

She could go by herself, but there was an advantage to having a police detective with her. People were less likely to shirk from answering her questions. Still, she hadn't got to be a successful inves-tigative journalist because she was afraid to interview witnesses alone.

Sighing, she pulled out her keys and climbed into her car.

Ted Wentworth lived in the same house he had twenty years ago. It was one block back from the square where the Christmas market had been held. The area was populated by start-ups, trendy cafes and warehouses offering communal working space.

Kenzie parked beside the square and stared at the spot in the middle where every year a giant fir tree was decorated with lights and baubles. She pictured the people whirling around, laughing, shopping, and drinking. The festive music. The smell of pinecones and chestnuts.

Had it really been twenty years?

She remembered running around, delighted by everything, excited to talk to the boys. Distracted from what was really going on. Blissfully ignorant. Back when all was right in her world. Little did she know everything was about to come crashing down.

Mr. Wentworth had said in his statement that he'd walked home from the Christmas market. He'd been drinking, but that didn't mean he hadn't seen her. A blonde woman. Average height. Red dress.

Kenzie remembered that dress well. It was a wrap-around in a soft, figure-hugging viscose material and fell to knee-level. Her mother had looked beautiful in it.

Red. Such a distinctive color and yet nobody had noticed her. Except possibly this man and the woman who owned the store.

Kenzie walked up the street to the road behind, following the route she thought Mr. Wentworth would have taken. The shops and surroundings would have been different twenty years ago, but it wasn't a long walk, and her mother could have come this way.

Mr. Wentworth's house was fairly run down with paint peeling from the siding and a worn porch in need of repair. It looked sad, like it had seen better days. Kenzie walked up to the door and pressed the buzzer. There was an answering shout and a moment later an elderly man opened the door.

"Mr. Wentworth?" she inquired.

"Yes, yes. You must be the young lady asking about... Well, yes. Come on in."

She hesitated, then entered the house. As a reporter, she was always wary about entering properties belonging to people she didn't know, particularly men. She kept pepper spray in her purse as a precaution but looking at the white-haired man with ruddy cheeks and an enlarged nose, she didn't think she would need it.

"Would you like a drink?" he asked.

"Oh, no thank you. I'm driving." It wasn't even noon yet.

He huffed, then gestured for her to sit down. The living room was cluttered with piles of newspapers and magazines. A television stood on a weathered table, which, judging by the dust, hadn't been cleaned in ages.

"Thank you for seeing me," she said, trying not to sneeze.

"I must admit, I was surprised to get your call. It's been a long time since anyone asked me about the missing woman."

"Who asked you before?"

He inhaled, his eyebrows rising at the same time. "A police detective. I can't remember his name now. It was too long ago."

"Vic? Vic Reynolds?"

He shrugged. "Could be. My memory isn't what it once was."

Great.

She noted the empty tumbler on the side table and wondered if he'd had a few already. "Mr. Wentworth, the woman who went missing was my mother. I'd like you to tell me what you saw that night. Could you do that?"

"There's nothing much to tell." His glazed eyes fixed on his empty glass. "I was walking home from the market. I'd gone to get some presents for my nephews, you see. They're all grown up now."

Kenzie nodded encouragingly.

"I was on my way home when I saw her."

Kenzie straightened her back. "What was she doing?"

"She was standing on the sidewalk. At first, I thought she was waiting for someone, but I didn't see anyone approach her."

"Could a car have picked her up?" Kenzie's pulse ticked up a notch.

"Maybe. I got home, went inside, and when I looked out of the window a few minutes later, she was gone."

Kenzie grimaced in frustration. "You didn't see where she went?"

"No, sorry. Like I said to that cop, I only saw her for an instant, and I only noticed her because she was standing right outside my house in that red dress. Very striking."

Kenzie caught her breath. The police had mentioned the dress in their appeal.

"When I saw the posters asking for information, I thought I'd better call it in. She seemed like a nice lady. She smiled at me as I walked past."

"She was a nice lady," Kenzie breathed.

She thought back to the police report. Reynolds and the other detectives working the case had dismissed this man's testimony as unreliable because he'd been drinking. Yet Mr. Wentworth seemed certain about what he'd seen.

"My wife had just left me," he blurted out.

"Excuse me?" Kenzie glanced up.

He gestured to the empty glass. "That's why I was drinking. It helped numb the pain."

"I understand," she murmured. "I'm sorry."

"I know the police didn't take me seriously," he went on, scratching the armrest with his fingernail. "I was in a dark place, and I looked up and there was this angel standing outside my house. An angel in a red dress. I didn't imagine it."

"I believe you," Kenzie murmured. "I believe you saw my mother."

Hannah Gibson was a slim, elegant lady in her sixties or seventies. It was hard to tell. Her grey hair was swept back off her face in a sophisticated twist, and she had a smooth complexion with a light smattering of make-up. She wore a matching skirt suit in powder blue with beige pumps. Kenzie wasn't sure if she always dressed like this, or if she'd made the effort because she was expecting a visitor.

"Thank you for seeing me," she said, when the woman invited her in. "You have a lovely house."

"Why thank you." Mrs. Gibson broke into a smile. "We moved

here shortly after that lady went missing in the square, the one you want to talk about."

"She was my mother," Kenzie said quietly.

The woman gasped. "Oh, I'm so sorry. I didn't know. I thought you were just a reporter."

Just a reporter. She was that too.

"That's okay. I should have mentioned it when I spoke to you on the phone."

"I'm guessing you never found her?" Kenzie read real sadness in Mrs. Gibson's eyes.

"No, I'm still trying to figure out what happened."

The old lady shook her head. "Well, I don't think I'll be much help, but I can tell you what I remember."

Kenzie eased into a straight-backed chair around a polished dining room table. Mrs. Gibson perched opposite her. "Shall I make us some tea?"

"No, I'm fine. Thank you. If you could just tell me what you saw."

"It was a warm night for that time of year. Very un-Christmassy." She smiled at Kenzie. "I once spent a whole December in Europe. Loved every minute of it. The snow, the markets, the festivities. It was wonderful."

Kenzie let her reminisce, but she was gritting her teeth. "I'm sure."

"I was working that night. We had a shop, my husband and me. We sold natural products, soaps, scents, oils, that sort of thing. Many were imported from overseas." She paused, a faraway look in her eyes. "Every year, we set up a stall in the Christmas market. It was a great way to maximize the holiday sales."

Kenzie could understand that. She didn't remember the stall, but she must have gone into it when she'd been searching for her mother. She'd run into every stall at the market.

"When did you see her?" she asked.

"She came in to browse. Lovely lady. I noticed her straight away because of her dress. It was a beautiful fire-engine red."

"That was her," Kenzie breathed.

"She remarked on my lavender body spray. It was always popular."

"What did she do then?" Kenzie leaned forward in the chair.

"She left. She said thank you and walked out of the door. I was a bit surprised, I thought she might buy something."

"Did she seem rushed or in a hurry?" Kenzie asked.

"No, not at all. She was browsing like she had all the time in the world."

Kenzie drove back deep in thought. On one hand, her mother had been seen in the street waiting for someone. That would indicate an assignation, planned or not. Maybe a car picking her up? Why else would she wait on the sidewalk in the street behind the market?

On the other hand, she'd been browsing contentedly in the market stalls, unrushed, enjoying the festivities. How could she be both?

She checked her phone. Still no word from Reid.

Frowning, she called him again using her car's Bluetooth function. It went straight to voicemail.

"Hey, Reid. Is everything okay? Call me."

It wasn't like him to maintain radio silence, not when they'd planned to meet up. On a whim, she diverted off the road she was on and headed toward his place. Perhaps he was sick, or hurt?

She put her foot down and sped along the north-south highway towards the Glades. Half an hour later, she pulled into the parking spot beside his house. His truck was missing. Now that was odd.

Just to be sure, she knocked on the door. No answer. She crept around to the back and climbed onto the deck. The silver water stretched out for miles in front of the cabin, mirroring the cloudy sky.

She peered through the closed glass doors, but it was vacant inside. Reid wasn't home.

Bizarre. She hoped he was all right.

Kenzie ducked back around the house to her car and was about to pull out when two police cars roared in and stopped behind her, blocking her exit.

"What the hell?"

She got out again. "Excuse me, what is going on?"

"Ma'am, step back please. We have a warrant to search these premises."

"What?"

She watched, horrified, as they rammed open the door and marched inside.

"Where is Reid Garrett?" she asked the officer standing at the door. "Why are you searching his premises?"

"Mr. Garrett has been arrested, ma'am."

"Arrested? What for?"

He gave her a terse look. "Murder, ma'am. He's been arrested for murder."

7

Reid was fuming. He'd tried to help these imbeciles and instead they'd arrested him on suspicion of murder. He'd spent the night in a stinking cell with three other guys, one of which snored like a trooper, another who'd paced up and down all night. Consequently, he hadn't managed to get a wink of sleep.

He put his face to the bars. "Hey! I want to make a phone call. I know my rights. I'm allowed one phone call."

He'd been here for sixteen hours, and nobody had asked him anything. They'd simply arrested him and thrown him into the holding cell. They'd get to him eventually, but from what he'd seen so far, Lieutenant Casillas and his crew did not inspire confidence.

He sat down to wait. Eventually, after what felt like an eternity, Casillas came to see him. He had a uniformed officer with him who unlocked the cell.

"Your turn." He gestured to Reid to follow him.

"I want my phone call," Reid demanded.

Casillas laughed. "All in good time."

Reid gritted his teeth. There was no getting around this moron.

He was led into an interrogation room and told to sit at a metal table in a chair bolted to the floor. He knew the drill. He was no stranger to the interrogation room, but never from this side of the table.

Casillas sat opposite him.

"We searched your cabin," the detective said. "We found a shirt with blood on it. It's gone to the lab. We suspect it's the victim's blood."

"It is," Reid confirmed.

Casillas's eyes widened. "Well, I appreciate you being so honest. Would you mind telling me how it got there?"

"Certainly. I was in Smiley's bar the night before last with my friend, Lieutenant Pérez from the Miami Police Department." Casillas's pupils dilated at the mention of Pérez's name. "We were having a drink when two guys got into a fight."

"What two guys?"

"The victim and another man. I don't know their names."

Barry, the brunette had said. But that was unverified.

"What happened then?"

"The lieutenant and I separated them. That's how I got blood on my shirt. The victim had a cut on his head from a broken beer bottle."

Casillas fixed his beady eyes on him. "It was a lot of blood."

"He was bleeding profusely. Head wounds do that."

"I don't appreciate your tone, Mr. Garrett. This is a serious matter. You have been apprehended in connection with a homicide."

"And I'm telling you I had nothing to do with it. The blood is from the night before at the bar. If you test it, you will find it is not fresh. You should be looking for the man who had the altercation with the victim, not me."

"Where'd you get the shiner?" Casillas ignored the mention of the other man.

"That was also from the fight in the bar. The victim elbowed me in the face when I tried to pull him off the other guy."

Casillas studied him for a long time. "I've only got your word that any of this happened."

Reid squeezed his hands into fists. He was tempted to beat some sense into this guy. "Call Lieutenant Pérez at the Miami PD. He'll vouch for me." There was also the barman and most of the patrons at the bar. A place like that would have a security video, for sure.

"In a minute." Casillas didn't want to let go of his one and only suspect. Reid got the impression this guy didn't like to go out of his way. He was cutting corners, taking the easy route, even if it meant convicting the wrong man.

"What were you doing at the crime scene?" Casillas asked.

"I live nearby. I saw the sirens and thought I'd check it out. I'm an ex-cop."

"Do you make a habit of hanging around at crime scenes?"

"Only when they're on my road." He shot Casillas a hard look.

"Can anyone vouch for you at the time of the murder?"

"What time was that?" He hadn't spoken to the CSI team, he didn't know when the time of death was.

Casillas snorted. "Between eight and ten last night."

He'd dropped Kenzie back home around nine, then headed back to the cabin. She could alibi him. His truck would have been picked up on CCTV cameras. He began to relax. "Yeah, I was with a friend. I dropped her off at home at nine o'clock."

"Friend's name?"

"Kenzie Gilmore."

He watched as the detective wrote out her name, painstakingly slowly. "Okay, we'll get her to give a statement."

Reid leaned forward. "Fine, but in the meantime, I want my phone call."

Sighing, Casillas eased himself out of the chair. "Okay. Follow me."

Finally.

Reid followed Casillas down the corridor back to the squad room. It wasn't a very large police station, and he was still handcuffed, so he didn't pose a threat. A few heads bobbed up as he passed. At the reception desk was a phone.

"Hey?"

Casillas turned.

"My hands?"

The lieutenant removed the cuffs and posted an officer to guard him. "Don't let the suspect out of your sight."

Suspect, my ass.

Turning his back on the police officer, Reid picked up the phone.

Twenty minutes later Pérez stormed into the Sweetwater police station. Reid, who was back in his cell, heard him yelling at Casillas and smiled. Everything was going to be okay.

"Thanks for coming," he said, when Pérez appeared outside the cell.

"Jesus Christ, Reid. What the hell happened?"

He rolled his eyes. "Remember the guys from the bar? The ones who got into that fight?"

"Yeah?"

"Well, one of them turned up dead last night outside the Gator Inn."

"Shit. You're kidding?"

"I wish I was. I told Casillas I knew the guy, and he arrested me."

Pérez took in Reid's dirty clothes, stubble, and black eye. "You been here all night?"

"Unfortunately. The bastard wouldn't let me make a phone call until now."

Pérez shook his head. "This isn't the most efficient police department in town. I've heard reports." He raised his eyebrows. "They're thinking about shutting it down. Part of the budget cuts."

"Well, to be fair, the victim's blood is all over my shirt."

"What?" Then Pérez understood. "He was bleeding when we broke up that fight."

"Yeah, but forensics should be able to show it isn't fresh blood. Not from the night of the murder."

"Thank God for that."

"Can you speak to them?"

"I'll see what I can do, but you'll most likely have to wait for the lab results before they let you go."

"I have an alibi for the night of the murder," he said. "Kenzie Gilmore. I only got to the crime scene after the fact."

"All right. You sit tight. I'll get you out of here."

"Thanks, LT."

Pérez gave a terse nod and stalked off down the corridor.

8

KENZIE WAS GOING MENTAL. Reid had been arrested for murder, and she had no idea what to do about it. She didn't even know where he was.

She called the Miami Police Department, but they had no record of him being brought in. She asked to speak to Detective Ryan, a female officer she'd met several months earlier and liked, but the rookie cop didn't know anything about it.

"Let me check the system," she said. "If he's been arrested, it'll tell me where he's being held."

Kenzie waited, her heart pounding. It must be some mistake. Reid would never kill anyone. He couldn't. Then she thought back to the time they'd bumped into Alberto Torres during the Strangler case. The drug kingpin had been coming out of an office high-rise as they'd been going in. According to Reid, Torres shot and killed his colleague and ex-lover. The look on Reid's face had been one of sheer hatred.

Okay, he might be able to kill him, but nobody else.

"Kenzie, he's at the Sweetwater Police Department. I can't tell you much more than that. I believe my boss, Lieutenant Pérez, is there with him. I'm not sure what the situation is."

"Okay, thanks."

She sat in her car wondering what to do. Should she go over to the station to see him? Would he want her to? Would they even let her see him? While she was deciding what to do, her phone rang. Fumbling, she pulled it out of her purse. The number was unrecognized.

"Hello?"

"Kenzie Gilmore?"

"Yes, who's speaking?"

"This is Lieutenant Pérez from the Miami Police Department. I'm calling in connection with Reid Garrett. He's been arrested, and we'd like you to come in and give a statement."

"A statement?"

"Yes, I believe you were with him yesterday evening?"

"I was, that's correct."

A sigh of relief. "Great. Could you come to the Sweetwater Police Department as soon as possible? We're waiting for you."

"Oh, sure. I'm on my way."

Decision made.

She turned the car around and got back onto the highway.

Sweetwater Police Department was situated on the west side of Miami in a mainly Hispanic area. The building was squat and uninteresting, just a long, brick rectangle. Kenzie parked in the lot and marched inside, pushing open the door.

A man came up to her, extending a hand. She recognized him as Reid's former boss, Lieutenant Pérez, the man who'd telephoned her. "Kenzie, it's good to see you."

"Thank you. I came as quickly as I could."

"Lieutenant Casillas is over here." He led her across the squad room to where an overweight man in jeans and a grey T-shirt stood, talking to a uniformed officer.

"Lieutenant, I have Miss Gilmore here to give her statement."

Casillas turned around. "Ah, Miss Gilmore. Please sit down."

He gestured to the desk in front of him. It was cluttered with papers, folders, and food wrappers. Kenzie sat.

Casillas squeezed into the chair opposite while Pérez stood, hovering over them like a hawk. She was glad he was keeping an eye on proceedings.

"Miss Gilmore, could you state where you were on August 23rd between eight and ten o'clock?"

"Yes. I was with Reid Garrett. He took me home after we went to see Captain Reynolds at the Miami Police Department."

Casillas cleared his throat. "I see, and what time did you get home?"

"Around nine o'clock."

"Did Mr. Garrett leave immediately afterwards?"

"Well, we spoke for a few minutes, then I went inside."

"He didn't accompany you?"

"No." She got the feeling that wasn't what Pérez wanted her to say, but it was the truth.

"Where do you live, Miss Gilmore?" Pérez asked, butting in.

Casillas looked annoyed but went with it.

She gave her address on Bay Harbor Island.

"And that's what? A forty-five-minute drive to Reid Garrett's house in the Glades?"

She saw where he was going with this. The time of death must have been between eight and ten. "Depending on traffic, yes. Sometimes it's even longer."

"Which means Mr. Garrett must have gotten home at about a quarter to ten."

Casillas tapped his pencil on the desk. "That still leaves fifteen minutes unaccounted for."

Pérez scowled. "Fifteen minutes to drive to the motel, shoot the victim twice in the chest, dispose of the gun, then get back to his home to shower and change before returning to the crime scene? I don't think so?"

"What makes you think he went home and changed?" Casillas asked.

Even Kenzie knew the answer to that one.

"Because he didn't have any gunshot residue on his hands or clothing when you picked him up," Pérez intoned.

Casillas was silent.

"Now you've heard his alibi, the lab results will prove the blood on his shirt was from the previous night, and Miss Gilmore has given a statement. You've got nothing to hold Mr. Garrett on. I insist you release him immediately."

Kenzie watched as disappointment then acceptance passed over Casillas's face. He was backed into a corner. He had to let Reid go. He issued the order to a young officer in uniform, then closed the folder on his desk.

"If I were you," Pérez barked, "I'd start looking for the man your victim fought with in the bar. There were plenty of witnesses. I'm sure if you asked around, you'd get a name."

"Thank you, Lieutenant, but we're on it." Casillas pushed himself to his feet.

Kenzie could see by Pérez's expression that he very much doubted it.

A few moments later, Reid was led into the squad room. She was so glad to see him, even with a yellowing eye and two days' worth of stubble. "Are you alright?" She touched his arm.

He shot Casillas a dark look. "I am now."

"I apologize for the inconvenience, Mr. Garrett." Casillas didn't meet Reid's eye. "Just doing my job. No harm done, eh?"

Reid grunted and went to the reception desk. "I'd like my watch and phone, please."

The duty officer handed them over. "Sign this, sir."

Reid scribbled his signature; then flanked by Pérez and Kenzie, marched out of the precinct.

.   .   .

"How about we all go out for dinner?" Pérez suggested, once they were outside in the parking lot.

"Sounds good to me," said Reid. "I'm starving."

They both looked at Kenzie. "Sure, why not?"

"I know a great place nearby. It's only four blocks away."

"I'll grab a lift with Kenzie. We'll see you there." Reid shook Pérez's hand. "Thanks again for your help."

"No problem. I just did what he should have done."

Reid grinned.

Kenzie unlocked the car and they got in. Reid had to put the passenger seat back, his legs were so long. Suddenly, her little Honda felt even smaller.

"I'm dying to hear what happened," she said, starting the engine. The car purred to life. They set off after Pérez, who was already accelerating down the road in his black SUV.

"I'll tell you at the restaurant," he said. "Thanks, Kenzie, for coming to give a statement. Sorry to ruin your afternoon."

"Please don't worry about it. I'm happy to help." She paused. "I had wondered why you stood me up."

He laughed. "I would have called, but they confiscated my phone."

"Fair enough."

Big Mike's Tavern was on the left and she turned in after Pérez and parked beside him. They went inside and got a table.

"I'll be right back," Reid said. "I've got to freshen up."

Kenzie smiled at Pérez. She'd met him for the first time several months ago at the Miami Police Department while working with Reid. He hadn't said much to her at the time, but to be fair, he'd had his hands full.

"Would you mind filling me in? I still don't know why Reid was arrested."

"Yeah, sure. It's a strange story." He told her about the fight at the bar and how they'd separated the brawlers.

She raised her eyebrows. "I can see why they thought he was responsible, especially if the blood was on his shirt."

"Unfortunate coincidence, that's all," said Pérez. "We left right after that."

"And the murder happened last night?" Kenzie asked.

"Between eight and ten," clarified Pérez. "That's when Reid was with you."

"I figured that much. Do you think this other guy did it? The one who hit him over the head with the bottle?"

"Possibly. He's the guy I'd be looking for. The fight gives him a motive."

"But you don't think Casillas is going to do that?"

"Casillas couldn't find an elephant in a giraffe enclosure," growled Reid, returning. He'd washed his face and run a hand through his hair, but he still looked like a ruffian with that bruised eye and days old stubble.

"That place has the worst closure rate in the whole county." Pérez shook his head. "I don't know what they do there, but it's not solving crimes."

"They need help." Reid sat down and opened the menu. "They'll never find out who did it if they keep arresting the wrong people."

The waiter came up and they ordered. Steaks and beer all around.

"Why don't you help them?" Kenzie suggested, glancing at Reid.

He scowled. "Why would I want to do that?"

"You just said they need help. You're not working at the moment, and you're familiar with the case."

Pérez pursed his lips. "She does have a point."

"No, it's a terrible idea. He arrested me. I can't work on a case I've been a suspect in."

"You weren't charged," Pérez argued. "That's entirely different. If I speak to the Chief, he could get you assigned as a consultant, like you did for us."

"He won't go for it." The waiter brought their drinks, and Reid reached for his. He downed half of it in one gulp.

"Well, at least think about it," Kenzie said.

He put his beer bottle on the table. "I'm not interested."

But she could tell by the look in his eye that he was already thinking about it.

9

WHERE THE HELL ARE YOU?

Kenzie studied the text from Keith, her editor at the Miami Herald, early the next morning. He wasn't one to mince his words. She sent back a response.

On my way.

What had got him so worked up?

She went straight to his office. "About time," he growled as she walked in.

"I told you I was taking a few days off," she said.

He grunted, clearly having forgotten.

"What's going on?"

"Budget cuts," he snapped. "Out of a hundred staff reporters, you and Clayton are the most expensive writers here. Together you managed to suck up a sixth of the budget last year. And you know what's worse? You're both doing the same thing."

A shiver went down her spine.

"What are you saying, Keith?"

He got up and stormed up and down his office. "I hate doing this, Kenzie, but one of you has got to go."

"No! You can't."

"I have to. Orders from above." Kenzie sometimes forgot there were other people running the newspaper besides Keith. He was always roaming around, shouting out deadlines, asking for more.

Dig deeper. The story is there, you just have to find it.

And they did.

"Who?" Her voice trembled. Clayton had been here before her, so if they were going on a last in, first out policy, she'd have to go.

"I haven't decided yet. Clayton's been here for eternity, but you —" He glanced at her. "You know I admire your work, Kenzie. You're a great reporter, but you've been distracted lately."

Crap. It was the investigation into her mother's disappearance. She'd been taking time off, disappearing for days, neglecting less important tasks. Now it was coming back to bite her.

"I'm sorry. I've had... a personal issue. It's over now. I'm back, a hundred percent."

He sat down again with a loud creak. "You'd better be, Kenzie. I've got to let one of you go at the end of the month and I'd hate for it to be you."

"I won't disappoint you." Adrenaline surged through her body. "What can I do? Give me something to work on. Anything."

He glanced down at his desk. She saw a Xerox of another newspaper article. On it was a photograph of a middle-aged man in a dark suit and tie. Hair greying at the temples, prominent cheekbones, a square jaw. He was looking up, one hand in his pocket.

"Who's that?" she asked.

"Don Ingleman, a Florida businessman slash loan shark, although they've yet to prove it."

"I can," she volunteered eagerly. "Let me prove it."

He chuckled. "Easy. He's been charged already. His trial begins tomorrow at the Miami-Dade County Courthouse. I want you to cover it."

"Sure, I can do that."

He gave a curt nod, her signal to leave. She rushed back to her desk, determined to do some research on Don Ingleman. By the time the trial started tomorrow, there was nothing she wouldn't know about the Miami businessman.

Kenzie stayed late at the office researching. To her annoyance, so did Clayton. She wondered what he was working on. Was it Ingleman? Were they both covering the same story?

Unfortunately, she didn't have the best relationship with Clayton. He didn't like her. Never had. Even though they'd worked together for nearly ten years, they had no relationship to speak of. Most of the time they covered different angles of the same story. He led and she was the follow up, or vice versa.

He felt she'd encroached on his beat, which she had, but it was nothing personal. She just wanted to get to the truth. She couldn't help it if she was a better investigator than he was.

Don Ingleman made for interesting reading. The guy was a multi-millionaire financier. He'd started his career crunching numbers for a major car financing firm, then quit to form his own company, Linwood Investments. Unlike normal loan companies, his clients were financial under-achievers with low-end credit scores. Many were struggling with bankruptcies, past repossessions, or limited credit histories—things that made them unattractive to traditional lenders.

Risky, but it also enabled him to charge an eye-popping rate of interest, more than double the average and just under legal limits. Rumor had it, he also ran a less legitimate side to his business offering credit to individuals that wouldn't qualify through normal channels, even his. One such character was an ex-con by the name of Barry Marshall.

Marshall had borrowed $20,000 to cover his gambling debts, and when he couldn't make the payments, was allegedly threatened. Fearing for his life, he'd gone to the cops. They'd offered to protect him if he testified against Ingleman. Racketeering was a felony, particularly when the rate of interest exceeded 45%, which in Marshall's case, it did.

Kenzie stopped reading as a crash of thunder made the lights in the office flicker. She looked out the window. It had started to rain. She hadn't noticed it at first, but now it was getting heavier. Frenzied spears clattered against the glass, creating a deafening roar.

"Goodness," she muttered.

At the end of the row, Clayton grunted. It was only the two of them left in the office. A two-man race to the finish. Kenzie turned back to her computer screen.

I'm going to win.

It was still raining the next morning when she arrived at the courthouse. Giant puddles had formed on the sidewalk and dirty water rushed down the gutters like mini rapids. She darted inside, then stopped to shake out her umbrella.

To her dismay, Clayton was already there.

Damn it. He was also working on the Ingleman story. Keith had them in direct competition with each other. She clenched her jaw and strode right past him. Everyone began to file in. Kenzie sat as close to the front as she could get. She didn't want to miss a word.

Once the visitors and press were seated, the jury filed in. Twelve somber-faced men and women who'd been carefully selected in a pre-trial process for their open-mindedness and non-judgmental opinions.

There was a shuffle from the side, and a door opened. The defendant, Don Ingleman, was led in. Kenzie studied him. He wore an expensive suit and wore it well. It fit his toned body perfectly. Tailor-made, she guessed. His shoes shone; his tie was straight. He held his head high and glanced around as if surveying guests at a house party. For a man on trial, he seemed surprisingly calm and self-assured. Perhaps that was all part of the act.

She glanced across at the prosecutor. He stood nervously, his head bowed, whispering with his colleague.

"All rise," came the familiar cry. They stood.

In walked Judge Heseltine, resplendent in his flowing robe. He had a neatly trimmed beard and hard, probing eyes. Kenzie shivered. He didn't look particularly lenient.

The lawyers began their opening arguments. The prosecution's team kept glancing at the door as if waiting for someone to walk in. Midway through the defense's speech, a steward of the court walked up to the prosecuting attorney and handed him a note. He read it, and the color drained from his face. It was not good news.

"Excuse me, Your Honor," he rasped. "May we approach the bench?"

"If you must."

The four lawyers went up to the judge. The prosecutor said something in a low voice that shocked the judge. The defense attorney argued a point, gesturing wildly to the court. After about five minutes, the judge stood up.

"I'm sorry to have to do this." He scowled at Ingleman. "But the primary witness for the prosecution was found dead yesterday. Since the prosecution's entire case depends on this witness's testimony, I'm going to dismiss the case. Mr. Ingleman, you are free to go."

He slammed his gavel on the desk and the court erupted. Kenzie sat glued to her chair, dazed. What had just happened?

Ingleman pumped his attorney's hand, then slapped him on the back. The prosecution filed out, sending bitter looks Ingleman's way.

Their key witness dead?

Kenzie's heart began beating faster. There was a story there, she could sense it. She just had to keep digging.

10

Kenzie dashed out of the courthouse after the frazzled prosecutor.

"Excuse me," she panted, catching up with him and his associate. "Could I ask you a few questions? I'm with the Miami Herald."

"I'm afraid I can't stop." He kept walking, collar up against the driving rain.

"Do you believe your witness was murdered?" She asked the one question that might get his attention.

He halted, his eyes darting to his colleague then back again. "How—How did you know?"

That was a yes.

She ignored the tiny spears that stabbed her face. "How did he die?"

"He was gunned down outside his motel." The lawyer gave her a curious look. "What's your name again?"

"Kenzie."

He stared at her.

Gunned down. Her mind was working overtime. "Where? Which motel?"

"I don't have all the details yet," he said. "We've only just heard."

"But it happened yesterday?"

"The day before, apparently. They had a problem identifying the body, otherwise we'd have known sooner."

"Okay, thanks." Kenzie stood frozen to the spot as they walked off, unbothered that she was getting soaked.

No way? It couldn't be...

She needed to see a photograph of the witness. Running back into the courthouse, she took out her phone and searched for Barry Marshall. Nothing came up.

She tried again.

Barry Marshall dead

Only one newspaper had the story, the Miami Post, and it was a few lines stating that a man identified as Barry Marshall had been shot to death outside his motel room in the Everglades.

Holy crap!

It *was* him. The same guy Reid had been falsely accused of killing.

She sent Reid a text message. "I'm coming over. Got news on the dead guy."

When she arrived, Reid was inside reading through the police reports on her mother's case. Hell, so much had happened, she'd forgotten to tell him about her day yesterday, visiting the two people who'd answered the appeal all those years ago. Never mind, she could fill him in later.

"You're never going to believe this," she said, shaking out her hair.

"Do you want a towel?" he offered. "You're making a puddle in my hallway."

She glanced down. "Oh, yeah. Sorry." His words barely registered.

"What's going on, Kenzie?"

"You know that guy who died outside the motel?"

He nodded.

"Well, he was supposed to testify in court today. He was an important witness for the prosecution in a racketeering case."

"He was a witness?" Reid frowned.

"Yeah. Ever heard of a guy named Don Ingleman? He's a wealthy financier. Lends people money for insane rates of return."

"I don't think so."

"Well, anyway. He was on trial for loan sharking, and I was sent to cover it. There we were, waiting for the first witness when they announced he was dead. I asked some questions, and it turns out it's the same guy."

"You're saying it was a contract killing?"

She sat down on one of the wicker chairs. "It looks like it. What do you think?"

"I don't know. The guy was shot twice in the chest, but it didn't look like a pro. The shots were messy. One above the heart, one on the other side. The guy bled out."

Kenzie swallowed. "His name was Barry Marshall. He was an ex-con and a gambler. He owed Ingleman thousands of dollars in interest payments."

"How do you know this?"

"I'm researching him for my article. Or series of articles. This is big, Reid. I can sense it. If Ingleman killed Marshall—" She blew air out from her cheeks.

Reid held up a hand. "Okay, back up for a second. What is your goal here? Are you trying to prove he did it?"

"I was supposed to cover the trial, but the case has been thrown out of court. No witness, no prosecution."

"Now you're going after this financier, Ingleman?"

She raised an eyebrow.

"Kenzie, do you realize how dangerous this is? I know guys like him. He's not the type you want to mess with. Loan sharks are not nice people."

She tilted her head. "I know that. I'll be careful, I promise."

"What about your mother's case?"

"Actually, I do have some information on that too."

He sat down opposite her.

"I went to visit those two witnesses who responded to the appeal. They both seemed legit. I think they really did see her."

"You're sure?"

"Mrs. Gibson spoke to my mother at her stall. She called her a nice lady who complimented her on her products. That sounds like my mother. She was always complimenting people. Mrs. Gibson said she didn't appear to be in a rush, that she was browsing the items on display."

Reid crinkled his brow. "Doesn't sound like a woman preparing to run away."

"Exactly." Kenzie sat back. "Then there's Mr. Wentworth. He saw her outside his house. An angel in a red dress he called her. That's pretty accurate. She had wispy blonde hair, lighter than mine, and she was wearing a red dress."

"Where does he live?"

"Close to the market. A few streets back. It's an easy walk. He said she looked like she was waiting for someone."

"Did he see who?" Reid leaned forward.

"No, and this is the really annoying part. He walked past her, she smiled at him, then he let himself into his house and when he looked out the window a few minutes later, she was gone."

"A few minutes?"

"Yes. What do you make of that?" She studied him, eager to hear his point of view.

"The timing makes me think it was a vehicle that picked her up, otherwise he would have seen her walking down the street."

"That's what I thought." She sighed. "But how could she browse the market stall and then, a short while later, wait on a sidewalk for someone to pick her up? It doesn't make sense."

"One of the witnesses could be mistaken?" he suggested.

"Or something happened while she was browsing in the market that caused her to walk up the street."

He nodded slowly. "Could she have seen someone? Arranged a meeting, perhaps?"

"I don't know." Kenzie grimaced. "I was too young to remember. I can't think who else was there that night, other than our immediate party."

"What about your friend, the one you were with? What was her name?"

"Bethany?" Kenzie pursed her lips. "I haven't spoken to her in years. Not since the incident."

"Perhaps you should? She might not remember anything either, but she's the only other person we haven't spoken to who was there that night."

Kenzie fell silent. He had a point, although it would have to wait.

"I've decided to put my mother's investigation on hold," she confessed. At his astounded look, she continued, "They're laying off people at work. I have to get this Ingleman scoop, otherwise I'm going to lose my job."

"You know that for a fact?"

She bit her lip. "I've been warned."

He leaned against the back of the chair. "I'm sorry, Kenzie. I didn't realize things were so precarious."

"I didn't either, but now that I do, I've got to pull out all the stops. I've got to find out who killed this witness, and soon, before the story dies out." Reid knew better than most how important it was to act while a case was still hot.

He shook his head. "I don't like it. This guy's dangerous. Look how his witness ended up."

She folded her arms. "Why don't you help me then?"

"I can't get involved." He glanced away.

Kenzie wasn't ready to give up. She knew Reid. He couldn't resist a case like this. And he was already involved, whether he liked it or not. "Reid, think about it. If you take the position at Sweetwater, we can work together. We work well as a team."

He had access to information she couldn't get her hands on, and she could go places he couldn't. She had feminine wiles, she could morph into other characters, other personalities. She could persuade, cajole, and manipulate people into telling her things, a skill he would never master. They complimented each other.

He stared out the window. The rain was still pelting down, the silver surface of the water pockmarked and uneven. The sound was strangely comforting.

"I know you want to find out who did this as much as I do," she whispered.

His shoulders tensed, the muscles in his neck flexed. She was getting to him.

Eventually, he turned back to her. "Okay, I'll do it. But only because those fools at Sweetwater aren't going to get there on their own, and I don't want to see another innocent man go down for murder."

Yes!

"Thank you," she gushed. "You won't regret it, I promise. We'll find the real killer, and when it leads to Ingleman, I'll have my scoop, and you get to send the guilty man to prison."

"And I can keep you out of trouble."

She grinned. "That too."

11

Reid put down the phone. "It's done. I'm now a bona fide member of the Sweetwater Police Department."

"The Chief agreed?"

"Yeah. It turns out Pérez had already briefed him. Captain Reynolds had a few concerns, but the chief overruled him."

Kenzie frowned. "Vic? What concerns?"

"My background. That business with Ortega. You know, the same old shit. It never goes away."

"But you have a great reputation," Kenzie insisted. "Nobody closes as many cases as you."

He gave a rueful grin. It was sweet of her to say so, but his failing in the undercover op where his colleague had died would forever haunt him. That had been his responsibility, and she'd died on his watch, even if it had been Ortega's fault.

"Casillas isn't going to like it," he said, thinking of the big man with the lackadaisical attitude who'd kept him locked up overnight without a phone call.

She rolled her eyes. "Who cares? He's an incompetent moron. I can't believe they put him in charge."

"He's the most experienced detective there," Reid pointed out. "The others are all rookies. That's why they made him lieutenant. The problem is Casillas wants an easy ride until he can retire. He probably thought the backwater police station was the place to do that."

"Until a dead body wound up on his turf and he had to do some work for a change."

Reid scoffed. "Fat chance of that happening."

"Now they've got you to kick them into shape." Kenzie smiled and reached for the last slice of pizza. They'd been going through her notes on Ingleman, and Reid was now fully up to speed. "What do we do first, detective?"

Detective Garrett.

It felt good to be back, even though he'd never admit it to Pérez.

"We need to go back to Smiley's and talk to the barman," Reid said. "I also saw a couple of working girls outside the motel who seemed to know the two guys."

Kenzie ran a hand through her hair. It was starting to dry now she was indoors. "You think the guy he fought with in the bar was the one who killed him?"

"I don't know, but we can't rule it out."

"A bar brawl is not the best way to assassinate someone." There was doubt in her voice.

"We don't know it was an assassination yet. It could have been a personal grudge, a dispute over money." He shrugged. "It might not be related to Ingleman at all."

"Seriously?" She shot him a look. "A witness about to testify against a dangerous loan shark is killed the day before the trial and you don't think it's connected?"

"It's suspicious," he conceded. "But I wouldn't be doing my job if I didn't consider all the options."

She studied him, her eyes shining. "Okay, fair enough. But let's not consider it for too long. I want to get on to Ingleman."

He sensed her excitement. Granted, Ingleman was the most

likely suspect, or someone he'd hired, but he couldn't rule out the altercation in the bar. That was the logical place to start.

"We could go now." He eyed her clothes. Jeans, a T-shirt and running shoes. Her hair was tied back in her normal ponytail, her face devoid of make-up. "Don't think I'm being sexist, but Smiley's is not the nicest place for a lady."

"Then I won't be a lady."

He grinned. He'd forgotten she could morph into anyone she chose. "Okay, then. Let's do this."

"I need five minutes." She jumped up and disappeared to the bathroom.

"Ready?" he called, a short while later, picking up his car keys.

"How's this?"

"Wow." He stared at her as she modelled up and down in front of him. Gone was the casual look. Instead, she'd tied her T-shirt in a knot at the waist exposing an indecent amount of bare midriff, her hair was loose and wild, and she wore a lot more make-up than he was used to seeing on her. Her eyes were positively luminous.

"Will I fit in?"

"Erm—" He pulled himself together. "You'll be fine."

Except he might have another problem on his hands. She looked so damn hot he was going to struggle to keep the other men away from her. Smiley's was a free-for-all after ten o'clock and could get pretty wild. Hopefully they wouldn't be around long enough for that to happen.

Reid parked outside the bar, and they went inside. To his surprise, Kenzie linked her arm with his. "I don't want anyone to think I'm single," she hissed. It was a good call, although it wouldn't stop the guys from trying.

The music was loud, much louder than last time he'd been here. The volume increased the later it got. Usually, he liked to get the hell out before it reached this stage.

"Hey handsome, wanna party?" A woman sidled up to him and put a hand on his chest. Kenzie shot him an amused grin.

"No thanks." They kept walking up to the bar.

"Want a drink?" he asked Kenzie, pulling out a bar stool for her.

"Thanks." She released his arm. And he was just getting used to her being there.

He looked around for the redhead and brunette he'd seen outside the motel the night of the murder, but either they weren't here yet or they were busy plying their trade. Maybe they'd come back later.

"Two beers please," he said to the barman. There wasn't much else to order in this place unless you liked the hard stuff. "Ant, right?"

"Yeah." The barman frowned. "Do I know you?"

"We met the other night, after those two guys got into a fight."

"Happens most nights," he retorted, getting two bottles out of the fridge and putting them on the counter.

"The one guy smashed a bottle over the other guy's head. Lots of blood. Me and my buddy pulled them apart."

"Oh yeah." Recognition dawned. "The guy who died outside the motel."

"That's the one."

The barman leaned over the counter. "Are you a cop?" His gaze roamed over Kenzie. "'Cos we don't like cops in here. Even one's with scorching hot girlfriends."

She laughed. "That's so sweet of you."

Reid frowned. He knew she was acting, but it still irked him. "Nah, just trying to find the guy who hit him, that's all."

The barman straightened up. "Can't help you. Didn't know him."

Reid gave an accepting nod.

"He's lying," whispered Kenzie.

"I know, but he's not going to rat out a customer. We're going to have to find some other way of getting the information."

Kenzie glanced around. "Who are the locals?"

Reid surveyed the crowd. "Those guys playing darts. They were here the other night. I can't recall anyone else."

She took a deep breath. "That'll do."

Before he could stop her, she picked up her beer and sauntered across the bar. He watched her hips move, a rhythm designed to show off her bare midriff. He wasn't the only one. Several other eyes were on her. She tossed her hair back and smiled, seemingly unaware of the sensation she was creating.

What the hell was she up to? This was a sure-fire way of getting hit on. Although, knowing Kenzie, she had a plan. He let her do her thing, but picked up his beer and followed, in case there was a problem.

She waltzed up to the guys playing darts and said something. They all turned to look at her. Some ogled while others leered. Reid began to feel uncomfortable.

Kenzie ran a hand through her hair and made a comment. They laughed. One of the guys offered to show her how to throw a dart. She giggled and took it from him, handing her beer to another guy to hold. Reid watched in amazement as the men instructed her on throwing techniques, then she attempted a throw. Unsurprisingly, she wasn't bad. The dart hit the board. They cheered and urged her to try again.

She tried a few more throws, then laughed and took back her beer. One of the men put his hand on her back. Another offered her a seat at the high top table nearby.

She accepted and Reid watched as she talked to them, her legs crossed, her shoulders back, thrusting out her bust. He shook his head. She was incorrigible. Still, the dart players were fawning over her like she was a princess.

Ten minutes later, she excused herself and went to the restroom. It would have been too obvious if she'd walked straight over to him. As she passed, she winked. "Got it."

Reid went back to the bar to await her return.

"His name was Reg Arnold," she said, grinning. "He's a swamper. Hunts pythons and the occasional gator. A good guy, by all accounts."

"A good guy?" Reid rolled his eyes. "He smashed a bottle over the victim's head."

Kenzie leaned in. "Because he stole his girl."

"What?"

"Yeah. Becca is a local here. A working girl, as you put it. Reg had his eye on her, as he often does after a few beers, but then this other guy, an out of towner—Barry Marshall—got to her first. Reg was more than a little pissed when she went off with him."

"So he hit him over the head?"

"That's the gist of it."

Reid glanced back at the men who'd gone back to their darts game. "They told you this?"

"Yeah." She gave him a 'why wouldn't they' look. "Mike—he's the one with the snake tattoo up his arm—said Reg was sweet on Becca. The others agreed."

He shook his head. "What did you say to them to get them to tell you this?"

"That I was here the other night when they fought, and Reg dropped his phone. I was hoping to return it to him."

He pursed his lips. "Very clever. Did you get an address?"

"Yeah."

He grinned at her. "Shall we go pay him a visit?"

"Hell yeah."

Reg Arnold lived in an unremarkable wooden house next to an alligator farm. It was little more than a big shed with a boat covered by a tarpaulin on a trailer parked outside. It was pitch dark and the reeds and other foliage murmured eerily in the breeze.

Reid took a flashlight out of the glove compartment.

"It looks deserted." Kenzie peered in through one of the front windows. "There aren't any gators around, are there?"

"Dunno. Might be."

She glanced around nervously.

He joined her at the window, shining the flashlight inside. "Can't see any sign of life."

"He might be asleep."

"At ten-thirty? No. I think he's gone."

"Gone where?"

"Run away. He heard that the out of towner was killed and he fled, fearing a reprisal. Either he was complicit in his murder, or he doesn't want anyone to think he is."

Kenzie sighed. "Running's just going to make him look more guilty."

"Yeah, but in the moment of panic, he won't think of that."

Kenzie glanced around. "There's not even a neighbor nearby, other than the gator farm, and I'm not venturing in there after dark."

Reid chuckled. "Probably wise. Let's come back tomorrow. We'll talk to them then. They might know where he's gone."

"Don't you have to work tomorrow?"

He grimaced. "Yeah, Sweetwater won't know what hit it. I'll call you. We can meet out here."

"Sure. I also have to go to work, but I can get away for an hour or two."

With that plan in mind, Reid drove them back to his cabin.

"You want to come in?" he offered. It was late, and he wasn't sure what she'd come in for, but part of him didn't want the evening to end.

She hesitated, then shook her head. "Thanks, but I'd better get home. I don't want to leave it too late. Besides, I've got to take this junk off my face before I crack."

"It worked," he admitted, making a point not to stare at her bare midriff.

She laughed. "It usually does. See you tomorrow."

He was looking forward to it.

12

Reid marched into the Sweetwater Police Department at precisely nine a.m. the next morning. A young Latino officer jumped up from his desk. "Er, can I help you?"

"No, thanks." Reid strode into the squad room and looked around. "Is this desk free?" It was piled high with folders presumably waiting to be filed away, boxes of printer paper and several used coffee mugs.

"Yeah, but..."

"Good." He picked everything up and dumped it on Casillas's desk before sitting down.

"Excuse me, sir," ventured the officer. "Who are you?"

"Detective Reid Garrett, Miami PD." He held up his badge. "And you are?" He didn't recall seeing the young officer last time he'd been here.

"Officer William Vargas, sir. But everyone calls me Willie."

"Well, Officer Vargas. Chief Gates has loaned me to your department to assist with the recent homicide at the Gator Inn."

"Police Chief Gates?" He swallowed nervously. "I'm sorry, sir, but we weren't informed."

"I'm informing you now. Feel free to clear it with the Chief." He pulled out his laptop and plugged it in. "I need to see whatever you've got on the Barry Marshall investigation."

The officer stood there, staring at him.

"Now, if you don't mind."

Vargas sprang into action. "Yes, sir."

He hurried towards a large filing cabinet at the back of the room. Within minutes, he'd located the relevant case file and brought it back to Reid. "We usually computerize everything, but as this is a new case, we haven't had time yet."

"Uh-huh." Reid didn't look up.

Willie Vargas hovered for a while, but then the phone rang, and he went back to his desk to answer it. A few more officers strolled in, then murmured in surprise at seeing Reid there. Clearly, Casillas didn't care if they were late to work. Reid glanced at his watch, it was close to a quarter to ten.

"Vargas," Reid called from across the room. The young officer hurried over, straightening his shirt. Out of everyone, he seemed to be the most disciplined. "Yes, sir."

"What time does your lieutenant usually get in?"

"Around ten." Vargas glanced at the door as if he expected to see the bulky figure of Casillas walk in at any moment.

"I see." He glanced around the room. The handful of officers that were there were staring at him with curiosity. He ignored them and sat back down.

There was a murmur as Casillas walked in. The lieutenant halted in his tracks when he saw Reid sitting at one of the desks in his squad room. His face reddened.

"What the hell are you doing here?" He stormed over.

Reid calmly looked up. "I've been tasked with helping you on the Barry Marshall case."

"You can't. You're a suspect. Get out of that chair now and leave the station."

Reid didn't move.

"I said—"

Reid stood up. He was a head taller than the overweight detective. The two men faced off. "I heard what you said." Reid kept his voice steady. "I think you'll find the Chief of Police has other ideas. I suggest you call him if you have a problem with my being here."

There was no mistaking the underlying menace. Out of the corner of his eye he could see the other officers murmuring to each other. Obviously, no one had questioned Casillas's command in a long time.

The lieutenant backed down. "Don't move until I've spoken to him." He moved away to his desk, then scowled as he saw the junk on it. He reached around a pile of folders and picked up the phone.

A tense lull fell over the squad room. Reid was the only one unconcerned.

"Uh, yeah. This is Lieutenant Casillas at the Sweetwater Police Department. I'd just like to clarify that Detective Garrett is..."

"Oh, I see." His face turned purple. "Yes, sir. I understand, sir."

His entire squad watched as he hung up the phone. "Make sure you stay the hell out of my way," Casillas growled. "And will someone clear this shit off my desk and get me a cup of coffee!"

Reid hid a smile and went back to working on his laptop.

The CSI report was in. Barry Marshall had been shot twice in the chest with a small caliber handgun. Neither shot would have been fatal, had he received medical care immediately, but because nobody had found him until almost an hour later, he'd bled out in the motel parking lot.

They'd removed both 9mm bullets, which had gone off to ballistics for further analysis. The gun hadn't been found at the crime scene.

Reid went up to Casillas, who'd managed to clear his desk and was now glaring at his computer screen. "What's the latest on the gun?"

"Huh?"

"The gun used to shoot Mr. Marshall. Did you conduct a search of the motel premises and the nearby vicinity?"

"We searched the motel parking lot," he said, still not looking at Reid. "The shooter got the hell out of there and took the gun with him."

"How do you know that? How do you know he didn't ditch the gun nearby?"

"Why would he do that?"

Was this guy for real? Reid raked a hand through his hair, aware that the other officers were watching.

"I don't know, to get rid of it, maybe? So he wouldn't be seen with it? He'd have gunshot residue on his hands and clothing, possibly even blood spatter. The autopsy report said the victim was shot at close range. There is stippling around the entry wounds. That's messy."

Casillas stood up. A hush fell over the room.

Reid didn't flinch. "I need you to send a team to the motel. Search every gutter, grate, and outhouse on the premises. Look in the dumpsters. Search the victim's motel room, if it's still unoccupied, and bag everything in there. Bring it all back here. Do you understand?"

"You can't give me orders. I'm the lieutenant."

"I can if you're not doing your job properly. Why do you think I'm here?"

That shut him up. He glanced around the room. "Pete, Sergio and Willie, take José and Luis and go back to the crime scene."

"Willie stays," Reid said. "I need him to come with me."

Casillas looked like he was about to complain, then stopped. "Fine."

Reid turned around to face the officers. "You're looking for a handgun, small caliber, probably a Glock or similar. Check every-where, and keep your eyes peeled for anything that looks like it might belong to the victim or the killer. Got it?"

There was a murmur of consent, a couple of 'yes, sirs' and a few 'yeahs.' Reid gritted his teeth. He was going to have to do something about the work ethic here. It stunk. Casillas had cultivated a culture of laziness and ineptitude. The place was rife with it.

"Time is of the essence," he urged. "This is an active homicide. We've already lost our window of opportunity. I want you to move on this."

He saw Vargas nod in agreement as the rest of the officers filed out. At least he had one supporter.

"Willie, I'm going to talk to Reg Arnold's neighbor. They own a gator farm out in the Glades."

"Who's Reg Arnold?" asked Casillas.

"Our prime suspect," Reid snapped.

"Since when?"

"Since last night when I found out who the guy was that got into an altercation with the victim the night before in Smiley's Bar. Any more questions?"

Casillas frowned. "How'd you find him?"

"It's called police work. You should try it sometime."

Reid nodded to Vargas and strode out of the station, leaving the lieutenant mouthing after him.

"How long you been at Sweetwater?" Reid asked Vargas as they drove out to the gator farm. He'd texted Kenzie to meet them there.

"Two years," he replied. "Since I graduated. I must say, it's not what I expected."

"In what way?" He didn't want to come right out and say how inefficient the place was.

"Well, I thought police work would be more interesting. Instead, nobody is very motivated. We sit around all day writing up reports. Not much actual police work gets done."

"That's the lieutenant's fault," Reid replied. "He's not running the place properly. It's not usually like that."

"I thought about transferring," Vargas said. "I put out some feelers, but no one will have me. I've got to get some experience under my belt before I can move." His face fell. Experience was not what he was getting at Sweetwater. Not the right kind, anyway.

"Consider this a crash course." Reid pulled off the dusty road and came to a stop outside the gator farm. A large wooden gate said, *Keep out. Trespassers will be shot.*

"We going in there?" Vargas asked.

"Yeah. We're the police. We can go anywhere."

Vargas gave a shy chuckle. "Yeah, I guess so."

Vargas jumped out to open the gate so Reid could drive through, then he closed it behind them. The driveway was long and curvy, the landscape uneven and lush. The pickup bounced along, kicking up a cloud of dust behind them. It wouldn't be hard to see them coming.

As expected, the owner, a beefy guy in denim dungarees with tattoos up both arms, stood outside holding a shotgun.

Reid got out of his car and held up his badge. "Police, lower your weapon."

The big guy's eyes narrowed. "How do I know you're telling the truth?"

"Because if you don't put your gun down, I'm going to shoot you," Reid replied.

The gator farmer put the shotgun on the ground. Vargas heaved a sigh of relief.

"I'm Detective Garrett and this is Officer Vargas. We're with Miami, I mean Sweetwater PD. We'd like to ask you a few questions."

"What about?"

"About your neighbor, Reg Arnold."

"I ain't seen Reg," he blurted.

"That's not what I asked, sir. I asked if I could ask you some questions about Reg."

"Uh, yeah. I guess."

"Thank you." Just then they heard tires on gravel and another dust cloud swirled up the driveway.

"Jesus, who's that now?" the farmer muttered.

Kenzie parked next to Reid's truck and climbed out. Today she wore skinny jeans and a longish striped shirt with boots. Her legs looked endless.

The gator farmer stared at her unabashedly. "Who are you?"

"Kenzie. I'm with him." She pointed at Reid, who nodded.

"She's my assistant."

Vargas looked surprised.

"Well, you'd all better come inside, then." The gator farmer walked into the house, leaving the door open behind him. They followed him in.

"I'm Kenzie," Kenzie said, introducing herself to Vargas.

"Wille," he replied, shaking her hand.

"Good to meet you, Willie."

They stood in the sparsely furnished living room. Reg's neighbor wasn't big on decor, but the place had a kind of manly comfort to it. A leather sofa and matching armchair stood around a low coffee table. The windows were shut and the air conditioning was on. A couple of flies buzzed around the light fixture, unable to get out.

He gestured for them to sit.

"What's your name, sir?" asked Reid.

"Troy Banner."

"Can I call you Troy?"

The big guy nodded. "Everybody else does."

"Troy, when did you last see your neighbor, Reg?"

"Couple of days ago."

"Could I ask where?"

"We went to Smiley's together."

"Was that the night he got into a fight?"

Troy looked down at his beefy hands. They were enormous, capable of wrestling alligators into submission. "Yeah."

"You were there?" he asked.

"I left before the fight, but I heard about it. I usually go for one or two after work, then I come home. The wife cooks dinner and I gotta be up early, you know."

Reid didn't, but he nodded. "You didn't see the altercation between the two men?"

"No, sir."

Reid sighed. Vargas sat upright beside him, hanging on every word.

"Do you know Reg well, Mr. Banner?" Kenzie asked. She was going for the polite approach.

"I guess."

"I mean, are you friends?"

"Yeah, you could say that."

"So you know him quite well." It was a statement rather than a question. "I wonder." She paused to nibble on her lower lip. Reid saw Troy's gaze drop to her mouth. "Is there anywhere he might go if he wanted to lay low for a while?"

"Um, I don't know." He seemed to be fumbling, nervous even.

Kenzie smiled at him. "I think Reg is scared," she said, almost as if she were confiding in him. "The man he had a fight with ends up dead. Obviously, the police are going to come looking for him, so he panics. He runs. The thing is, Mr. Banner. We know he's innocent."

Troy's eyebrows shot up.

"You do?"

Vargas frowned, but Reid glanced at him and shook his head.

"Yes, we just want to ask him if he saw anything. He could help us with our investigation. The more he runs, the longer this will drag on."

Troy contemplated this for some time. "How'd you know he's innocent?" he eventually asked.

"Good question." Reid took over. "We have evidence that this was a professional hit. We know Reg isn't a contract killer, is he?"

"Hell no. He shoots gators, that's about it."

"Exactly. That's how we know."

Kenzie picked it up again. "If you have any idea where we can find him, Mr. Banner, it would be really helpful. You'd be helping your friend, too."

Troy shifted uncomfortably, then cleared his throat. "He has a place down in the Keys. He could've gone there."

13

KENZIE HUNG her arm out of the window. The aquamarine ocean stretched away on both sides of the highway. The breeze was warm, and the clouds were faint brush strokes across the sky. She'd left her car at Reid's house, content to let him drive the 165 miles to Key West where Reg Arnold supposedly had a fishing cabin.

"According to the real estate agent," she said. "He bought the lot back in 2009 for next to nothing. She thought he'd put a manufactured home on it, but she couldn't be sure. She said the plot is big enough to build a comfortable four- or five-bedroom house, with a garden and space for a boat."

"Impressive." Reid kept his eyes on the road. It appeared endless, shimmering into the distance as far as the eye could see.

"Do you really think Reg Arnold killed Barry Marshall so he couldn't testify?"

It had been bugging her. Reg seemed like a simple guy, a man who made his living from the swamp. His house had been basic, nothing special. He hung out at Smiley's Bar, he wasn't married, but had a thing for a local hooker. "He doesn't strike me as the type to kill anyone."

"Money's a powerful motivator," Reid said.

"But Reg got into a fight with his mark the day before he was supposed to kill him." She shook her head. "How dumb is that?"

"Maybe it wasn't a fight," Reid said. "Maybe he was trying to kill him, but it failed."

"With a bottle?"

Reid snorted. "Yeah, I know, but it's the best I've got. Granted, it's a long shot, but he was mad when he left the bar. Trust me, I was there. I saw the look he gave Marshall. It didn't look like a fight over a girl."

Kenzie was silent for a moment. If it wasn't about the girl, why'd he hit him? Perhaps Reid was right. There could be something else going on here. They needed to dig deeper and find out what beef Reg had with Barry Marshall.

"I did some research on the victim," she said. "Or rather I tried. There isn't much out there on him."

"No?"

"He's not on social media. I couldn't find any reference to him online other than an article describing how he was arrested for aggravated assault in 2011. He did five years, but only because the guy he hit had an epileptic seizure and had to be hospitalized.

"That's tough."

"Yeah, apart from that, he's clean."

"Except for his ties to Don Ingleman, right?"

Kenzie enjoyed the warm air lifting her hair off her neck. Reid wasn't driving too fast on account of the traffic, so she was able to keep the window open. The radio played in the background, but it was low enough so they could still talk. It helped break the silence between conversations. The trip to Key West would take them roughly three and a half hours.

"Barry Marshall borrowed twenty grand from Ingleman to pay off a gambling debt, or that's what the court records said. When the interest payments got too steep, he defaulted and according to his statement, was threatened by Ingleman."

"Ingleman himself?"

"No, a henchman. A guy called Andrei Malkovich.

Reid raised an eyebrow. "Never heard of him."

"Serbian enforcer, apparently. He's Ingleman's Operations Manager, whatever that means."

"That's why he went to the cops? He got threatened?" Reid sounded surprised. To be fair, most ex-cons would run a mile rather than talk to the cops.

"It surprised me too," she said. "But when I looked into it, I discovered Marshall had worked as a snitch while he was in prison."

"He ratted out someone on the inside?"

"His cellmate. A guy called Alonzo Capó. Apparently Capó was some sort of drug kingpin and was orchestrating deals from the inside. They wanted to shut down his organization, so they had Marshall join his crew and report back on him."

"How do we know this Capó didn't have him shot?" Reid asked.

"We don't." Kenzie pursed her lips. "But Capó is still in prison, and it's been three years since Marshall was released. Why would he bother now after all this time? If he was going to take him out, he would have done it as soon as he found out he was an informant. In other words, right after he was released."

Reid grunted. "Unless he only found out now."

Kenzie thought about this. "I'll look into it."

"No, let me put Vargas onto it. He's desperate to learn. It will be easier for him to track down Marshall's handler."

"Okay."

Reid made the call putting the phone on speaker.

"Yes, sir. I understand," Vargas said. Kenzie could hear the enthusiasm in his voice.

"He's keen."

"Very. He'll make a good cop if Casillas doesn't ruin it for him."

They drove on for another couple of hours. Kenzie told Reid about Don Ingleman and what she'd been able to dig up on him.

"He stays just inside the law," she explained. "And to make sure of it, he's hired a whole team of lawyers from one of Miami's largest law firm."

"Except for the Barry Marshall investigation," said Reid.

"Yeah, that's the first witness the Feds have found where he's exceeded the legal interest limit. They know there's more, but they've never been able to prove it."

"They won't now," Reid mused. "Not since their star witness turned up dead. It's going to frighten off any other possible whistle-blowers."

He was right. This had been the prosecution's one chance to nail Ingleman, and they'd blown it.

"They should have taken better care of him," she said. "That motel is hardly a safe house. And what about bodyguards? Why didn't they have people watching him?"

"Yeah, that is strange. Perhaps they thought the Glades was far enough out of the way to be safe."

Kenzie grunted. "Maybe."

They kept going, the sun reflecting off the azure surface far below. "I've never driven down here before," she remarked. Crazy since she'd lived in Florida all her life.

"I've done it a few times," he said. "But not recently."

She wondered who he'd come down here with. It was such a romantic spot, the Keys. Was it a girlfriend? Someone special? Bianca, maybe?

None of her business.

Eventually, they got to Key West, and the endless highway ended. A large lagoon opened up on their left, while a neat row of townhouses poked their heads above a line of trees on the right.

"What was the name of the street?" Reid asked.

"Roosevelt Drive." She glanced at her phone. "It's in the middle of the island."

Reid headed in a westerly direction.

"Turn left here," instructed Kenzie, who was directing him via Google maps.

He turned into a wide avenue with coconut palms lining both sides of the street. The houses here were on big plots of land, set back from the road.

"Very nice," commented Reid.

It was a bushy neighborhood, with lots of vegetation separating the properties.

"That's it." Kenzie pointed to a broad expanse of lawn. "The house before was number 24, so this must be 26."

Reid pulled over and cut the engine. They surveyed the plot. It was large, easily the size of a football field, with a small, rectangular manufactured home on the top section furthest from the road. It had been positioned behind a grove of trees and only the roof was visible.

"It's not what I expected," she admitted.

"Fishing shack," said Reid. "That's what his neighbor said. This looks like a fishing shack to me."

There were trailer marks on the lawn where a boat had been parked. Kenzie stared down at them. "I think he's gone fishing."

Reid walked up and down the lawn, stretching his legs. "We'll just have to wait, then."

Kenzie's stomach rumbled.

"I'm starving," she said. "He could be gone for hours. Are we going to wait here the whole time?"

Reid grinned. "I spotted a parade of shops as we drove into the area. We could always go back there and pick up some snacks and a coffee."

"That sounds great."

Half an hour later they were back, armed with burgers, chips, and soft drinks. "Now this feels like a stake-out," she mumbled.

He laughed. "You watch too many cop movies."

"You're probably right. I wanted to be one, remember."

"Yeah, I know. I'm sorry that didn't work out for you." He knew about her accident.

She smirked. "Isn't it funny? You're a cop and don't want to be one, while I desperately want to, but can't."

"I guess it is kind of ironic, although to be fair, I said I didn't want to go back to the Miami PD, not that I didn't want to be a cop."

"Oh, so you do still want to be in law enforcement?"

She was teasing him, but she could tell by the twinkle in his eye that he didn't mind. "I don't know what I'd do if I wasn't catching bad guys."

"You could always be a reporter, like me."

He shook his head. "God, no. I can barely string a sentence together, and I've got none of your communication skills. I'm not good at manipulating people."

"You think I am?"

He studied her, his gaze warm. "You know you are. I've never met anyone who can change their personality as quickly as you. One moment you're the intrepid journalist, the next a celebrity groupie or a hard-drinking, dart-playing woman in a swamp bar."

She laughed. "Okay, you got me there."

They'd just finished their burgers when a maroon pickup truck rolled in pulling a metal trailer carrying a dripping fishing boat. It ramped the sidewalk and parked on the grass in front of the shack. A man got out wearing shorts and a Hawaiian shirt. He was well built, like most swampers were, although his belly was fat.

"That's him," Reid murmured, opening the door. He got out of the truck and approached the man. "Mr. Arnold?"

The man didn't turn around.

Kenzie frowned, coming up behind Reid.

"Mr. Arnold, we'd like to speak with you about Barry Marshall," Reid said. "I'm with the Sweetwater Police Department."

Reg turned around. "Stay where you are! Don't come any closer or I'll shoot."

Kenzie gasped. Reg was holding a gun and pointing it directly at them.

14

Reid heard Kenzie gasp and took a step in front of her. "Put the gun down, Mr. Arnold, we're only here to talk."

"I didn't kill him," he said. "I don't know what you heard, but I didn't do it."

"I know," Reid said. Drastic action was called for and even though he'd told Kenzie he was a bad communicator, he now had to prove himself wrong.

Reg hesitated. Reid saw fear in his eyes, real fear. "Who are you? Cops?"

"Sweetwater PD," Reid said. "But I'm not here to arrest you."

Not yet.

"You're not?"

"No, why don't we go inside and talk?"

"I don't think so." Reg kept the gun pointed at them. It wasn't steady, though. The man was shaking like a leaf. Given half a chance, Reid figured he could probably take him before he pulled the trigger. This man didn't want to shoot anyone, but he also didn't want to go to jail.

"Okay, let me tell you what I know." Reid kept his hands where

Reg could see them. "I was at Smiley's the night you and the victim had a fight. I pulled you off him, remember?"

Reg's brow furrowed. "Oh, yeah."

"Anyway, the next night that same guy turns up dead."

"I had nothing to do—"

"I know that." Reid interrupted. "But you can see how it looks."

There was a pause as Reg pondered this.

"Why don't you tell me where you were the night that guy was shot, and I can take you off my list of suspects. All I need is your alibi."

"That's the problem." Reg's voice was tight with tension. "I don't have an alibi. I was at home, by myself."

Shit.

"You didn't see anyone?" Reid persisted. "Not a girlfriend, not your neighbor?"

Reg shook his head. "You see? That's why I ran. That's why I came out here. Who's going to believe me?"

"I believe you," Reid reiterated, seeing the gun drop a little more. "I know you didn't shoot the victim with your gun." He looked pointedly at the weapon in Reg's hand.

Reg did too. "That's right. This is the gun I use to shoot gators or hogs in the swamp if I come across 'em. I gotta have it for protection."

"That's a way you can prove your innocence," Reid said. "If you let us test your gun, the bullets won't match those in the body."

He wavered. "You think?"

"Well, if you didn't do it, the bullets won't match."

"That's right." His shoulders sank in relief.

"Do you think you can put the gun down now?" asked Reid. "I'd hate for it to go off by accident."

"Oh, sure." Reg stuck the gun back in his pants.

Kenzie heaved a sigh of relief.

"Thank you." Reid stayed where he was. He didn't want to spook the guy, not after he'd gotten this far. "What are we going to do, Reg?"

"What do you mean?"

"Well, you need to come back to the police department and tell your side of the story. If you don't, people will think you're guilty."

He frowned. "I ain't going to no police station."

"Why not?" Kenzie stepped out from behind Reid. "You're innocent, right?"

"Yeah."

"Then you've got nothing to worry about. If you don't go in, you'll have to worry."

"They'll come after you, Reg. They'll bring you in handcuffed like a criminal. Either way, you have to come in. Don't make it the hard way."

Reg ran a hand through his hair. It was an impossible situation. Reid almost felt sorry for him, but he'd been in the same position.

"You know the same thing happened to me, right?" He tried a different tack.

Reg surveyed him. "They came after you?"

"Yep. Sure did. I was at the crime scene. I said I'd met the victim, and they searched my house and found the shirt I was wearing the night of the bar fight. It had his blood all over it."

"Shit." The swamper gazed at him with newfound respect. No, not respect. Something.

"I had to go into the police station and give my side of the story. That's how the system works. They arrested me, I got stuck in a cell for a night, and then when I told the lieutenant my story, I was released."

Okay, that wasn't exactly how it went down, but close enough.

"You were cleared?"

"I'm here, aren't I?

Reg sighed. "Okay, I guess I have no choice."

"That's the way," said Reid. "Also, they're more likely to go easy on you if you come in voluntarily."

"You promise I'll get out?"

"Once they've cleared you, they'll have to let you go." He hoped he wasn't going to eat his words.

Kenzie smiled in agreement. "They're after the guy who did it, not you. Once they rule you out, or rather your gun out, you'll be free to go home."

"Okay, then." He took the gun out and tossed it onto the grass. Reid pulled a glove out of his pocket and put it on. Then he picked up the weapon.

"You're doing the smart thing, Reg. I'm going to drive you there myself, okay? I'll be with you every step of the way."

"It's a relief," Reg said, once they were back in the truck and heading toward the highway. "I was really scared. I knew I couldn't stay here forever. I knew someone would track me down."

"Running is never the answer," Reid said. "Not if you're innocent."

He only hoped the gun would prove it.

15

KENZIE WAS in the office before the sun came up. She buzzed herself in and meandered down the rows of empty desks towards her own. God, she needed a coffee.

They'd got back to the police station late last night, and an officer had given her a lift to Reid's house so she could pick up her car. He'd had to stay and process an anxious Reg Arnold.

She paused briefly beside Clayton's desk. It was clear. He'd taken his laptop home with him. No telling Post-it Notes, no revealing names on a scratch pad. He was being careful.

He would have found out by now that the key witness had been gunned down and would be looking to prove it was related to the trial. In other words, a hit put out by Don Ingleman.

But how? What angle was he working?

He couldn't know about the suspect, Reg Arnold. She had the edge on that one—even if it turned out to be a red-herring. It was still newsworthy.

Kenzie sat down and opened her laptop. She wanted to get this article typed up for tomorrow's edition. Keith was expecting it. He knew she'd been following up a lead yesterday, which was why she hadn't been in.

The story was percolating in her mind, the words falling into place. By the time she'd made herself a coffee and returned to her desk, she had the first paragraph figured out. It would cover the background on the murdered witness, Barry Marshall, the altercation at Smiley's, the hunt for the man he'd fought with and the subsequent arrest.

She did feel a twinge of regret for tarnishing Reg Arnold's reputation. She didn't for a moment think he'd done it. He was running scared, but he wasn't a killer. Still, he lived in the swamp, he hunted pythons and gators for a living. He wouldn't be affected by one little article, particularly when she cleared him in the follow-up.

Besides, she was just reporting what had happened. That was her job.

She'd just started typing when Clayton walked in. He sat in front of her in a huddle of four desks with the news blogger, a junior reporter, and a guy named Larry who did the horoscopes.

"You're in early." He frowned as he pulled out his chair.

"Wanted to get an early start."

He took off his backpack and sat down. Kenzie glanced up, but she couldn't see his screen from where she sat, just like he couldn't see hers. She gritted her teeth and got back to work. He was not going to beat her to the finish line.

Keith got in shortly after eight. He glanced at them both, then went to his office without a word. She wondered if he realized the chaos he'd created when he'd pitted them against each other.

Kenzie had the article done by midday. She put it on Keith's desk.

"Thanks, Kenzie. What am I reading?"

She sat down opposite him. "The witness at the Ingleman trial, Barry Marshall, was gunned down outside a motel room in the Everglades the day before he was supposed to testify."

"Ingleman?" Keith asked. He didn't sound surprised, which meant Clayton had already briefed him on that much.

"Most likely."

"Got any proof?"

"Better. I've got a suspect."

He smiled at her. "I thought as much. Who is it?"

"A swamper was seen having an altercation with the victim the night before the shooting. He hit him over the head with a beer bottle."

"Hit him over the head?" Keith frowned, his newsman's instinct telling him something didn't feel right. "Are you sure this is the shooter?"

"No. Actually, it's unlikely this guy is the killer, but the police have him in custody. Do you want the story or not?"

"Yeah. If they've got him in custody, we can write about it. Do we know if they've charged him?"

"I'll find out," she said, "but it won't be before the deadline."

She knew Reid would have kept Reg in a cell overnight and interviewed him this morning. It was standard procedure when an arrest was made late at night. Suspects required some downtime to rest before interrogation, and Reid would have needed to regroup. He'd driven over 300 miles yesterday.

"Okay, we'll run with what you've got."

She got to her feet. "Oh, what's Clayton working on?"

"Same as you, the Ingleman trial."

"Isn't there anything else going on?" she asked. "It doesn't make sense having us both on the same story."

"We're covering this from multiple angles," he said. "Clayton's working on Ingleman, you're going after the witness."

Crap, she knew it.

"Okay, so who's getting the front page?"

"Clayton this time. His story is bigger news. Ingleman's been linked to various other loan-sharking deals."

Kenzie's heart plummeted. "Does he have proof?"

"He's working on it. Ingleman's a multi-millionaire. He owns a soccer team. People know who he is. Nobody knows your witness.

Sorry, Kenzie, I'm putting you on page three as a follow-up to the trial."

Shit. Shit. Shit.

Page three wasn't going to get her the senior news reporter position. She had to find out more, dig deeper.

Deflated, she went back to her desk. How was she going to do that? She needed an in, someone on Ingleman's team she could tap for information. Reg Arnold didn't kill the witness. She knew it and Reid knew it. He had to follow all lines of enquiry, he was a detective, but she didn't.

The only way she was going to find out who shot Barry Marshall was by going straight to the source. She was just figuring out how to do that when her phone rang.

Vic Reynolds.

She answered it, keeping her voice deliberately low so that Clayton would think she was onto something. It was petty, she knew, but it irked her that he was getting the front page and she wasn't.

"Hi, Vic. How are you?" She listened for a moment. "Yes, sure. That would be great. When?"

She waited for his answer. "Okay, I'll meet you there."

She hung up. In her peripheral vision, she saw Clayton staring at her. He'd think she had a lead. If only it was true.

She finished up what she was doing, then told Keith she was leaving early. "I'm going to meet a source."

He gave her a distracted wave.

Vic was waiting for her at an Italian restaurant close to where she lived. It was one of her favorites. The seafood linguini was to die for. Tonight, though, she had no appetite. All she could think about was her job.

I've got to let one of you go. I'd hate for it to be you.

She couldn't lose this. The *Herald* was one of the top newspapers in Miami. She didn't want to go to *The Post* or worse, one of the local presses. It was bad enough she'd had to lose her first job before it had even begun, she didn't want to lose this one too.

"Kenzie, you're miles away. Is anything wrong?"

"Sorry, Vic. Work's just getting to me."

"I asked how your investigation into your mother's disappearance was going."

Oh, God, she'd forgotten all about that. Bethany. She had to find out where Bethany was. But it would have to wait.

"It's been put on hold." Guilt gripped her, making her feel slightly ill. Her mother would understand. The case had been untouched for twenty years, a few more months wouldn't hurt.

"I'm sorry to hear that. What happened?"

"It's this story I'm covering at work. It's pretty intense, and I don't have time to concentrate on both."

"Well, it's probably for the best." He reached across the table and took her hand. "I know how much your mother's case means to you, but I don't want you to be disappointed."

"I know." She withdrew her hand. "I have realistic expectations. Anyway, you don't have to worry, like I said, it's been shelved for now."

"And Garrett?"

"He's working with Sweetwater PD on a case." She didn't go into detail.

"Yes, I heard about that. The motel shooting, right?"

Kenzie raised her eyebrows. "Yes, that's right." Then she remembered he'd had some concerns about Reid taking the role. "He's doing a great job at Sweetwater."

"Is he? I've had a Lieutenant Casillas on the phone complaining about him."

"He's just jealous because Reid took over as lead detective on the case."

Vic signaled to the waiter. "A bottle of red, please."

"Yes, sir."

Kenzie didn't bother to point out he'd forgotten to ask her if she was happy with red.

"I believe he was arrested for the shooting?" Vic picked up the conversation.

"That was a misunderstanding. Reid knew the victim and Lieutenant Casillas brought Reid in before he could explain himself."

Then kept him overnight, refusing to hear his statement.

Vic gave a tight nod. It was clear he didn't think Reid should be in charge either.

"Have you heard anything about Ingleman organizing the hit?" she asked him.

He gave a wolfish grin. "You know I can't talk about it, Kenzie."

"I know." She'd been hoping he'd be able to give her a lead. That was the only reason she'd agreed to come tonight. Unfortunately with Ortega, her previous source, suspended, she had no one to sneak her information. Ortega had looked up arrest warrants for her, given her DNA results. But then, they'd been friends, once upon a time.

"You're working this case too?" Vic said.

"For the paper, yeah. I'm looking into a possible Ingleman connection."

"I see."

"I was at the courthouse when the prosecution found out their key witness had been murdered."

"I heard." The waiter brought the wine, and they paused while he poured. "Judge Heseltine is a friend of mine. He filled me in on what happened. Terrible business."

"Not for Ingleman," Kenzie said. "The case was dismissed."

Vic shrugged. "That's the way it goes, unfortunately."

"It doesn't seem right." Kenzie felt herself getting worked up. "Why wasn't the witness given better protection?"

"That wasn't my decision," he told her, taking a sip. "The Feds oversaw him. We had nothing to do with it. We didn't even know who the witness was."

Until he'd been shot.

She studied her father's old friend and partner. He'd aged well. He'd always been a big guy, but he'd kept a decent physique, his face was tanned, and he sat upright, sporting an air of confidence. A man who knew his worth. "What do you think of Ingleman?"

Vic thought for a moment. "He's a wealthy man. Successful. Worked his way up from nothing. You have to admire that."

"Do you know him?"

"We've met once or twice, but I don't know him personally."

"What's he like?"

Vic looked at her. "Kenzie, I don't want to see my name in a news article."

"This is off the record. I promise."

He took a sip of his wine. She hadn't touched hers. "He's an affable guy. A bit rough around the edges, but he's got a certain charm. He knows how to get what he wants."

"Is he dangerous?"

"I don't know him well enough to say." Vic picked up the menu. "But I'd watch my step around him, Kenzie. I'd hate to see anything happen to you."

If that wasn't a warning, she didn't know what was.

Unfortunately, it wasn't going to stop her from trying to infiltrate Ingleman's circle.

16

REID SAT ON HIS DECK, a half-drunk beer beside him, and stared out over the dark water. It had been a hell of a day. Reg Arnold had been accommodating, until Reid had told him he had to spend the rest of the day in lockup.

"I shouldn't have trusted you," he'd bellowed from his cell. "You lied to me. You said if I told the truth I'd be released."

He hadn't charged him, there wasn't enough evidence. Even though Reg didn't have an alibi for the night of the shooting, he didn't have the gun either. The weapon Reg had been holding wasn't the same one that had fired the shots that had killed Barry Marshall. None of his clothes had gunshot residue on them, neither did his hands. That stuff took a few days to come off.

The only problem was Reid didn't have any other suspects.

Casillas insisted they charge him. Reid said no. In the end, the decision was to hold Reg for the maximum time before they let him go—forty-eight hours—to see if anything else came up.

The air had cleared after the downpour the other day and the humidity hadn't kicked in yet. The water was still and glassy and inky black. Every now and then he heard a rustle of grass or a muted splash. The creatures of the night were on the move.

He thought about Barry Marshall's shooter. He was still out there, walking free. With the heat on poor Reg, the killer must be thanking his lucky stars. He couldn't have found a better scapegoat if he'd planned it.

Reid's thoughts turned to Kenzie. He'd left her quite abruptly when they'd got back to the station. He'd arranged for one of the uniformed officers to give her a lift back to her car, but it had been fairly late. He'd meant to call her today, but he'd been so busy, he hadn't had time.

He glanced at the time. Ten-fifteen. She might still be up.

He was about to call her when his phone buzzed. It was a with-held number. That meant it was work related. For some reason government organizations always hid their numbers. It made them so easy to read.

"Detective Garrett."

"Sir, this is Nancy from the forensic lab. We're handling the ballistics on your shooter."

He sat up straight. "Have you got something?"

"We have sir, that's why I'm calling you at home."

"Go ahead." He held his breath.

"We have matched the bullets to a gun," she told him, the words music to his ears. "The only problem is we don't know which gun."

"I don't understand."

She cleared her throat. "What I'm trying to say, detective, is that we've matched the bullets to a gun that was used in another homicide. The bullets are identical to those we pulled out of a victim two years ago."

His pulse leaped. "You're sure?"

"One hundred percent, sir. The bullets are an exact match."

"But you don't have the gun?"

"No, the gun was never found."

There was a pause as Reid let this sink in. "Where was this other homicide?" he asked.

"Here, in Miami. The victim was a twenty-seven-year-old woman. Gina Downing. She was shot during an attempted burglary. That's all I know."

"Do you have a reference number?" He could look up the police report. It would be in the system.

"Yes, sir." She read it out and he wrote it down.

"We could be looking at the same killer," he thought out loud.

"Could be," Nancy replied. "But it's more likely the gun was sold or passed on to someone else who used it in your shooting. The new owner probably wasn't aware of the gun's history. If he was, he would never have used it."

She had a point. Guns were too easy to trace back.

"I need to find the previous owner," he murmured. "Did they catch the burglar?"

"I'm sorry, I don't know. You'll have to check the police report."

That he could do, first thing tomorrow.

Reid downed the rest of his beer. This was great news. Finally, he had a lead.

Gina Downing had arrived home to find a burglar in her house. That was the theory, anyway. She'd surprised him, he'd shot her, and run away. Nothing had been taken.

The lock on the front door had been forced. Gina had probably walked in behind her killer, confused as to why the door was open. She hadn't used her key to get in. They'd found it on the floor near her body.

She'd collapsed in the middle of the living room where she bled to death. The bullet had hit her in the neck, severing her carotid artery. The medical examiner's report stated she would have bled out in less than a minute.

He cringed. It was a terrible thing to have happened. Gina looked like a happy and healthy young woman. She was blonde, slim, and athletic, a bit like Kenzie, actually. The photos on file showed her in gym wear with her hair up in a ponytail, the way Kenzie liked to wear hers.

Neither the perpetrator, nor the gun were ever found.

Shit.

He'd been hoping for a conviction, then he'd have been able to interview the perp in prison and ask him about the gun.

Still, all was not lost. He could have a chat with the detective in charge of the case and get his take on it. Sometimes they had their suspicions, but without proof, the perpetrator couldn't be brought to justice.

The jurisdiction was Miami PD. That made things easier. It would have been just after he'd left the department. He scanned the report to see who the detective in charge had been.

His heart sank.

Ortega.

17

Kenzie checked her reflection in the restroom mirror.

"Who are you today?" she whispered.

The woman who stared back at her was confident, efficient, and bubbly. She had a wide smile, sparkling eyes and just the right amount of make-up to make her features stand out. She wore running shoes, jeans and a tight, pink T-shirt, her hair up in its usual ponytail.

Being a waitress wasn't a difficult job, but it was tiring. She'd be on her feet for eight hours per shift, and would have to deal with demanding customers, which would require a great deal of patience —not necessarily her strongest trait.

She'd waited tables in high school and had quite enjoyed it back then. Now she was doing it to befriend Simone Gerlach, Don Ingleman's girlfriend.

Ingleman had been seen with several high-profile women in recent years but was currently "slumming it"—their entertainment correspondent's words, not hers—with a waitress from Indigo's, a contemporary Asian restaurant in the upscale neighborhood of Wynwood.

Luckily, she'd been able to secure an interview. They were hiring.

"You're overqualified for the job, Kaylee." The manager, a tall, stylish woman named Marg, told her. "Why do you want to work here?"

When using an alias, Kenzie tried to stick as close to the truth as possible. The lies came easier that way.

"I've been let go," she confided, letting her shoulders slump. "Budget cuts. I've decided to freelance from now on, so I'm looking for a way to supplement my income."

It might very well be true next month.

"How do I know you won't leave us in a couple of weeks once you find another job?"

"Oh, I'm not interested in working for anyone else." A calm, practiced smile. "I want to work for myself."

"Hmm." Marg scanned the rest of her resume, then looked up. "Okay, Kaylee. We'll give you a trial run. Can you start tonight?"

"Yes, of course. Thank you so much."

She was in.

"Good. Be here at five to run through a few things. Your shift starts at six."

"Okay." She beamed and pumped the woman's hand. "Thank you again."

Simone was a stunning brunette with oval-shaped eyes, a smooth, olive complexion and a figure worthy of a catwalk model. She could see why Ingleman was attracted to her.

"Excuse me, could you show me how to work the register?" An embarrassed smile, wide eyes, eager to please.

Simone tossed her silky hair over her shoulder. "Sure, you're new here, aren't you?"

"Yes, I'm Kaylee."

"Simone."

They smiled at each other.

"How long have you been here?" Kenzie asked.

"Almost a year. It's a fun place to work. Tips are good, so is the food." She shot her a cheeky grin. "I recommend the seared tuna salad."

"I'll remember that."

Simone demonstrated how to put an order through the register, and then how to total up at the end of the meal.

"Got it." Kenzie grinned. "Thanks."

"You're welcome. Good luck and let me know if you need anything. It can get chaotic here."

"I will."

Simone wasn't kidding. After seven-thirty, the restaurant got really busy. They were fully booked most nights, and tonight was no exception. The hostess was running a waiting list with walk-ins having drinks at the bar.

At nine o'clock, a group of men walked in. Kenzie saw from Marg's body language that they were important. She craned her head to look, while balancing two dishes on each arm.

It was Ingleman. He was here.

Marg beckoned to Simone who smiled and welcomed her beau and his three friends. There was no attempt to hide their relationship. He kissed her on both cheeks, then she led them to a table—their best table. He must have come to see his girlfriend in action.

There were a few murmurs from other diners as people recognized him. He'd been in the media a lot lately, thanks to his arrest and subsequent trial. The dismissal had also been front page news. Another tick for bloody Clayton who'd covered it while she was away working on her mother's case.

Simone took care of Ingleman, but Kenzie didn't miss the discreet hand on her back, or up her leg when she bent over to collect the plates. It was amazing she kept her cool.

Vic had been right. The multi-millionaire financier was suave and charming. He flattered Marg who flushed when she went to check on their meal. He entertained his guests, who listened with rapt attention and laughed in the appropriate places. And he sent

Simone appreciative glances and made no secret that he adored her.

Kenzie didn't get a chance to talk to Simone again. All the wait staff were swamped until last orders at eleven. By then Kenzie was ready to drop. Perspiration dripped between her breasts and her feet ached. When she finally got a break, she collapsed against the wall outside with a little groan.

"It gets easier," Simone said, joining her. She looked annoyingly fresh, no smudged eyeliner or hair out of place. Ingleman had just left in his flashy Lamborghini, and she was done for the night.

To Kenzie's surprise, she lit up a cigarette. "Want one?"

"Sure." She didn't smoke but wanted to bond with the leggy waitress and this seemed like a good opportunity. Kenzie took a cigarette from the proffered box and put it to her lips. Simone took out her lighter and lit it for her.

"Thanks." Kenzie inhaled. "I don't know how you do this every night."

"You get used to it." She took a drag of her own cigarette, then tilted her head back and exhaled, sending a spiral upwards into the night sky. "I only work four nights a week. I'm a model, so I need my days free."

That was understandable.

"I'm a reporter," Kenzie told her. "Or rather, I was."

God, she hoped she'd never have to say those words.

I'm a police officer, or rather, I was going to be, before a car accident ended it all.

"Sorry. It's tough out there."

"Yep, it sure is."

Kenzie drew on the cigarette, trying not to cough. It made her throat itch. "Who was that man that came in? I recognized him but couldn't place him."

"Don Ingleman. You probably recognized him because he's been in the papers recently."

"Oh, that's right." Kenzie frowned. "Wasn't he arrested on some bogus charge?"

"That's right." Simone warmed to her. "It was dismissed. He was innocent."

"I'm so glad," she said. "Do you know him? Sorry for prying, but you looked like friends."

She laughed, a deep throaty sound. "You could say that. We've been seeing each other for a while now." Was that pride in her voice?

"How exciting," Kenzie gushed. "He's very suave, isn't he?"

"Yeah, that's what I like about him," Simone said. "And he treats me like a princess."

Kenzie smiled enviously. "What more could a girl want?"

Simone finished her cigarette. "We'd better get back."

"Yeah."

Kenzie crushed her cigarette underfoot and followed the model inside. That had gone better than expected. They weren't bosom buddies yet, but it was a start. She was one step closer to Ingleman.

18

Reid stood outside the house on Virginia Street, where Gina Downing had been murdered. It was a neat two-story painted a pale blue with darker blue shutters. There was no garage, but a space outside for two cars, and an automatic gate that was open. The gate must be a new addition. He didn't recall seeing it in the crime scene photographs.

He rang the doorbell. At first, nobody answered, and he was about to leave when someone pulled back the latch. The door opened a crack and an elderly voice asked, "Who's there?"

"Detective Garrett from Sweetwater PD, ma'am. I'm looking for Mr. Downing."

The crack widened. "Oh, I'm sorry, detective, Mr. Downing doesn't live here anymore. He moved out two years ago."

"I see."

Damn.

"Is this about his wife?"

"Er, yes. Did you know her?"

"Lovely girl. I knew the family, you see. I was friends with her parents. Sadly, they've both passed now. Probably a good thing, considering what happened."

He gave a sage nod. "Mrs.?"

"Mrs. Peters. Do you want to come in?"

"Please, if you don't mind."

She opened the door to give him access. He hadn't shown his badge or warrant card, and she hadn't questioned his identity. Mrs. Peters was a trusting person.

"Can I get you anything? Coffee? Tea?"

"I'd love a cup of coffee, if you've got it." He wasn't in a rush, and he wanted time to analyze the living room where Gina had been shot.

"Okay. Take a seat. I'll be right back."

He surveyed the room. It was roughly twenty by twenty wide with windows on two sides. One overlooking the street, the other the side alley leading to the backyard. The carpet was different, but it would have been replaced after the murder.

"Tell me about Gina," he said, when she got back with the coffee. It was freshly brewed, smelled good too. The rich aroma wafted across to him.

She gave a sad shake of her head. "Gina was a delightful girl. Always happy. Kind too. She used to check in on me every week. We'd talk about her parents." She put the coffee tray down. "They died when she was a teenager, and she liked to ask about them."

"I'm sorry to hear that," he said, taking a sip.

"Car accident on their way to the Florida Keys for a vacation. It was such a tragedy. Gina was sixteen at the time."

That was the highway they'd taken to Key West to find Reg Arnold. "What happened to her?"

"She moved in with Matthew's parents. They were already dating back then."

"Matthew being her husband?" he inquired.

"Yes, poor boy. They got married straight out of high school. They were very young, but she needed him, I think, and he was smitten with her. He was devastated when she died."

"I'm sure. Didn't they look at him for the shooting?"

She scoffed. "Briefly, but he was cleared—and rightly so. Matthew would never harm a hair on that girl's head. He adored her."

Reid looked at the place where Gina had fallen. He could see the crime scene photo in his mind. She'd been facing the door, then fallen backwards as the bullet hit her in the neck. The report said the shooter had most likely been trying to escape when he'd fired the fatal shot.

"I had the carpets replaced." Mrs. Peters' gaze lingered on the imaginary spot.

He nodded. "Did Matthew sell you the house?"

"He did. He gave me a special deal too. He was very kind. I think he just wanted to get out."

"I can understand that. Excuse me for asking, but didn't you mind that there'd been a murder here?"

She contemplated this, then shook her head. "My own Ted passed away shortly before Gina, and I couldn't afford the mortgage on our house. We'd over extended. When Matthew offered me this one, I didn't feel like I could refuse. Also, I was very fond of Gina. Knowing she died here, well it makes me feel closer to her, if that makes any sense."

It did, in a weird way.

"Well, I'm glad it worked out for you." He hesitated. "Do you know where Matthew is now?"

"I believe he lives on Hialeah Drive. I don't know the number or anything. He had to downscale since he lost his job."

"He lost his job? Was that because of what happened?"

"I think so, but I'm not sure. He may have quit. Like I said, he was devastated when Gina died."

"What did he do for a living?"

"He worked in IT. That's information technology," she told him with a sharp nod.

He couldn't help but smile. "Thank you."

"He worked with computers. He was very good at it too. He fixed my ancient laptop several times."

"Do you know the name of the company?" It might make it easier to locate him.

"Some big firm downtown." She wrung her hands. "I'm sorry, I can't remember the name."

Another dead end.

"Last question, Mrs. Peters. You don't happen to know what he does for a living now, do you?"

"No, detective, I don't. It's been a while since I've seen him."

Reid finished the rest of his coffee. It was too good to waste. Then he got to his feet. "Thank you for talking to me, Mrs. Peters, and thanks for the coffee."

"Will you tell Matthew to call me if you see him?" She got up to show him to the door. "I have a box of his things here. I found them in the spare room after he left."

Reid followed her into an unused bedroom. It was mostly a storage area filled with old furniture, a rolled-up rug, and a worn antique display cabinet filled with model airplanes.

"Most of this is my husband's," she said sadly. "I didn't have the heart to get rid of it after he died, but I will one day."

"This it?" Reid asked.

The cardboard box was taped up with no label or markings on it. It had been pushed to one side of the room, out of the way.

"Yes, that's it. I've been meaning to give it to him, but he doesn't come around anymore."

"I'll take it to him." Reid picked up the box. It wasn't heavy, and he'd have no problem carrying it to his car.

"Why, thank you." She smiled at him. "That's kind of you."

"Not a problem."

He picked it up and carried it outside. Mrs. Peters stood at the door, watching. Balancing the box on one hip, he unlocked the truck and placed it on the passenger seat.

"I'll tell Matthew you say hello."

She smiled and waved as he drove off down the street.

Once he'd rounded the corner, Reid pulled over and cut the engine. He sat for a minute and stared at the box.

How was he going to find Matthew Downing? All he knew was he lived on Hialeah Drive, and that was a long road. Sure, he could search the DMV database, but where was the fun in that? Especially when there might be something in the box that could tell him where he lived.

He tore off the tape. It was very well wrapped. Matthew hadn't wanted anyone opening it by mistake. When he was done, he opened the flaps and peered inside. It was work stuff, mostly. He took out an old keyboard, some folders containing IT system specs, and a bunch of stuff he didn't understand. He laid them aside and delved back in.

More folders and documents. He inspected each one but there was nothing with an address or anything else that might indicate where he'd moved to.

At the bottom, he found a large manilla envelope. Inside were a bunch of photographs. He went through them one by one. Family snaps. Gina and him on vacation, Gina in the garden, Gina holding a glass of champagne, Gina in the driver's seat of a new car.

Lots of Gina. Very few of Matthew. Mrs. Peters was right, he'd been very much in love with his wife.

He continued flicking through the photographs until he got to one of Gina walking down the street. He paused and studied it. The way she was walking, her head bent down like that. She seemed unaware that the photo had been taken.

In the next one, she was having coffee at a street side cafe, a magazine in front of her. She was staring off into the distance, lost in thought. The shot had been taken from across the road. It was a surveillance photograph.

There were several more in the same vein. Each time, it was obvious Gina had no idea she was being photographed. Reid separated the surveillance photos from the other snaps and studied them. Same size, taken with the same camera.

Taped to the back of one of the photographs was a handwritten receipt. The name at the top was Danny Caruso. There was also an address.

Had Matthew hired a private investigator to spy on his wife?

19

REID REPACKED THE CARDBOARD BOX, sealed it the best he could, then called Pérez.

"Reid, how's the case going?"

"I've hit a stumbling block," he said. "I hoped you could help me out."

"Oh, what's that?"

Reid told him about the bullets from the missing gun and how they matched those in another homicide. "I'm trying to track down the husband of the murdered woman, Matthew Downing. Ortega was the detective in charge. Since he's on suspension..."

"Frank Walker." Pérez cut in. "You need to speak to Frank. He was Ortega's partner. They worked that case together."

"Thanks, LT."

"Good luck. Let me know what you find."

"Will do."

He called Walker and arranged to meet. The name wasn't familiar. He didn't think Walker had been there when he'd done his temporary stint with the Miami PD a couple of months back.

"Paternity leave," Walker explained. They met at a pop-up cafe near the precinct. Walker was an athletic African American with a firm grip and an easy smile. "I took three months off to help Fiona with the baby."

"How's that going?" Reid asked, more to make conversation than anything else. Kids had never featured on his radar.

"It's getting better." The detective rolled his eyes. "The first few months were hell."

Reid laughed.

"Pérez said you wanted to talk to me about a case?"

"Yeah, it's going back a few years. Gina Downing, remember her?"

He scrunched up his forehead. "Oh, yeah. The housewife who was shot in her living room. If I remember correctly, she disturbed an intruder."

"That's the one. I'm trying to trace the weapon that was used to kill her. It's come up in another homicide, one I'm working on at Sweetwater."

He tilted his head to the side. "Same gun?"

"Yeah. Same bullets."

Walker whistled under his breath. "I wish I could help you, but we never found the gun. If you want my guess, the intruder ditched it when he fled, and it was found by someone else."

That was the most likely possibility.

"What about the husband?" he asked. "Was he ever a suspect?"

"Yeah, we brought him in for questioning, but he had an alibi. He was bowling when his wife was killed. His buddies confirmed it."

Reid remembered reading that in the report. "Okay, but if I wanted to pay him a visit?"

Walker shrugged. "He moved shortly after it happened. I'm not sure where to. Sorry I can't help you, man."

"That's okay. I'll track him down. Thanks anyway."

Reid shook Walker's hand and went back to his truck. It was time to put Vargas to work again. He needed an address for Matthew Downing.

. . .

Vargas came through for him, and in record time too.

"Thanks, that's great work." It had taken the youngster less than twenty minutes to trace Gina's husband.

"How are things over there?" Reid asked.

Yesterday, they'd spent the better part of the day sorting through the evidence Casillas's team had brought back from Barry Marshall's motel room and the parking lot. Not wanting to miss anything, they'd brought him every scrap of paper, every cigarette butt and every used bottle and can they could find.

After sifting through the junk, they hadn't found anything of value other than a $1000 casino chip from the victim's motel room. While probably not important, it did suggest that Marshall hadn't ditched his gambling habit.

"Fine. Casillas has been on the phone trying to get you thrown off the case."

That wasn't a surprise. Having Reid there was showing the others how ineffectual he was. It meant he had to get off his fat ass and do some work for a change.

"Anything else?"

"Yeah." Vargas lowered his voice. "I found out who Marshall's handler was while he was in prison. A cop called Redding out of Miami-Dade. They offered to cut Marshall's sentence if he spied on his cellmate for them. Thanks to Marshall's intel, they shut down the drug distribution network in the prison."

"Good work. Did the drug kingpin ever find out who ratted on him?"

"Redding doesn't think so. There's been no word on the inside."

"It couldn't have been him then," Reid muttered. "I thought three years was a long time to wait to get revenge."

"Some of those guys have nothing but time." Vargas sounded almost philosophical, but he was right. They couldn't discount it just because Marshall's handler didn't know about it. "Okay, thanks

Vargas. Here's what I want you to do. Look into the drug dealing cell-mate. Find out who his crew is on the outside. There must be someone he trusts. A deputy or lieutenant. Let's see what we find if we come at it from that angle."

"Yes, boss." He heard the eagerness in Vargas's voice.

"Thanks, Vargas, but I'm not your boss." Casillas had that honor.

"Yes, sir."

Reid smiled as he hung up.

It was late afternoon, and the traffic was getting heavy. Reid contemplated going to talk to Matthew Downing now, but the bowling alley was closer. It would be better to check out the husband's alibi before he went to speak to him. That way he'd know if there were any holes in his story.

Bill's Bowling Alley was in full swing when he got there. Reid was assailed by the familiar roar of the balls rolling down the alley and the crash as they smashed into the pins.

"The after-work crowd," the guy behind the bar told him. "Thursday's a big day for bowling."

"I'm looking for the manager."

"That would be Ben, Bill's son. He's over there by the shoe rack."

Reid spotted a stocky man in a striped shirt talking to a group of guys sitting around a table celebrating their team's win. High fives and beers all around. His back was to Reid but his head was as smooth and shiny as one of his bowling balls.

"Thanks." Reid walked over to them. "Sorry to interrupt. You Ben?"

"Yeah, who wants to know?"

"Detective Garrett, Sweetwater PD." He flashed his badge. "Mind if I ask you a few questions?"

Ben gave the group of guys an apologetic shrug. "Sure, let's go to my office."

He led Reid behind the shoe rack to a wooden door beyond

which was a cozy office. There were several trophies on a shelf, along with lots of framed photos of bowling teams from bygone years.

He gestured for Reid to sit, which he did. Ben took a seat behind the desk, cluttered with invoices and statements. "Sorry, I was doing the accounts." He hurriedly piled them on top of each other.

"Don't worry on my part." Reid waved his hand in the air. "I'm here to talk about one of your customers, Matthew Downing. He used to play here a couple of years back."

Ben nodded slowly. "I remember him. It was his wife who got killed."

"Yeah, that's right. He used this place as his alibi for the night of her murder. Did you know that?"

"Yeah, I knew his friends had been questioned."

"I don't suppose you have any records of who was here that evening?"

"No, I don't. We wipe the tapes every year. No point in keeping them." He shrugged. "But I do recall that night."

"Oh?"

"Matthew was here with his buddies. They had a weekly thing going on. Three on each team. Two of the guys still play here from time to time."

Reid's heart sank. "He was here the whole evening then?"

"Yeah, till closing."

Shit. So much for that theory.

"Okay, well thanks for your time." He pushed himself out of his seat.

"He arrived late, though." Ben said, not getting up.

"What?" Reid sank down again.

"I remember because his teammates waited for him. They had a drink at the bar. When they started the game, they shuffled the playing order around. Matthew always bowled first—he liked it that way. But that night he bowled last. I saw him rush in after the others had started."

Now that was interesting.

"How much after?"

"I couldn't say exactly, maybe close to an hour."

"How did he look? Was he upset? Agitated?"

Ben shrugged. "Not that I noticed. He said hello like he always did, then went to join the others. Said he'd been held up at work."

There was a pause as Reid let this sink in.

"I have to say, I was surprised the cops didn't ask me about it." Ben scratched his bald head. "I mean, at the time."

"They didn't come here to question you?"

"No. Not a peep."

"Okay." That was unusual. Ortega and Walker should have checked out his alibi. Come to think of it, he didn't recall reading anything about it in the original police report. "Thanks again, Ben. It was good talking to you."

Ben got up. "Say, did they ever catch the bastard who shot his wife?"

"No," Reid replied, heading for the door. "Not yet."

20

KENZIE WAS GETTING USED to the frantic pace of the restaurant. The evening ebbed and flowed with waves of customers, and when she wasn't rushed off her feet, she tried to grab a few moments alone with Simone.

It was on a smoke break that Kenzie had a breakthrough. Simone was talking about an upcoming party on Saturday night at one of the most exclusive clubs in Miami. "I'm so excited," she gushed. "I bought a Gucci off-the-shoulder dress for the occasion. Don likes me to dress up." Kenzie caught a flash of something uneasy in Simone's eye, but the next instant, it was gone. She wondered how Simone could afford designer party dresses. It must be Ingleman, unless she made a ton of money modeling. Except then why would she be working here?

"Wow, that sounds so glamorous," Kenzie sighed.

Simone gasped as a thought occurred to her. "You should come."

"Oh, no," Kenzie said hastily. "I don't want to intrude."

"You wouldn't be. There'll be lots of people there." Did Simone want her to come? Did she need support? A friend in a sea of sharks?

Kenzie didn't want to give in that easily. "I wouldn't know anyone."

"You'd know me." She gave Kenzie a conspiratorial wink "Besides, there'll be lots of eligible men there. There always are at Don's parties."

"It does sound fun." She hesitated, unsure.

"Oh, come on. It'll be a blast."

"All right."

Simone gave a little jiggle, then inhaled the last of her cigarette. "Excellent. Give me your number, and I'll send you the details."

She was in! On Saturday night she'd meet Ingleman.

When Kenzie finished her shift, she checked her phone. Two missed calls from Reid. They hadn't spoken in a couple of days, not since they'd got back from Key West. She wondered how he was doing.

It was after midnight when she got home. Too late to call. Or was it? The last message had come through at ten-thirty. Reid sometimes stayed up late working when he was on a case. Like her, he had no off-switch when the scent was strong.

She decided on a text message. That way, if he was sleeping, it would go unanswered, and hopefully not wake him up.

You awake?

A minute later. *Yeah.*

She called him. "Hi. I'm sorry I've been out of touch. I've started a new job."

"A new job?" She heard the confusion in his voice.

"Yes, but it's not what you think. I'm working an angle."

A pause.

"You're going after Ingleman."

He was astute, she'd give him that much. "How'd you know?"

"I know you. When you go off the radar, it's usually because you're up to something. We didn't have much luck with Reg Arnold, so now you're going after the man himself."

She laughed. It was true, he was getting to know her. He could anticipate her actions, as she could his. The realization made her both warm and uncomfortable at the same time. "I'm waitressing. I got a job at the restaurant where his girlfriend works."

"Ah, I see."

"I've been invited to a party on Saturday night."

"Ingleman's place?"

"No, it's at Gold Dust."

"What's that?"

She smiled to herself. "It's a club." Only the most exclusive club in Miami, but he didn't need to know that.

"Oh." A pause. "Are you going with Ingleman?"

Did she detect a note of jealousy? She must be imagining things.

"No, his girlfriend invited me."

"Kenzie, I don't want to sound condescending, but are you sure that's wise? What if he finds out you're actually a reporter? He's not going to be pleased."

Not jealousy. Concern.

"I'll be fine, don't worry. There are hundreds of other people going. It's a nightclub."

"Hmm..." He wasn't happy about it, she could tell.

"I'll be perfectly safe."

"Ingleman is a dangerous man, Kenzie. Look what happened to the witness."

That gave her pause.

"I know, but I'm not going to testify against him."

"No, you're just going to bust him wide open in the national press. How's that any different?"

She lowered her voice. "I know what I'm doing, Reid. This isn't the first time I've gone undercover."

"Okay, fine." He gave in. "But keep your wits about you. I know how impulsive you can be."

"Impulsive? Me?"

He chuckled. She was glad he wasn't going to push her on this.

And he was right. She did tend to be impulsive, especially when she was after a story, and this was a big one. The scoop of her career. She needed it to keep her job.

"How's the case going?" It was time to change the subject.

"All right. I'm chasing up a lead on the gun used to kill Barry Marshall. I'm hoping it'll steer me to the shooter."

"Really? That sounds promising." Her ears pricked up. The shooter would make another great page three article, but she was after page one.

"It's a bit of a long shot to be honest."

"Can I have an exclusive if you find him?"

She pictured him grinning into the phone. "I'll think about it."

"Thanks, Reid. I'll let you know if I find out anything on my side."

"Be careful, Kenzie. I mean it. This guy went to great lengths for this not to get out. He won't appreciate you digging around."

"Let's not go there again. I promised I'd be careful. You worry too much."

"That's your fault," he growled good humoredly. "Take care, Kenzie."

"You too."

21

MATTHEW DOWNING LIVED in a run-down condo at the not-so-great end of Hialeah Drive. His second-floor balcony overlooked the street below and despite it being mid-morning, there was a permanent smell of fried food in the air. It was a step down from his Virginia Street suburban home.

"Mrs. Peters told me where you were," Reid said, by way of introduction. "She says hello, by the way." Matthew ignored the reference to the old woman and surveyed Reid. He had a heavy-lidded gaze with something in it that Reid didn't like. He was average height, but stocky, and looked like he could handle himself in a fight.

"What do you want, Detective Garrett?"

This guy wasn't into small talk. Okay, fine. It wasn't his strong suit either. "I want to ask you some questions about the night your wife was murdered."

"I went through all this with the cops at the time."

"I know, and I apologize for bringing it up again, but I need to clarify some details."

"What details?"

Reid glanced around the sparse apartment. He couldn't see a

single photograph of Gina. Couldn't he stand to look at her? Was it too heartbreaking or was there some other reason? An open laptop and a notepad lay on the sofa. Matthew had been doing some work before Reid had arrived, although what that was, Reid had no idea. "I spoke to Ben, the manager of Bill's Bowling Alley. I believe you know him?"

No reply. Just a stony-eyed stare.

"Anyway, he told me that on the night of the break-in, you arrived late to your weekly game. The guys had started without you. Is that right?"

There was a long pause.

Reid thought he might have to repeat the question when Matthew cleared his throat. "That was two years ago." But he was thrown. His initial hostility had been replaced with indecision. He hadn't been expecting that.

"I know, but if you could cast your mind back, it would be really useful."

Matthew sighed and shut his eyes as if it hurt to think about it. "Yes, I was late that night. I got tied up at work."

"At Intel Logistics?"

"Yeah." He opened his eyes. "How'd you know that?"

"It's in the original police report."

Matthew didn't respond.

"And you didn't stop anywhere else on your way to the bowling alley? You didn't go home first?"

"No, Jesus. Why would you think that?" He glared at Reid, his hands balling into fists. This guy had a short fuse.

He wouldn't hurt a hair on that girl's head.

"I didn't have anything to do with my wife's death."

Reid held up a hand. "Okay, okay. No one's saying you did. I'm just trying to get the facts straight."

Matthew clenched his jaw. He was at the point of throwing Reid out.

Reid walked to the window and back to ease the tension, get the air moving around the room. It worked. Matthew relaxed his shoulders and unfurled his hands. "You see, I checked with your ex-company, and you clocked out at ten past five that evening. You used your swipe card to get out of the building."

"I must have stopped at a shop or something," the IT guy muttered. Then his eyes narrowed. "Why are you interrogating me? My wife was killed by an intruder."

That was another thing Reid didn't understand. The way she'd fallen... as if she'd been facing the front door. If the intruder was already in the house, the bullet would have come from a different direction. He didn't buy the "shooting-as-he-was-leaving" scenario. It made no sense. If the burglar was running for the door, there'd be no reason to turn and shoot. It just turned attempted burglary into attempted murder. No one would take that risk. Not unprovoked. And the one-hundred-and-thirty-pound Gina was hardly a threat.

"Some aspects of the investigation didn't add up for me," he said.

"Well, I had nothing to do with it. I can't remember why I was late. That night is a bit of a blur, as you'll appreciate. I must have had an errand to run or something. I didn't go near the house, and when I got home later that evening, I found my wife lying in a pool of blood."

He looked haunted by the fact. The faint lines around his mouth and his lips were pulled back in a semi-snarl. Even after two years, it was still raw.

"I apologize for intruding," Reid said. There was nothing to be gained from antagonizing him. "I'll leave you in peace."

He made for the door. Matthew followed, momentarily pacified.

"Oh, I almost forgot." Reid turned around. "Mrs. Peters gave me something to give to you. A cardboard box. It's in my truck." He watched Matthew's face for a reaction, but apart from a minuscule flicker, there was nothing. "I'll just go and get it."

Reid took the stairs down to his pickup, got the box and went back up. Matthew met him on the landing. He didn't want Reid back in his apartment.

"You open this?" Matthew snapped, eyeing the loose duct tape.

"Nope. I was given it like that." He didn't think Matthew would call Mrs. Peters to check. "I did have a poke inside though when I was looking for your address."

Dark daggers glared at him.

"Yeah, I couldn't help but notice some of the photographs in that box are of your late wife. It looks like she was under surveillance. Is that something that you arranged?"

"I think it's time you left," Matthew growled, closing the gap between them.

Reid stood his ground. "Were you having her followed, Mr. Downing?"

"Get out," he hissed. "I've said all I'm gonna say."

Reid backed up. Unless he arrested Matthew Downing, he couldn't keep interrogating him. It could be seen as harassment.

To be continued...

"I'm going."

As he left, he spotted Mathew at the window staring down at him, an indecipherable expression on his face. The time of death was reported to be between six and eight that night. The timing fit. Matthew Downing could have murdered his wife.

22

Donny Caruso's office wasn't hard to find. It was squeezed between a high-rise and a parking garage, off Brickell Avenue. The squat single-story building seemed out of place between the two tower blocks, as if it had been slotted in the gap like a Lego brick.

The sign on the door read: *D. Caruso. Private Investigator.*

The PI stood up as Reid walked in. He looked him over. Dirty blond hair, a pale complexion, and a paunch. He didn't inspire confidence. "What can I do for you?"

Reid showed him his badge. "I'd like to ask you a few questions about a job you did a couple of years back."

The PI frowned before sitting down again. "I'm not comfortable talking about my clients. I have a confidentiality agreement to uphold."

Reid approached the desk. "Would you prefer if I arrested you? Then you can answer my questions down at the station."

"What was it you wanted to know?"

Reid took a seat. The office was sparse and smelled like detergent. Hardly any sun filtered through the tinted-glass storefront, and

Caruso had the desk lamp on despite it being the middle of the afternoon.

"Matthew Downing," Reid said.

Surprise flickered over his face. "Yes, I remember Mr. Downing. He thought his wife was screwing around."

"Was she?"

He hesitated. Reid waited.

Eventually, Caruso sighed. "Yeah, she was."

"You get a name?"

"Of course. That's what he paid me for."

Reid leaned over the desk. "I want everything you've got on him."

"Thanks for meeting me."

Frank Walker gave a quick nod. "No problem, but I don't have long. What did you want to ask me?" Reid had met Ortega's partner at the pop-up Cuban café across the road from the police station. Walker's, not Reid's.

He got straight to the point. "How come nobody checked Matthew Downing's alibi?"

"What do you mean?" Walker frowned.

"At the bowling club. On the night his wife died, Matthew was nearly an hour late. He said he'd been held up at work, but he hadn't. I checked."

Walker stared at him. "I don't remember that."

"Yeah, his team started the game without him." Reid leaned forward. "Gina Downing was killed between six and eight o'clock, according to the pathology report. Matthew got to the bowling alley shortly before seven. That gives him a window of opportunity."

Walker ran a hand over his head. "Are you saying Matthew Walker had something to do with his wife's death?"

"I'm saying he could have."

Walker exhaled. "Shit."

Reid waited, letting the silence draw out. Eventually Walker said,

"I checked with his bowling buddies, they vouched for him. Said he was with them all night, till closing."

"He was. They were right about that, but he got there late. They didn't tell you that?"

"No, sir."

Reid rubbed his stubbly chin. Walker seemed legit. It was possible he'd missed it. That he and his partner, Ortega, hadn't interviewed the owner of the bowling alley. An oversight, for sure, but not necessarily intentional.

"Did you know Matthew was having his wife followed?"

Walker balked. "He was?"

"Yeah, I saw a bunch of surveillance photographs in a box left at his old house. I don't suppose you know why?"

"No idea." He looked genuinely perplexed.

"He didn't mention anything about it during the investigation?"

"No, he said they were happily married."

"Did you believe him?" Reid watched Walker's face twitch.

"I had no reason not to."

Reid was about to push him, then changed his mind. He didn't want to get on Walker's bad side. "Okay, thanks."

Walker seemed hesitant to leave. "What are you going to do now?"

"Not sure."

He was going to do what Walker and Ortega should have done the first time around. He was going to talk to Matthew's bowling buddies and find out why they failed to mention that Matthew was late to the game that night. Had they genuinely forgotten to mention it, or were they covering for him?

Luke O'Hara lived in a middle-class suburban neighborhood not far from where Matthew and Gina used to live. According to what they could find online, he was married with two grown kids, both of whom were away at college.

"I haven't seen Matthew for a couple of years," he confessed once Reid had explained why he was there. "Not since that awful business with his wife."

"Poor Gina." His wife came into the room and stood beside her husband. "Gunned down like that in her own home. It's too dreadful to think about."

"When was the last time you saw him?" Reid asked.

Luke thought for a moment. "It must have been just after it happened. I went over to ask if there was anything I could do. I mean, the guy was a wreck."

"Did you stay long?"

"No, he wasn't in the mood for talking. Understandably. He went to pieces after Gina died. It was tough to see. He lost his job, stopped coming to the club, didn't see anyone."

"We lost touch," his wife said, lowering her gaze.

"Mr. O'Hara," Reid said. "I'd like you to cast your mind back to that night at the bowling alley, the night Gina was shot."

His pale blue eyes fixed on Reid. "Okay."

"When the detectives in charge of the investigation asked you to confirm Matthew's alibi, you said he was at the club all evening."

"That's right."

"But he arrived late, didn't he? Ben told me he was the last to arrive, and you had already started the game."

Luke scratched his head. "Oh, yeah. That's right."

"But you didn't tell that to the police?"

"I think I did." He clicked his fingers. "In fact, I'm sure I did. I remember that detective asking how late he was. It must have been nearly an hour after we'd started the game. Matt got tied up at work."

"Do you remember which detective it was?"

"Um, no. Sorry."

"Was it a big African American? Detective Walker?"

"No, that wasn't it."

"Ortega? Shorter, Hispanic, good looking?"

"Yeah, that's more like it."

Reid frowned. If Luke had told Ortega that Matthew Downing had been late, why wasn't it in the report?

Reid left the O'Hara's house and drove toward the port. He needed time to think and driving helped him do that. He also had an ulterior motive for coming out here.

Alberto Torres.

Earlier in the year, and without a warrant, he'd set up a surveillance camera opposite Torres's dockside warehouse. The warehouse was part of the drug dealer's logistics business and from what Reid could make out, was legitimate.

But lately, the footage had shown something unusual. The delivery of several used cars. A stream of them had been driven into the garage and left there. He didn't know what Torres' men were doing with them. Overhauling them, perhaps? Kitting them out for drug distribution around the state? Either way, it was suspicious.

Reid had been waiting for an opportunity to catch Torres for years, ever since the douchebag had gunned down Bianca, his undercover operative, in Little Havana. He didn't want to get him on a measly drug charge, though. Not after he'd committed cold-blooded murder. But setting up a drug distribution network might work. It came with a harsher sentence and would mean a lot more jail time.

Torres was the Morales cartel's Head of Operations and a very important figure in the cartel hierarchy. He was arguably the most powerful member in Miami, other than Federico Lopez—"The Wolf" —who hadn't been seen for so long that it was rumored he'd gone back to Mexico.

Reid pulled into the office parking lot a block down from the warehouse and turned off the engine. Only Torres's car remained, but it was after five o'clock. Sometimes Torres worked late, other times he knocked off early. He wasn't a stickler for routine.

The used cars were still inside the garage. They'd been there for nearly a week now, according to his surveillance app. It would take that long to adjust them for drug smuggling. They'd have to rip out certain sections and replace them with hidden compartments, then smooth it over so any cop doing a routine check wouldn't notice.

He could raid the warehouse, but all they'd get were some altered vehicles. No crime in that. So, he was prepared to wait. Wait until the drugs were delivered, and then he'd act. Torres wouldn't get away from him a second time.

23

KENZIE WALKED into the exclusive club and looked around. It was a whirl of designer cocktail dresses and finely cut suits. Champagne bubbled in crystal flutes while the guests smiled and air-kissed their way around the room.

Simone had left her name at the door, so Kenzie had no problem getting in. Standing on her tiptoes she tried to spot the model and her infamous beau, but there were too many people, and the lighting was too dim to make them out.

"I'll have a martini," she told the bartender, pausing to sweep a hand over her hair. She'd taken extra care with her appearance tonight. It was important she caught Ingleman's eye.

A DJ was working his magic in a caged pedestal at the end of the club under alien-green lighting, while people mingled around, not quite dancing yet, but nodding and tapping in time to the music. In another hour the dance floor would be heaving.

"There you go." The barman winked at her. He was cute, in an easy-going, scruffy kind of way.

She was glad her effort was having the desired effect. "Thanks."

On a raised section where the VIP booths were located, she spotted Simone, or rather her glossy head and striking face. She seemed to glitter from across the club.

She began walking in that direction.

"Hey, your drink?" the barman called after her.

As she got closer, Kenzie noted the off-the-shoulder dress in a white silk.

"There you are!" Simone embraced her. "You look stunning."

She'd certainly tried her best. The slinky gold dress clung to her curves and plunged at the cleavage. She'd had her hair done professionally, because she didn't have the patience or the know-how to get it to twirl around her face in messy spirals.

"Thanks." She did a little pirouette. "I'm glad you approve."

"Approve? You look amazing. Hey, let me introduce you to Don."

Kenzie's stomach flip-flopped. This was the moment she'd been waiting for, the whole reason she got the job at the restaurant and befriended Simone.

"It's a pleasure to meet you, sir." She let him encase her small hand in his large, rough one.

His dark eyes roamed over her from head to toe. "The pleasure is all mine."

He was suave all right, with his silky voice, knowing eyes and lips that curled up in a sardonic smile.

"Kaylee works with me at the restaurant," Simone explained.

"Ah, indeed." He held her hand a fraction too long, but Simone didn't notice, or maybe she was used to Ingleman's behavior. He struck her as the type of man who did whatever he liked when he liked it. She met his gaze and smiled.

"Kaylee, won't you join us?" Ingleman patted the seat next to him. Simone flittered on his knee, reaching over for the champagne.

"Here, you must have a glass." She poured one for Kenzie.

"Thanks." Kenzie accepted the flute of dancing bubbles and took a much-needed sip. Expensive.

Ingleman was watching her. "Are you a model too?"

She laughed. "Oh, no. Just a waitress."

"You're far too attractive to be just a waitress."

"Thanks, I am actually looking for another job."

"In what field?"

"Admin, secretarial, that kind of thing. I have a broad skill set."

"I'm sure you do." He kept his eyes on her face. Curious, probing. She was half expecting them to drop to her cleavage, but they didn't. He liked to read people, that's what he was doing to her.

She gave him a coquettish smile. "You wouldn't happen to have any vacancies at your company, would you?"

"I'll have to check." He wrapped an arm around Simone's waist. "You know what it is I do?"

"Oh, yes. I know exactly who you are, Mr. Ingleman. I was pleased your case was dismissed."

His eyes narrowed. "You were following the case?"

Another rehearsed smile. "It was in all the papers."

He accepted that. "I was lucky the witness didn't show up for court."

Because he was shot dead in a motel parking lot.

"Did they ever find him?" Wide eyes gazed into his.

"Not that I know of."

Liar.

He knew very well what had happened to Barry Marshall. He'd orchestrated the hit.

"Well, I'm glad you're free." She held up her glass. "Cheers."

"Shall we dance?" Simone asked her. The DJ was getting into a rhythm and a few people had started to move around the dancefloor. Kenzie would have preferred talking with Ingleman, but she didn't want to arouse suspicion. Tonight, she was the fun-loving waitress. The flighty, uncommitted, attention-seeking wannabe with a provocative smile and teasing eyes.

"Sure."

She felt Ingleman's gaze on them as they made their way to the dancefloor. "I'm so glad you're here," Simone raised her voice above the music. "Don doesn't like to dance, but I adore it."

"Does he have many parties?" Kenzie asked.

"Quite often," she admitted. "He says it's good for business. They're all lavish affairs and go on for most of the night. I usually leave around one or two in the morning. Don has tremendous staying power; he can keep going all night."

He was drinking whiskey and pacing himself, Kenzie noted. She smiled in his direction. He gave her a curious nod. She'd sparked his attention, just like she'd planned. The only problem was now that she had it, she wasn't sure what to do with it. Her initial strategy was just to meet him, to see what kind of man he was. Was he capable of putting out a hit on Barry Marshall? Well, she'd achieved that. The answer was yes.

His dark gaze lingered on her, and a shiver went down her spine. Definitely dangerous. Then a man approached him, and he turned away.

Kenzie danced with Simone for a few tracks, then suggested they go back to sit down. "I could use another drink," she shouted above the beat.

Ingleman and the man were still deep in conversation, so Kenzie and Simone sat opposite him in the booth and refilled their glasses. They laughed and joked and talked about men and other silly things, until Kenzie once again felt Ingleman's eyes on her. She shot him a sultry smile, after making sure Simone was facing the other way.

He slid a business card across the table. "I might have something for you at one of my companies. Call my PA tomorrow to set up an appointment."

"That would be amazing,'" she gushed. "Thank you, sir."

His smile was akin to a predator, circling its prey. "Please, call me Don."

"Okay, Don."

. . .

The night progressed. Kenzie was introduced to several successful men, all friends, or acquaintances of Don's. Harold or Harry for short, was a trendy dresser with a wide smile and crinkly eyes. He gyrated with her on the dancefloor, bought her drinks and talked to her about the best restaurants in Miami. She was bored stiff.

The club got very crowded. Someone spilled red wine over Simone's dress. It immediately spread out like a blood stain, seeping into the fine, white fabric. With a plaintive yelp, she ran off to the lady's room.

Kenzie got up to follow her when Don grabbed her arm. "Stay."

One word. A demand.

She sat down again.

He brushed her hair aside and whispered, "You're the most beautiful girl here tonight."

Her plan had worked too well. She now had his full and undivided attention. He'd had several whiskies and instead of getting blustery like some men, he only seemed to get more intense. His arm snaked around her back and she felt his fingers caress her bare skin.

"I'd like you to come and work for me," he murmured.

"I'd like that."

Out of the corner of her eye, Kenzie noticed a well-dressed man in his forties watching them. He had dark hair, greying at the temples, a lithe, slim physique, and an impeccably cut suit complete with vest. She wondered who he was.

Simone came back, flushed and embarrassed. Ingleman dropped his hand.

"I'm going home." She collapsed next to Kenzie. "I can't walk around like this. My dress is ruined." She looked like she was about to cry.

"I'm so sorry," Kenzie said, reaching for her purse. "I'll come with you."

"No, stay. You're having fun. I saw you flirting with Harry."

"He's sweet," she lied.

Simone gave a conspiratorial wink. "Go for it. He's a great guy. Drives a Lotus, too."

Harry was, in fact, watching Simone, disappointment etched on his craggy face. Kenzie secretly thought he might be into her. Still, she wasn't in the match-making business, she had a job to do—and Ingleman was in play.

"Would you like some champagne?" Kenzie offered, once Simone had gone. "I can pour you a glass."

Don shook his head. "I'm fine with this."

He wasn't going to be persuaded. Despite the charm, he was guarded and controlled.

"How is the finance business these days?" Kenzie gave him a dazzling smile.

He chuckled. His hand was back, idly stroking her shoulder. "I think you're putting me on, Kaylee."

Her heart skipped a beat. "What?"

"I think you planned this from the start. You're not interested in all this." He waved his hand around. "You have a hidden agenda. You're after a job. Am I right?"

She laughed, relieved. He'd read her correctly, she did have a hidden agenda, but it wasn't a job. "You got me. I admit, I was eager to meet you. When Simone invited me, I thought it would be the perfect opportunity."

That was all true.

"I think we can work something out." He idly stroked her shoulder.

"Why did they arrest you?" she asked, her eyes wide. "Did you do something bad?"

His gaze dropped to her lips. She hoped he wasn't going to try to kiss her. "Because I push the boundaries," he murmured. "And the authorities don't like that"

"You mean the boundaries of what's legal?"

"All sorts of boundaries." He leaned closer and whispered in her ear. "Would you like to find out?"

Her heart thumped in her chest. Shit, now what? If he took her home with him, she could poke around his house, have a look for incriminating evidence, but how would she get away? She had no intention of sleeping with him, but he didn't look like the type of man who'd take no for an answer. Every instinct was telling her this was a bad idea.

He took her lack of response as a positive. "Come on, let's go."

She allowed him to help her to her feet. Now. She had to say something now, make an excuse, anything not to go back to his place.

Simone. She'd use Simone.

"You know, I don't feel right about this. Simone is my friend."

He smiled. "We aren't exclusive."

Double shit.

He led her out of the VIP area and across the floor.

"Kaylee, is that you?"

Her head spun around. Nobody other than Simone and Ingleman knew her by that name. The man in the finely cut suit who'd been watching them throughout the evening stood there.

"Um, yes. Who are—?"

"Darling, it's so good to see you. It's been ages." He embraced her and whispered in her ear. "If you know what's good for you, you'll play along."

Ingleman stopped. Annoyance flashed across his face. He didn't like being interrupted when he was homing in on his prey.

Kenzie gasped. "Oh, my gosh. How *are* you?"

"I'm well. Can I buy you a drink?"

"She was just leaving," came Ingleman's growl.

The stranger met her gaze. It was up to her.

"Oh, I'm sorry, Don. I haven't seen my friend for a long time. Do you mind terribly if we stay?" She knew he wouldn't. His ego wouldn't let him.

He released her hand. "This is your friend?"

"Why yes, do you know each other?"

Don shook his head. "I might have known."

The stranger gave a curt nod. "Don. Good to see you."

"Likewise."

Then, before Kenzie could say goodbye, Ingleman strode out of the club. Bemused as to the turn of events, she faced the stranger. "Who are you?"

24

"Carlisle Harrington." He shook her hand. It was smooth, unlike Ingleman's, but his grip was firm.

"Kaylee, but you already know that."

He tilted his head. "Don't you mean Kenzie?"

Now she was really confused.

"Mr. Harrington, I don't mean to be rude, but have we met?" She didn't recall the name. Yet how did he know who she was? Music pulsed from the overhead speakers making it difficult to hear.

"Shall we go outside?" he suggested.

She nodded.

He led her into a courtyard with twinkling lights, an outdoor bar, and coconut palms. The music was muted out here, bearable. They stood in the corner, away from the other club-goers. Kenzie took a good look at him. He was handsome in a distinguished way, with salt-and-pepper hair, an angular face, and deep-set brown eyes. They reminded her of a Labrador's.

"That's better. Would you like a drink?" His accent was hard to place. English, maybe, but with the slightest twang.

"I'd like to know who you are and why you've been watching me."

He seemed delighted she'd noticed. "I told you who I am. I'm sorry to hijack you like this, but you looked like you needed rescuing."

Was it that obvious?

"Good call, by the way. I've known Don for a long time, I know how he treats his women." He shook his head.

"What do you mean?"

"Let's just say he likes it rough."

I push the boundaries. Would you like to find out?

She pursed her lips. "How do you know this?"

"I know women who've been with him. I've seen the bruises."

She shook her head. "That can't be right. I know his girlfriend, Simone. She adores him. Apparently, he treats her like a princess."

"He's not like that with his bona fide girlfriends, only the one-night stands. The nobodies. No offense."

Then she got it. She was a fling, a nobody. Someone he could discard the next day. A waitress without a real job. Someone who wouldn't report him to the authorities. He probably had no intention of giving her a job.

Well, Ingleman had almost made the biggest mistake of his life.

Problem was, so had she.

"How do you know Don Ingleman?" she asked. The way Ingleman had greeted him, they didn't look like friends.

I might have known.

"I've known him for years. I helped kick-start his career."

She frowned. Ingleman had been around ever since she'd started at the newspaper, and that was almost a decade ago. "*You* kick-started *his* career?"

Ingleman was the financier. It was usually the other way around.

"He needed startup cash, and he came to me. I got it for him."

"How?"

"I put him in touch with some backers."

She was beginning to understand. "You're a fixer?"

"Crude term, but yes. I facilitate deals."

"I see."

That was why Don had backed off when Carlisle had appeared. He was wary of him. Carlisle was obviously very well connected. Powerful even. Ingleman could boss around most people, but not the man who'd given him a start in life.

She gazed at him with newfound respect. "Well, thank you. You're right. I was in a tight spot."

"You don't have to thank me, but maybe you could do me a little favor?" His brown eyes flickered in the fairy lights.

"A favor? What kind of favor?"

"You work for the Miami Herald, right?"

She stared at him. "I'm sorry, but how on earth do you know that?"

"I've seen you in action once before," he said mysteriously. "I was at a Christian Delacroix's party, almost a decade ago, when you helped the police figure out who shot him. That was a brilliant piece of deduction, by the way. Very impressive."

Her mind tumbled backwards into the past. The Miami mansion. The dead film star, shot at his own fundraiser. "That was a long time ago." It was the case that got her promoted to the crime beat.

"I recognized you when I saw you with Ingleman. When you introduced yourself as Kaylee, I was initially surprised. Then I realized you were playing a part." There was that mysterious smile again.

"Why were you watching him?" she asked.

He shrugged. "I like to keep tabs on people."

A suitably vague answer. She addressed his earlier question. "What favor?"

"What if I asked you to add a quote by a prospective client in the next article you write about the city's economy."

"I'm not the economics editor, I'm an investigative journalist. I have no sway over what he writes."

"But you could contribute a quote?"

"I could," she said slowly. "But why would I do that?"

"Because I'm trying to set something up, and I need a little help. I'd like to portray this client in a certain way."

"You mean boost their reputation?"

"Something like that, yes."

"In order to facilitate a deal?"

He grinned. "Exactly."

She sighed. "I don't know if I can do that."

"Could you try? It would help me enormously."

Kenzie's journalist brain was working overtime. Carlisle was obviously a good man to know, a useful source. He was well connected. He knew things about people. She could use him in the future.

"Okay. I'll see what I can do."

"Excellent." He beamed at her. "Now that's out of the way, are you sure I can't get you a drink?"

She pursed her lips. "I might be persuaded, if you tell me everything you know about Don Ingleman."

He laughed. "I see we're going to get along famously."

25

REID KNOCKED on Kenzie's door.

No answer.

He checked his phone. Eleven a.m. Her office had said she was working from home today. Her car was in the lot reserved for residents, so she hadn't gone far, unless it was with someone else. He turned and gazed over the landscaped lawns and down to the water's edge. No lone blonde figure. He was about to leave when he heard the latch being pulled back.

"Ah, there you are." She looked like she'd just rolled out of bed. Tousled hair, smudged eyeliner, adorably disheveled. She wore leggings and a long T-shirt. He couldn't resist a grin. "Big night?"

"You could say that. Come in." She turned away, leaving the door open for him.

"Ingleman's party?"

"Yeah." She ran a hand through her hair, but it got stuck, so she gave up. "I need coffee."

He followed her into the kitchen. "How was it? Did you find out anything?"

"Yes and no." After the coffee was on, she sat down at the kitchen table. "I learned that he's arrogant, self-assured, cocky, and doesn't believe in monogamy."

Reid stared at her. "You didn't—?"

"Of course not. He hit on me, that's all."

Reid sat down opposite her. "With his girlfriend there?"

"She'd gone by then."

Reid didn't know what to say. "I hope you weren't contemplating doing anything stupid."

She tilted her head. "Define stupid."

"Kenzie...Ingleman's dangerous. I don't want you alone with him."

She blinked at him. "*You* don't want? Isn't that my decision?"

"That's not what I meant." Shit, he wasn't explaining himself very well. The last thing he wanted to do was sound like an overprotective boyfriend. He knew he had no right to dictate what she did or who she saw—except he cared about her. More than he wanted to.

"I'm worried about you, that's all."

That was the truth.

Ingleman was a shark, a hunter, and he didn't like the thought of her in his sights. It wasn't anything other than that.

She got up to pour the coffee. "Want one?"

He gave a distracted nod.

"Look, you don't have to worry. I know where to draw the line."

"Okay, good. I apologize. I didn't mean to come off as—"

"Reid, it's okay. I know you're concerned, but really, I've got this." She flashed him a tired smile as she put down his coffee.

"Thanks."

"I did meet someone else, though." She took a sip and briefly closed her eyes. "Aah, that's good."

He waited for her to go on.

"An associate of Ingleman's. Now he *was* interesting."

"Oh?" Reid frowned. "What's his name?"

"Carlisle Harrington. Have you heard of him?"

He rolled the name over in his mind. "Can't say I have."

"Neither had I, so I Googled him. Couldn't find a single mention of him anywhere. Not even a reference. It's as if he doesn't exist."

"Maybe it's a false name?"

"It's possible. Anyway, he knows Ingleman from way back, and he told me a lot about him."

"Like what?"

"Like how he started the business. He had a wealthy backer, a lawyer who acted as a silent partner. When the company took off, Ingleman bought him out."

"Nothing suspicious about that. It happens every day."

"True, but Ingleman paid much less than it was worth. The lawyer was running for governor at the time. Interestingly, a few weeks later, he dropped out of the race. He said it was because of family commitments." She rolled her eyes.

"You think Ingleman threatened him?"

"I wouldn't be surprised. There were rumors this lawyer was gay. That's nothing these days, but when you're supposedly happily married and running for governor, it could be career ending."

Reid raised an eyebrow. "And here I thought you'd just got up."

"I've been Googling for hours, researching everything Carlisle told me. So far, it all checks out."

Why wasn't he surprised? "What's your next step?" It was a real shame that she hadn't become a detective. She was damn good at it.

"I keep digging. Ingleman is the type to put out a hit on the key witness in his trial, no doubt about it. I've just got to find proof."

"Ingleman won't like you sniffing around," he warned her. "Sooner or later, he's going to catch on."

She stiffened her shoulders. "I need this, Reid. I have to go after Ingleman. Anything less and I'm going to lose my job."

Shit, he'd forgotten about that.

"It's between me and Clayton. There's only room for one."

He didn't know what to say. She was in a tough situation, but she was giving it her best shot, even if it meant putting herself in harm's way to do it.

"That's why I have to pull out all the stops." Her eyes begged him to understand. He wished there was something he could do to help. "I've got to get the scoop."

Reid thought for a moment. Maybe there was. "There might be another way."

"What do you mean?"

"What if we could get into Ingleman's house and have a look around?"

"You'd break in?" she whispered.

He chuckled. "No, I'd get a search warrant."

"Oh, right."

"Rather than you poking around and putting yourself in danger, why don't we do this the official way?"

She rubbed her forehead. "How long will it take to get a warrant?"

"A couple of hours. Ingleman's the prime suspect in Barry Marshall's murder."

She grinned, her face losing some of its tension. "Then I'm in."

He took out his phone and made a quick call. Warrant was in the works. After he'd hung up, she said, "How's your side of the investigation going?"

"It's long winded. I'm still trying to track down the gun. I've linked it to a homicide that happened two years ago, but after that..." He shrugged.

"Do you know who the original shooter was?"

"I think so. All the evidence points to the husband, Matthew Downing." He sighed. "But it's all circumstantial. I can't prove it."

"What evidence?" She sipped her coffee, her legs curled beneath her on the chair.

"He was having her followed, his alibi didn't check out, and he's being hostile and uncooperative."

"Isn't that enough?"" she asked.

"No, unfortunately not. Besides, it's not my case."

If it was, he'd get it reopened, but he couldn't see Walker doing that, not with Ortega on suspension. Pérez wouldn't be keen to dedicate more resources to a case they couldn't solve two years ago. Not when they were so stretched.

"Okay, so let's say this guy, the husband, did kill his wife, what do you think he did with the gun?"

"That's what I'm trying to find out." He threw up his hands in frustration. "The most likely scenario is he ditched it and it was found by someone who sold it to the guy who shot Barry Marshall. No link. In which case, I'm wasting my time. Or—and this is a stretch —Matthew Downing killed the witness too."

"Would he be stupid enough to use the same gun twice?" Kenzie asked.

Reid shrugged. "I doubt it. Although, he may not have known it was in the system. After all, it was never found."

Kenzie nodded slowly.

"It's more likely he ditched it, which makes my job even harder," Reid continued. He liked talking to her about his cases. That wasn't something he'd ever had with a girlfriend before. Shit, not girlfriend. Friend. Colleague. Crap, he didn't know what the hell she was. "It's like looking for a needle in a haystack. The worst part is I can't ask him, because he's never going to admit to killing his wife." He downed the rest of his coffee. "Maybe I am wasting my time. Perhaps I should be going after Ingleman, like you."

"That's the great thing about working together." Her eyes twinkled. "Once that search warrant comes through, you can do both."

26

Don Ingleman lived in a Spanish-style villa backing onto an exclusive country club. The property was surrounded by a spiked, six-foot wrought-iron fence entwined with bougainvillea. Pretty, but lethal.

Kenzie stood behind Reid, a young detective called Vargas, and two uniformed officers, one female and one male. They were all wearing forensic gloves so they wouldn't compromise any potential evidence. Vargas was shifting nervously from foot to foot.

"First time?" she asked him.

He nodded. She remembered Reid telling her most of the officers at Sweetwater were recent graduates. "I don't want to miss anything important."

She gave him a reassuring smile. "You won't. Don't worry."

Reid outlined the plan of action to his team. "We go in, I'll present the warrant and then we'll split up. Look for anything that connects Ingleman to the shooting of Barry Marshall. Any devices, suspicious documents or anything unexplained."

Granted, it was a long shot. Kenzie didn't think Ingleman would be stupid enough to leave evidence of his involvement lying around.

Any shady deals would be done via burner phone or encrypted texts. Still, Reid had offered, and she wasn't about to turn him down.

A uniformed maid let them in.

"Mr. Ingleman isn't home," she stammered, when faced with the team of police officers.

"That's okay." Reid handed her the warrant. "You can give him this when he gets back." He turned to the others. "Let's go."

As Kenzie walked past, he muttered, "You've got fifteen minutes max before he gets back. She's going to call him now."

Kenzie gave a terse nod. "Where do we start?"

"The study."

They located Ingleman's study in the west wing of the sprawling villa. It was a spacious room, very modern and minimalistic. The ceilings were high with recessed lighting in addition to the floor lamp positioned beside his desk. A glass arch led out onto a terracotta tiled patio. Outside, flaming bougainvillea and glowing hibiscuses out of giant urns.

"It's not what I expected," Kenzie admitted, looking around. Ingleman was so present, so forceful, and this was almost zen-like. Perhaps it counteracted his intensity.

Reid was inspecting the filing cabinet. "I'll take the desk," she said, going over to the sleek steel and glass table.

She scanned the top of it. Bills, documents, and contracts lay in plastic folders with yellow Post-it notes stuck to them. Ingleman was surprisingly orderly. There was nothing here that looked suspicious. She thumbed through them but didn't spot any familiar names.

To the side was a leather-bound diary. It appeared well-used. The leather was crinkling along the spine and the pages were curling at the corners. Inside were appointment dates and times, phone numbers, and random scribbles she couldn't make out. Still, it might be worth a further look.

"Can I have an evidence bag?"

"Found something?"

"I don't know. Maybe. It's his appointment book. I'd like to have a closer look through it." He handed her a see-through plastic bag, and she placed the diary into it.

Reid opened one of the lower drawers of the filing cabinet and let out a low whistle.

"What?" Kenzie looked up. "You got something?"

"Yep." He stood back so she could see. There were three discarded phones in the drawer and two more still in their boxes.

"Burner phones?"

"Looks like it. Let's bag 'em." He reached in and placed the phones in an evidence bag. "We might be able to find out who he's been talking to."

They kept going until there were no more drawers to check. Then they moved on to the other rooms off the hallway. There was nothing of interest.

Reid wrapped up the search. As they were leaving, a sports car screeched up the drive.

Reid glanced out of the window. "Shit, that's Ingleman. He's back."

Kenzie gripped his arm. "He can't find me here."

"I'll distract him. You slip out the back. I'll meet you outside the gate."

The gate?

How on earth was she going to get outside the property? Even if she was Catwoman, the spikes on the wrought iron fence made that a no-go area. She'd have to find another way.

Kenzie ran into the kitchen and out the back door. It led onto a small patio where the trash cans were located. Scanning her surroundings, she looked for a way out.

The golf course lay behind the house, separated by the lethal fence but also lots of lush, green foliage for privacy. It was particularly thick and leafy in one section. While Reid was dealing with an irate Ingleman, she wriggled behind the foliage. At least if she couldn't find a way out, she would remain hidden.

The ground dipped beneath her feet. Looking down, she realized there was a natural ditch, and the fence wasn't quite touching the ground. If she lay flat on her belly, she might be able to wriggle under it.

A trickle of water lay at the bottom, but she didn't care about that. Ingleman finding her on his property was much more of a worry. He'd know she'd lied, that she wasn't who she said she was.

Not a nobody.

Not dispensable.

And she needed him to keep thinking that for their next meeting. If there was one.

Gritting her teeth, she lay on her stomach and leopard-crawled along the muddy ditch.

"Ouch," she muttered, as the bottom of the fence caught her hair. It was a tight squeeze. She sucked in her breath and wriggled through. She could feel the bars clawing at her back, her buttocks, and her calves. Then she was through.

Breathing a sigh of relief, she got to her feet and dusted herself off.

Oh, what was the use? She was covered in dirt.

Four men with golf push carts walked past and stared at her. She smiled and waved, as if she were just out for a pleasant stroll.

Reid was waiting at the end of Ingleman's street with the engine running. The other police car had returned to the station. He took in her disheveled state. "Trouble finding an exit route?"

She pulled a face. "That fence goes all the way around. I had to crawl under the darn thing."

He chuckled. "Sorry, I tried to distract him for as long as possible."

"How did he take it?" she asked.

"Not well, but there was nothing he could do." The corners of his lips turned up. He was enjoying this.

"I'm sure it's not the first time his premises have been searched," Kenzie pointed out. "He was arrested after all."

"Yeah, I'm surprised he had those phones lying around."

"Maybe he didn't expect it again," she said. "The case was dismissed, after all."

"Could be. Hopefully it'll give us something to work with."

"What can I put in my article?" She studied her reflection in the visor window and grimaced.

"That's up to you. If you put in too much, he'll wonder how you got the information. Kenzie, Kaylee, it's not too far from the truth."

That was true.

"I'm not going to say I was there, obviously, or what we found. I don't want to warn him off."

"It's too late for that. He'll be taking precautions as we speak," Reid warned her. "Whoever he called on those burners will be compromised. He'll be giving them fair warning."

That was a shame. They'd probably hit a brick wall with the phones then.

"I'll just say the authorities are looking into him for the murder of the key witness at his trial, and a police search was carried out on the premises. That's vague enough. There's no photograph attached to my byline, so hopefully he won't make the connection."

She'd never told him—or Simone—her surname. Only Marg, the manager, knew it.

"Probably wise."

They drove on, Reid expertly dodging the traffic, one hand on the wheel, the other resting on the open windowsill. The cool breeze was welcome, although she could feel the mud drying on her skin.

"Can I come back to the station and look at the diary?"

He glanced across at her. "Sure, don't you want to get changed first?"

"Oh, yeah. I suppose I should."

He grinned. "I'll see you back at the station. You can inspect the diary if an officer sits in with you—we need to maintain the chain of custody. Anything you find, you share with him."

"No problem."

. . .

A couple of hours later, a freshly dressed Kenzie walked into the Sweetwater Police Department. Reid led her into a side-room where the diary, still in the evidence bag, lay on the table. A uniformed police officer went in with her.

"This is Officer Diaz." Reid introduced them. "She's going to inspect the notebook with you. Anything you find will get noted and followed up on."

"Got it." Kenzie smiled at the female officer who gave her a single nod back. She obviously didn't think Kenzie ought to be sitting in on the investigation.

"Kenzie knows Ingleman," Reid pointed out. "She might recognize something important."

Diaz gave a reluctant nod. Kenzie shot him a grateful smile, and the two women proceeded into the room. "You need to wear these." Diaz handed her a pair of latex gloves.

Kenzie pulled them on and took a seat at the table. She left the head for Diaz, who pulled the diary toward her.

"What exactly are you looking for?" Diaz asked.

Kenzie shrugged. "I'm not sure. I'm hoping I'll recognize it when I see it." If there was anything there to be found.

They went through it page by page. Diaz jotted down any phone numbers they came across. Kenzie knew Reid would ask her to look up who they belonged to. They got to August without finding anything that struck a chord, then the entries stopped.

"That's it," Diaz said. "The rest of it is empty."

Kenzie took the book from her. She closed it and looked at the cover. Wrinkled from use. It looked like it had been opened more than once a day. The last page of the book was covered with smudge marks. Why was this page touched more than the others?

She tilted the book to the side and inspected the back cover. Sure enough, it wasn't flush against the page. She gently peeled back the leather. "There's something in here."

Diaz leaned forward as Kenzie reached in with her forefinger and slid out a folded-up sheet of paper. She glanced at the policewoman. "He was trying to keep this hidden."

Diaz watched as Kenzie unfolded the note. It was a list of names handwritten one below the other with a monetary amount next to each one.

"Who are they?" whispered Diaz.

"I'd say it's an unofficial client list," Kenzie murmured.

She scanned the list, stopping when she got two-thirds of the way down. Her head jerked up so fast, it startled Diaz.

"What?" the policewoman asked.

Kenzie tapped her finger on the paper. "I recognize that name."

27

REID GAVE KENZIE A PUZZLED LOOK. "His name was Matthew Downing. Why do you ask?"

"Because he's on the list we found in Ingleman's diary."

"List?"

"Of clients. Or at least I think they're clients." She handed the paper over to Reid. Diaz stood beside her, nodding.

"It was tucked inside the back cover."

Reid's eyes flickered down the list, then they widened. "Holy shit. That's him."

"What does it mean?" Diaz asked.

"It means Matthew Downing owed Ingleman money." He ran a hand through his hair. "This changes everything" he breathed.

Kenzie met his gaze. "Do you think Matthew Downing killed the witness for Ingleman?"

Reid shook his head. "I don't know. I need to think."

He massaged his forehead, thoughts swirling through his mind. He'd been looking for the gun, when perhaps it hadn't been disposed of at all. Was it possible Matthew Downing had shot Barry Marshall?

"Ingleman could have offered to clear Downing's debt if he took care of the witness."

"Quite a risk," remarked Kenzie. "Using the same gun."

"Downing was never a suspect in his wife's murder. It was pinned on the intruder. He probably didn't think this would lead back to him."

It was only because he'd been looking into the home shooting that he suspected Downing. Nobody else had. Certainly not Casillas.

He frowned. Was the lazy lieutenant also on Ingleman's payroll? He scanned the list but didn't see his name. Nor any others he recognized. That didn't mean he wasn't accepting bribes, though. He'd get Vargas to look into it in more detail.

It would explain why Casillas was so keen to pin the shooting outside the motel on the first guy who came along. In this case, him. And with the victim's blood on his clothing, he'd made a perfect scapegoat. Thank God Pérez had been there to set the record straight.

"So now what?" Kenzie inquired.

"Now, I'm going to have to bring Downing in for questioning. Ortega is going to go ape-shit."

"Ortega?" Kenzie blurted out. "What's Xavier got to do with this?"

"Gina Downing's murder was his case. Him and his partner, Walker."

"I see." She frowned.

Reid knew there was history between Kenzie and Ortega, but he also knew Kenzie had ended all ties with the police detective after he was revealed to be the one who'd leaked the information that had led to Bianca's death.

"Isn't he still on suspension?" Kenzie asked.

"Yeah, but that doesn't mean he won't hear about it. He and Walker are pretty tight." Partners usually were.

Kenzie peeled off the latex gloves and handed them back to Diaz. "Okay, well I'd better get to work. Keith's going to think I've gone AWOL if I don't make an appearance."

Reid shot her a warning glance. "Remember what we discussed."

"I know. Only the general details. Nothing that will compromise the investigation."

He nodded.

"Thanks, Reid. I appreciate you helping me out. I've got to get the edge on Clayton."

"Good luck. And great work on finding the list. We've got a lot to follow up on."

She flashed him a dimpled smile and left the station. Diaz went to put the diary back into evidence.

"Should I issue an arrest warrant for Matthew Downing?" Vargas asked. He sat next to Reid and had overheard everything. "Willie" Vargas was turning out to be a conscientious and hardworking young officer.

Casillas had taken sick leave, his way of letting Reid know he wanted no part in the investigation. He wasn't going to be second in command at his own police station. Or perhaps he was too scared to go up against Ingleman.

Either way, it suited Reid just fine. The guy got in the way, and his officers were eager to learn when he wasn't around. Clearly, his lazy-ass attitude had filtered down, as it always did.

He looked at Vargas. "Yeah, let's do it, but there's something we have to do first."

Reid walked into Miami PD, a wide-eyed Vargas behind him.

"I've always wondered what it was like here," he said, as they stepped out of the elevator into the busy squad room.

"Same as Sweetwater, only bigger," Reid said.

He nodded to Pérez, who looked up from his glass office in the back. He'd given the LT a courtesy call on the way here, to let him know what he was doing.

Pérez wasn't happy about it, but there wasn't much he could do.

"Walker, can we have a word?"

Walker frowned. "What's this about, Garrett?"

"I'll explain everything, but not here." He gestured to one of the interrogation rooms where they'd have privacy.

Walker got up and strode across the room. A couple of officers glanced up. Once they were inside with the door shut, he turned to Reid. "What's so important we need to discuss it in here?"

Reid made sure the camera and audio equipment were off. "I'm arresting Matthew Downing," he said. "In connection with Barry Marshall's murder."

"Barry Marshall?" Walker stared blankly at them. "Who the hell is that?"

"The witness in the Don Ingleman trial. The motel shooting out in the Glades?"

"Oh, yeah." He shrugged. "Why are you telling me this?"

"Because Downing was your case. Yours and Ortega's. The gun that killed Gina Downing was the same gun used in the motel shooting."

There was a pause as Walker thought this over. "That doesn't mean he did it. No offense, Garrett, but it won't stand up in court."

"Downing also owed money to Ingleman. Big money. I think this was a way for him to settle his debt."

"By committing murder?" Walker blinked.

Reid shrugged. "Yeah, why not?"

Walker's eyebrows rose as the pieces fell into place. "You're saying Downing killed his wife?" It was a good act, but Reid wasn't fooled. Vargas said nothing, just watched the interchange, his eyes darting to whoever was talking.

"I am."

Walker frowned. "He was cleared. We've been through this before. Downing had an alibi."

"And I told you it didn't add up. You didn't question the manager at Bill's. If you had, you'd have known that Downing arrived late to his weekly bowling game. It would have been in the report."

Walker shifted uncomfortably.

"Why didn't you talk to him?" Reid pressed.

"We talked to all his friends, there was no need to question the guy at the bowling alley too."

"His friends confirmed he arrived late, and that wasn't in the report either. I spoke to a Luke O'Hara who told me Downing was nearly an hour late for the game. Was there a reason you and Ortega neglected to mention that?"

"What are you implying?" Walker's hands balled into fists.

Vargas swallowed, but Reid kept pushing. "I'm simply asking if there was a reason you failed to mention that Downing was late to the game?"

"He was held up at work. For God's sake, Garrett."

"He wasn't," barked Reid. "I checked with his employer. He left a little after five. I have the computer data to prove it."

Walker lowered his gaze.

"Ortega purposely left it off the report, didn't he?" Reid said.

"You don't know what you're talking about." Walker's tone was aggressive, a sure sign he was cornered.

"I think I do." Reid went in for the kill. "Ortega left it out because you were having an affair with Gina Downing. Her husband found out and that's why he shot her. You were worried that if suspicion fell on Matthew Downing, he'd divulge his wife was sleeping with you."

Vargas gasped. Reid hadn't told him what he'd discovered.

Walker stared stonily at him. "That's bullshit."

"Is it?"

Reid opened the folder he'd brought with him and pushed several photographs across the table. "These were found in Matthew Downing's belongings. Surveillance photos of his wife. He was having her followed. This one's particularly interesting."

He tapped a photograph of Walker and Gina at a hotel lobby. They were getting a room. It was one of the shots Donny Caruso had given him.

Walker picked it up and swallowed.

"The hotel confirms you booked a suite in your name. It's all on record. There's no point denying it."

Walker brought his fist down on the table. "Fuck!"

Vargas jumped, but Reid sat stoically, staring at Walker, letting the silence draw out.

Finally, Walker's shoulders slumped.

"Okay, fine. We were having an affair. We met a couple of months before that photograph was taken, when she was a witness in a hit and run."

Reid frowned. He hadn't picked that up, but then he hadn't been looking at Gina Downing, only her husband. He shook his head. He ought to have checked her out too.

Walker stared at his hands. "We began seeing each other. Gina wasn't happy with Matthew. They'd married young and... well anyway, it's not important. He was obsessed with her. I should have known he'd—" He clenched his jaw.

"Do you know what really happened that night?" Reid asked. Vargas was taking notes now.

"I can guess." Walker stared stonily at the pad Vargas was writing on. "Matthew found out about us. He had quite a temper. He must have gone home, confronted Gina and when she admitted it, shot her."

"I don't think so," Reid said softly.

Walker rubbed his eyes. "What do you mean?"

"Matthew planned to kill her. The whole thing was premeditated. The way the body was positioned, the blood spatter—everything points to him walking in the door and firing his weapon within seconds of entering the house."

Walker gaped at him.

"You missed it because you were so busy covering up your involvement. I'm guessing Ortega agreed to go along with it since he was your partner."

Walker nodded.

"I read the forensic report," Reid continued. "Gina was in the living room when Matthew let himself into the house. He kicked in the door to make it look like a forced entry."

Walker's eyes were hard.

"Gina wasn't expecting him back so soon, since he had a bowling game on Thursday night." Reid pictured the sequence of events. "As she turned around, he shot her from the doorway. She fell where she'd been standing. The bullet nicked her artery and she bled to death. It didn't take long."

Walker was breathing heavily.

"Then Matthew turned and left. He didn't have to worry about prints since they'd be all over the door anyway. He drove to the bowling alley and joined his team, acting as if nothing had happened." It was a cold, calculated murder. "It was only when he got home later that night and found his wife dead on the living room floor that he called 911."

The muscles in Walker's jaw flexed, but he didn't speak.

"You knew it was Matthew all along, didn't you?"

Still no answer.

Vargas stared at Reid with wonder.

"I have to tell Pérez," Reid said. "There'll be an internal investigation."

Walker sighed, resigned. "Let me do it."

Reid studied him. The muscular shoulders were slumped in defeat.

"Okay. I'll give you ten minutes."

Pérez wasn't happy. "Walker just confessed. Damn it, Reid. Now I'm down another detective."

"Yeah, sorry LT."

Earlier in the year he'd got Ortega suspended and now Walker. He couldn't help that they were both corrupt. Ortega had leaked information that had gotten an operative killed and Walker had obstructed the course of justice. He'd be lucky if he didn't get jail time.

Pérez shook his head. "This is why we need you back, Garrett. Who's going to lead this motley crew now Walker's gone?"

"Jonny Silva is a good detective," he said. "So is Ryan."

"Yeah, but they're young."

"They'll learn."

"It would be better if they had a mentor." He shot Reid a sideways glance.

"Jonny doesn't need a mentor. Besides, I told you before. I'm not coming back." Not to the Miami PD anyway. Too much water under the bridge. Besides, Ortega wouldn't be on suspension forever, and there was no way in hell Reid was working with that dickhead.

"Fine, so where does this leave us?" Pérez slumped back in his chair. "I'm going to have to reopen the Gina Downing investigation and bring the husband in."

"Not before I question him in relation to Barry Marshall's murder," Reid said. "After that, he's all yours."

"Deal." Pérez got to his feet. "I'll send Jonny over to Sweetwater to collect him when you're done."

The two men shook hands.

Pérez gave a tight grin. "And don't forget, if you change your mind, you know where to find me."

28

"Kenzie, a word," called Keith as she walked into the *Herald's* office, laptop under her arm. She bypassed her desk and went into his office.

"What have you got?"

Kenzie sank into the chair opposite him. "Quite a lot, actually."

She told him about the gun being linked to another murder, and how that suspect had owed Ingleman money. "It looks like he committed both murders," she explained. "First his wife, and then the witness in the trial."

Keith raised his eyebrows.

"It all comes back to Ingleman," she said with a flourish. "I think Ingleman offered to clear his debt if he took out the witness before the trial."

"Can we corroborate it?" Keith asked.

"Well, the suspect's been arrested in connection with both murders. Whether they can prove it or not..." She shrugged. Reid had his work cut out for him.

"Excellent work." Keith rubbed his hands together. "We'll lead with this tomorrow."

Kenzie glowed. Clayton lost his front page advantage. She looked across the open-plan office at him now. Head down, typing furiously, eyes glued to his screen.

"What's Clayton working on?" she asked.

Keith didn't look up. "Another angle. He's got something on Ingleman."

Kenzie frowned. Ingleman probably had his fingers in a lot of different pies, although he also had a legitimate business, a business that would suffer if he was proven to be a crook. Had Clayton found someone else to come forward? Or was it something other than the loan sharking?

She thought about the list of clients. Reid and his team would be chasing down those individuals to testify against Ingleman in court. He wouldn't let her use them, she knew him well enough not to even ask. By exposing more of Ingleman's illicit clients, she'd be putting them in danger and giving the loan shark time to silence them.

But had Clayton somehow managed to track one of them down?

"I want it by five," Keith called after her as she went back to her desk. That would give her enough time to write up the article and get to the restaurant for her shift. It was important to keep up her friendship with Simone.

She filed the article and was about to pack up when she remembered she had made a promise to Carlisle. He'd texted her the relevant information about his prospective client.

"Hey, Nick." She walked over to the economist's desk. "I need a favor."

He raised a bushy eyebrow. "I'm not going to be your wingman at some sketchy joint, Kenz. Last time I did that, we got kicked out of Razzles." She'd been questioning a customer who'd complained to the management, who'd thrown them out of the strip club.

"This isn't like that," she reassured him. "I just need to insert a quote in your piece on local Miami businesses."

"By who?"

"No one you know. It's for a source."

Nick sighed. "You know what? I don't want to know. I'm going for a smoke break. You've got five minutes." He got up and walked away from his desk, patting his pockets.

Kenzie slipped into his chair. She scanned the article he was working on. It was a run of the mill piece on how the recent budgetary changes were affecting the local businesses. She inserted a made-up quote and referenced Carlisle's client. Anyone reading the article would think he was a respected figure in the community.

"Reputation duly boosted," Kenzie mumbled as she hit save.

"Done?" Nick was back.

"Yep, thanks. I owe you one."

"Yes, you do." He winked at her and sat down.

Kenzie glanced at the office clock. Shit, it was past five.

She grabbed her bag and ran out of the office. There was no time to go home, which meant she'd be changing in the car. Being late wasn't an option. She couldn't afford to lose this job. It was her only real link to Ingleman.

Carlisle called Kenzie while she was on the way to the restaurant.

"It's done," she told him, putting the phone on speaker. The traffic lights turned red, so she searched in her purse for her make-up bag. "It'll be in tomorrow's paper. Page four. Business section."

"Much appreciated, Kenzie." His voice was smooth like caramel down the line. Not growly like Reid's. "But that's not why I called."

"It's not?" She took out the eyeliner.

"No, can we meet?"

"I'm a bit busy tonight," she said, applying it in the rearview mirror. "How about first thing tomorrow morning?"

"I think you're going to want to hear this."

"That's mysterious. Can't you tell me over the phone?"

"I'd rather not."

Intriguing. Her interest was piqued.

"I've got to work at the restaurant tonight. How about I make you a reservation and we can talk then? It's the best I can do under the circumstances."

"A noisy restaurant." She heard him thinking it over. "Sounds perfect. Send me the details."

Kenzie made the reservation as soon as she got in. "He's a friend," she told Marg. "I'll look after him."

The manager nodded. She didn't mind the girls soliciting business for the restaurant. In fact, she encouraged it, particularly when that business included the likes of Don Ingleman.

To Kenzie's surprise, Carlisle arrived with a glamorous woman who he introduced as Chloé. She wondered if they were a couple. Carlisle was so refined, so detached, it was hard to imagine him in a relationship with anyone.

"Chloé doesn't speak English," he explained with a cool smile.

When they were seated and had the wine list, Carlisle said, "Thank you for the article. In return, I thought I'd offer some free information on your friend's trial."

Free? This wasn't free. This was him paving the way for future "favors." That was okay, she was happy to cultivate a relationship with Carlisle. They could use each other.

"Ingleman?"

He tilted his head in acknowledgement.

"But the case was dismissed."

"Indeed, and I know why."

"So do I. It was because the witness didn't show up." She kept her voice low so only he could hear it.

"That wasn't the only reason."

"It wasn't?"

Marg walked past, eyeing her friend, so Kenzie straightened up. "I'd recommend the Lieu Dit Chenin Blanc."

Carlisle smiled. "Sounds perfect."

When Kenzie got back with the wine, Carlisle and his date were talking in hushed voices. She was loath to interrupt them.

"Would you like to taste?"

He gave a slight nod, and she poured a smidgeon into his glass. He took a sip, swirled it around his mouth in a practiced motion, then swallowed. "Excellent choice."

As she poured, he said, "Judge Heseltine has a little gambling problem. Texas Hold 'Em. He plays every Friday night in a suite at the Delano. He's had a bad losing streak recently."

Kenzie blinked. What did this have to do with the trial?

Then she gasped. "Are you saying he borrowed money from Ingleman to pay off his gambling debt?"

"Over fifty thousand dollars, if my source is correct. The interest on that will be pretty high."

Kenzie froze. That was one hell of an incentive.

"Are you sure?" she whispered.

"Oh yes."

Kenzie tried to get her head around it. Could the judge have dismissed the case in return for clearing his own debt? Holy crap. Was everyone in this guy's pocket?

"How do you know this?" she asked.

"Like you, I don't divulge my sources," he retorted. "You can look into it yourself. Suite 49. There are cameras in the lobby."

29

"How DID you say you found out about this?" Reid asked as they walked past a pair of enormous gauzy white curtains into the voluminous lobby at the Delano boutique hotel in South Beach. It was a little before eight in the morning, but the hotel was already bustling. Trendy guests wheeled designer luggage in and out while others ambled across the hardwood flooring to the dining room.

"You know I can't reveal my source."

"I might need to question your source," he grumbled.

"He won't speak to you. Anyway, I don't even know how to get in touch with him."

"It wouldn't happen to be your mysterious friend from the club, would it?"

She smiled. "I can't say."

Reid grunted but didn't argue. A lead was a lead. Whether it panned out or not was another matter. They'd know soon enough.

Reid showed his badge to the receptionist. "I'd like to speak to the hotel manager."

"Sure, one moment, sir." She picked up the phone and pressed a single button. After a few soft words, she hung up. "He'll be with you in a moment. Please take a seat."

They turned around to find an oversized lime green sofa positioned against the wall. They sat down and waited.

"I believe you wanted to see me?" A stocky man with a severe buzz cut stood there looking at them. From his posture and expression, he looked more like an army drill sergeant than a fashionable hotel manager. Reid got to his feet.

"Yes, thank you. I'm Detective Garrett from Sweetwater Police. I'd like to review your security footage from last Friday night." There wasn't enough evidence for a warrant.

"What's this in aid of?"

He hadn't said no. Reid took this as an encouraging sign and pushed on. "It's to do with a crime that was committed on that night. We want to check out someone's alibi."

"If they were here, they're in the clear," Kenzie added, smiling.

"We don't have cameras in the rooms," he said. "But if it's general footage you're after, we may be able to help."

"How about the lobby?" Reid inquired. "And if you have any in the corridors, that would be good too."

The man gave a curt nod. "We have that. Follow me."

Kenzie gave him a thumbs up. The manager seemed like a reasonable guy, and Reid was willing to bet he'd served in the military or some form of law enforcement. By rights, he didn't have to show them anything.

They followed him into a security room off the main lobby. Reid watched while the manager punched a series of numbers into a keypad, then pushed open the door.

"Solly, please help these detectives," he said, his voice authoritative. "They want to see some security footage."

"Yes, sir."

Even his staff treated him with respect. Reid was beginning to like this guy.

"I'll leave you with Solly," he said. "I hope you find what you're looking for."

"Thank you," Reid said, and meant it.

Solly brought up the footage of the night in question. He fast-forwarded through it until Reid caught sight of Judge Heseltine entering the hotel.

"Stop!" he exclaimed. "That's him."

Kenzie inhaled. "He *was* here."

They watched as the judge walked across the lobby toward the elevator. He was with another man who he appeared to know well. They laughed as the judge pressed the button. Once the elevator doors opened, they stepped inside and disappeared from view.

"Which floor?" breathed Kenzie.

They watched as the numbers above the elevator lit up. It didn't go very far.

"Can we see the footage for the fourth-floor corridor?" Reid asked.

Solly had preempted them and was already pulling up the footage. Reid was impressed by his initiative. "Here you go."

He wound the file to the same time as the men had left the lobby.

"There," whispered Kenzie when they came into the picture. The camera was positioned at the end of the hall, so they only saw the men once they'd stepped out of the elevator. They walked to the end of the corridor then stopped. The judge knocked on a door.

"Which room is that?" Kenzie asked.

Reid squinted at the screen. "I can't read it."

"Forty-nine," Solly supplied. "It's at the end of the corridor on the right. Ten rooms on every floor."

"Thanks." Reid glanced at Kenzie. "Well, Heseltine was at that game. Your source was right."

. . .

"I must admit, I never saw this coming," Kenzie mused a short while later as they left the hotel and walked back to their cars. "I mean, the judge of all people!" She shook her head.

"Just because he likes to gamble, doesn't mean he's corrupt," Reid pointed out.

"True," she acknowledged with a small nod. "But even if he was, how would we prove it? There's no evidence he knew Ingleman, or that they colluded to dismiss the case."

Reid frowned. "I don't recall seeing his name on Ingleman's list."

"*He* wasn't, but there was a Martin Judge," Kenzie said, remembering. "That could have been him. Ingleman might not have used his real name, just in case."

"That's not conclusive either," Reid muttered.

"I'll just have to get proof some other way," Kenzie said. "If the judge did dismiss the trial because of pressure from Ingleman, he shouldn't be allowed to remain on the bench."

Reid got a bad feeling in his gut. "Kenzie…"

"Don't worry, I'll be careful."

"What are you going to do?"

"Research. I'm going back to the office to look into Heseltine."

He exhaled. "Okay, fine. I've got to get back too. We're bringing Matthew Downing in today for questioning."

"Good luck. Oh, by the way, I managed to track down my old school friend, Bethany Greene. You know, the one who was with us that night in the market square. She lives in Palm Beach. I thought I'd visit her this weekend."

"Want me to come?" Reid hadn't forgotten about the investigation into her mother's disappearance. It had been put on hold when this case had exploded, and he'd been hauled in as a suspect.

"No, it's probably better if I speak to her alone."

"Fair enough. Call if you want to talk."

"Thanks, I will."

He shot her a parting smile and went back to his pickup. Downing would be at the station anytime now. A squad car had been dispatched to collect him this morning. It was time to find out what he had to say about Barry Marshall's murder.

"I don't know what you're talking about," he fumed.

Reid sat opposite a disheveled Matthew Downing, the cold, steel interrogation table between them. On it was a photograph of the deceased, Barry Marshall, outside the Gator Inn. It was pretty graphic, and Reid noticed Downing avert his eyes. He didn't want to look at it.

Vargas sat beside him, taking notes. Sweetwater didn't have the funds for a video link that showed the live footage on a camera in the squad room, but they were recording it and could play it back later.

Matthew had refused his right to an attorney, stating he hadn't done anything wrong and didn't know what this was about. "That's your prerogative," Reid had told him. It was better for him this way. Attorneys, in his experience, just got in the way.

"Are you sure you don't know this man?" Reid asked.

"I told you. No." A pause, then, "Who is he?"

"His name's Barry Marshall. He was supposed to testify at Don Ingleman's trial, but he never got the chance."

Matthew swallowed. "Well, I don't know him."

The flatness of his voice confused Reid. "Where were you on the twenty-third of August, between the hours of eight and ten in the evening?"

Matthew scrunched up his face. "Hell, I don't know."

"Think." Reid shot him a hard look. "It was a Friday, if that helps."

"Okay, okay." He closed his eyes. "I stayed in and played my game."

"Can anyone vouch for you?"

"Yeah, my team and the pizza delivery guy."

"I'm going to need their details."

"Seriously? I play online. I only have usernames for you."

Reid sighed. Another task for Vargas. "Give me whatever you've got. And the pizza delivery company."

"Sure." He shrugged. "I didn't do that."

"Except he was shot with the same gun you used to kill your wife."

Matthew's head snapped up. "I did not shoot my wife."

"The evidence proves otherwise." Reid leaned forward. "What did you do with the gun, Matthew? Did you keep it in case you ever needed it again?"

He glared at Reid, saying nothing.

"How do you know Don Ingleman?"

"Who?"

Reid smiled. "Very good. We know you owed Ingleman money. Your name was found on his client list. There's no point in denying it."

He gnawed on his lip for a moment, then muttered, "So what?"

"Well, you can see how it looks. You have an outstanding debt you can't pay. Ingleman needs a witness eradicated. You strike a deal."

"Fuck, no!" Matthew thumped his fist on the table. "You aren't going to pin this on me. I had nothing to do with that man's death."

"Then prove it," Reid said. "Tell me what you did with the gun after you shot your wife. Who'd you give it to? Because whoever bought it used it to take out Barry Marshall. And unless you tell us, it's going to fall on you. Are you ready to go down for a double murder?"

He was trapped. Damned if he did, damned if he didn't.

To escape the double murder rap, he had to confess to the first one.

"I think I need a lawyer," Matthew mumbled.

Reid nodded. "I thought you might."

30

An hour later they were back, but this time Matthew Downing had his lawyer present. She had hard eyes, a pinched face, and an expression that said she didn't want to be there. In addition, he'd called Jonny Silva from the Miami PD to sit in as the Gina Downing case now fell to him.

"My client is willing to make a deal," she said.

Reid fixed his gaze on Matthew. "Are you confessing to the murder of Gina Downing?"

He glanced at his attorney.

"My client wants assurance that if he assists you with your inquiry into Barry Marshall's murder, he'll receive leniency."

"Is he confessing to his wife's murder?"

"Only if you agree."

Jonny inhaled sharply. There it was. Matthew Downing had shot and killed his wife.

"It will be noted that your client cooperated," Reid said. "I can't speak for my colleague here, since the Gina Downing investigation is his case, but I'm sure he'll do what he can."

"We'll take your cooperation into account," Jonny promised.

"Let's begin with Gina Downing's murder," Reid suggested. He wanted to jump straight to what had happened to the gun, but it was logical to start at the beginning. He'd just have to be patient.

Jonny took over. "Talk us through what happened."

Matthew had a sulky expression on his face, like a child caught doing something naughty. "I knew Gina was having an affair." He kept his gaze low, refusing to look at anybody. "It killed me. I loved her so much and to think that she could...she could do that." He petered off.

"Did you talk to her about it?"

Matthew sniffed. "I confronted her. I begged her to stop seeing him, to come back to me." Reid almost felt sorry for the guy. "But she wouldn't listen. She said she was in love with him and wanted a divorce. I couldn't believe it. After all I'd done for her."

Reid knew he was referring to her parents dying and her moving into his family home.

"Is that when you decided to do something about it?" Jonny asked.

A sour nod. "I bought a gun, paid cash and gave a false name. He didn't ask questions. After that, I went to the house. All I could think about was how she was going to leave me."

"And you couldn't have that?" Jonny asked softly.

"I couldn't bear it." Reid heard the strain in his voice. Even now, two years later, it still hurt. "All I could think about was making her pay."

Reid stared at him. How you could think that about someone you loved, he had no idea. Even if they had threatened to leave you. There was something not quite right about Matthew Downing.

"I got madder and madder as I drove home. By the time I got there, I was furious. I was shaking so hard I could hardly hold the gun."

Neither Jonny nor Reid said anything. The lawyer still had her pinched expression, like she'd heard it all before.

"I kicked the door in. My aim was to go inside and make it look like a burglary, but I messed up. I was too consumed with rage."

"You shot her from the doorway," Reid said.

"Yeah, I saw her immediately and pulled the trigger. She collapsed onto the carpet. I couldn't believe what I'd done. I'd killed her."

Reid pursed his lips.

"I panicked. I didn't even go into the house. I just turned and ran." He sucked in air through clenched teeth.

"But you still made it to the bowling alley," Jonny said. He'd studied up on the previous report, and Reid had filled him in on the gaps.

Matthew stared at his hands. "I was going mad. I needed to go somewhere normal, to pretend it hadn't happened."

"Except you still had to go home afterwards," Reid said.

Tears filled his eyes. "Yes, I couldn't stand it. I called 911 from the car. I couldn't go back inside. Not with her lying there like that. Not knowing I'd killed her."

Jonny raised his eyebrows at Reid. That was it. He had what he needed. Now it was his turn. Reid gave Matthew a moment to compose himself, then he said, "Now can we talk about the gun."

Matthew swiped at his eyes, sniffed loudly, then raised his head. "I got rid of the gun. There was no way I wanted to see that thing ever again."

Reid leaned forward. "What did you do with it?"

"I wiped it clean and threw it in a dumpster downtown."

Shit. All this for nothing.

He wanted to yell, scream, hit something.

"How do I know you're telling the truth?"

Matthew's eyes widened. "I—I don't know. I made sure nobody saw me."

"Where was this dumpster?" Reid asked.

"I can give you the address," Matthew said helpfully.

Reid pushed a piece of paper across the table to him. "And the date. I want to know exactly when you threw the gun away. If you're lucky, we'll be able to pick you up on CCTV in the area." Matthew bent his head and started writing.

"Tough break," Jonny said, once they'd left the interview room.

"Yeah, I was hoping for a bit more than that." Reid strode back to his desk. "At least you got your confession. LT will be happy."

Jonny grinned. "Easiest case I ever worked."

Reid patted him on the back. "Glad to be of service."

After Jonny had left with his suspect, Reid called a team briefing. "Now, I know this isn't the way you've done things in the past, but we need to work together here. Matthew Downing disposed of a handgun in this dumpster two years ago." He pointed to the map he'd stuck on the wall with a small red sticker on it. "As you know, this weapon was used to kill Barry Marshall, our victim. I need to know what happened to that gun. What we need to do is collect all the CCTV footage we can of that area. Much of it won't still exist, but we have to try. Shops, restaurants, city CCTV, we need to scrutinize it all."

He was expecting moans, but instead all he got was eager faces and silence.

"Our window is from February 9 to February 12. After that, the garbage would have been collected. Let's see who finds that gun."

There were nods all around and the officers went back to their desks. This wasn't a bad department, it just had a rotten apple at the top.

Vargas stayed behind. "What shall I do, boss?"

He'd given up telling him not to call him boss. "We need to confirm that Matthew Downing really did get rid of that gun. Let's do it fast, because I'd hate for everyone to be trawling through reams of CCTV footage for nothing."

"I'm on it."

Reid was about to get back to work when a text message came

through from Kenzie. It hadn't been long since she'd left. Frowning, he opened it.

Got invited to a fancy party on Ingleman's yacht tonight. Judge might be there. Could be what we're looking for. Will keep you posted.

Hell no.

He dialed her straight back, but it went to voicemail. The little minx wasn't answering because she knew he'd try to talk her out of it. And she was damn right. Kenzie alone on a yacht with that snake. He shivered at the thought.

Even with the other guests there, it was too dangerous. Anything could happen at sea, and Reid didn't trust Ingleman one bit. Kenzie was in too deep, but she couldn't see it.

He sent her a message.

Call me. This is a bad idea.

But of course, he didn't get a response.

He let out a defeated sigh. She'd go anyway, no matter what he said. Kenzie wasn't the type to back down. Not if it meant finding out the truth.

31

KENZIE DRESSED CAREFULLY. She wore a dove grey dress with a silver shimmer that clung to her waist then fell past her knees in soft waves. She'd paired this with silver heels that sparkled as she walked down the pier to the waiting yacht.

Simone looked exquisite in a midnight blue gown that made Kenzie feel gaudy by comparison.

Reid had called twice that afternoon and left two voicemails on her phone, neither of which she'd listened to. He was trying to convince her not to go to the party.

If he knew Ingleman had asked Simone to call and invite her, he'd be even more concerned. Either it meant the loan shark knew she'd searched his house and found his diary, or he had designs on her after their last meeting at the club. Either way, it wasn't good.

Still, if she wanted to find out if he knew the judge, then she had to go.

"You look amazing," she told Simone, embracing her.

"So do you." Was it her imagination or was her friend's greeting slightly frosty? "Come on, let's go on board. The party's warming up."

Kenzie followed her up the short flight of stairs to the stern of the yacht. This area was reserved for boarding and disembarking and consisted of a wide flat area upon which sat a jet ski and a motor launch covered with a tarpaulin. Laughter and music wafted down from the upper deck.

"This way," Simone said, leading the way.

Kenzie recognized a few people from the club, but there were others she didn't know. Guests sporting platinum Rolexes and dripping with diamonds. Expensive boob jobs and plastic smiles. This was a wealthier, more exclusive crowd than at the last party. She wondered again why she'd been invited.

A shiver ran down her spine. Perhaps Reid was right. Maybe Ingleman was on to her.

And there was the man himself, standing near the bow, a glass of champagne in one hand, the other resting on the bow rail. He looked immaculate in a perfectly cut suit and freshly shaved with a satisfied grin on his face.

"Ah, Simone." He held out an arm. "You've brought your lovely friend, I see."

No surprises there.

"Mr. Ingleman. It's a pleasure to see you again."

"You're welcome. Please, call me Don, and help yourself to a drink. Simone, see to your friend."

Simone smiled indulgently and led Kenzie to the bar on the upper deck. "Don likes you. He said you two talked at the last party."

"We did." She kept her voice even. "He's an interesting man. I asked him about his businesses. I'm hoping he'll offer me a job at one of his firms."

The flash of jealousy she'd seen in Simone's eyes diminished. Thank goodness. She didn't want her friend to get the wrong idea.

"Oh, I'm sure he'll be able to help you. He employs a ton of people."

"Who's here tonight?" Kenzie asked, glancing around. "Anybody famous?"

"I don't know about famous," Simone replied. "But there are a lot of rich, important people here tonight."

"Like whom?" Kenzie played dumb. She'd already clocked a football manager, a record producer, the head of a big children's charity and a man she thought was linked to the Chicago Mob, but she couldn't be sure.

"That's Phil over there with the bald head. He's a sweetie although his wife is a pain, which is probably why he's brought his mistress tonight, Clarity. She's a blast." Her eyes roamed over the crowd. "That's Felicity Jacobs. She's one of Miami's top clothing designers. I've got a cream silk tunic of hers."

The other people Simone mentioned were either female or a designer of some sort. No one of interest. Then she saw him.

The judge.

He was standing on the port side of the yacht smoking a cigar and talking to a man she didn't know. Her heart fluttered in her chest. They were friends. Or something. Now she had to wait for him to talk to Ingleman, so she could get the money shot.

She took out her phone and pretended to check her messages. While she had the phone upright, she took a picture of Judge Heseltine. It wasn't the best photograph, but it verified he was on the yacht. She was sure to get as much of the boat in as possible to make it easy to identify.

"That's it," she murmured under her breath, as Heseltine made his way towards the bow. "Go and talk to the host."

"I want you to meet someone," Simone said, dragging her in the opposite direction. Kenzie grimaced but followed, slipping her phone back into her purse.

"This is Marc Anthony. He's the face of Avenci."

"Marc Anthony?"

"Real name," he said, displaying an array of disturbingly white teeth. She could swear they were glowing in the soft light on deck.

"Oh, right. Well, it's good to meet you, Marc. I'm Kaylee." Heavens, she almost said Kenzie. That would have been a disaster.

Simone beamed. It was clear she admired the male model. He was very good looking. Everything a model should be. Chiseled jaw, straight nose, full lips, and eyes that were always smiling. But somehow, he lacked depth. She thought of Reid's grisly jaw, strong features and penetrating gaze and found she much preferred them.

"What do you do, Kaylee?"

"She works with me, silly," Simone chastised him. "I've already told you that."

Had she?

Kenzie wasn't paying attention. She positioned herself so she could watch Heseltine's movements. He was very near to Ingleman now, although they hadn't spoken yet. Ingleman was surrounded by a group of men who looked like used car salesmen complete with greasy hair and slightly desperate stances. Perhaps they were pitching him something.

Then it happened. Heseltine moved into Ingleman's circle.

"Excuse me," said Kenzie hastily. "I'll be right back."

Simone was only too happy to be left chatting to Marc, while Kenzie ran down the stairs and along the port side of the lower deck to the bow. While she was moving, she took out her phone and clicked on the camera function.

Holding it by her side, she took several snaps in their direction, hoping she'd get one or two good ones of them together.

Another group of guests moved in front of her.

Crap, now she couldn't see. She maneuvered around them, raising the phone a little.

Snap.

That was a better one.

She lowered her arm just as Ingleman glanced over. He smiled, but it was more of a smirk.

Uh-oh.

Kenzie clocked his expression, and her heart skipped a beat. *He knew.* She was sure of it.

Turning around, she hurried inside in search of the restroom.

With shaking hands, she dialed Reid's number. It didn't connect. She glanced at her phone. No reception.

Shit.

Glancing out of the bathroom window she saw nothing but inky black sky. They were miles out to sea. Land was a flickering blur in the distance and getting hazier by the minute.

"Dear Lord," she muttered. Now what?

It's okay. She took a few deep breaths. *You're fine. This is a crowded party. He can't hurt you here. Not with all these people watching.*

What if he searched her? What if he demanded her phone?

She had to get rid of the evidence.

Quickly, she scrolled through the photographs of Heseltine and Ingleman and selected the best one. Then she texted it to Reid and emailed it to herself. They wouldn't go through until she had a signal, but at least they were on their way.

Then she deleted them off her phone.

Kenzie checked her makeup in the small mirror, and taking a deep breath, went to find Simone.

"Oops, sorry." She'd bumped straight into a man standing outside the restroom.

He gripped her arm.

"Hey!" She tried to wriggle free, but he held her in a vice-like grip.

Before she had time to cry out, she felt a prick in the side of her neck and the world went black.

32

REID TRIED Kenzie for the third time that evening, but her phone went straight to voicemail.

Shit.

She'd definitely gone to that party on the yacht.

He paced up and down his wooden deck, pausing every now and then to stare moodily out over the swamp. He had none of the details. He didn't know where the boat had set out from, where it was going, or when it would be back.

The edgy feeling he'd had since this afternoon was getting worse. He debated calling the Coast Guard, but they were busy and couldn't go chasing after a multi-millionaire's yacht for no reason. How would Kenzie react if he turned up, sirens blaring, and interrupted the party?

He pictured her face and almost grinned. Almost.

Damn it.

The least she could do was reply to his texts and let him know she was okay.

Cell phone reception was sporadic at best off the Florida coast. He could try to ping her phone, but she wouldn't appreciate that. He raked a hand through his hair. There was nothing he could do but wait. Wait until she got off that damn boat and called him.

Midnight, and still no reply. She must not be back yet. How long did these parties go on for? All night? He had no idea.

Reid tried to sleep but it was impossible, so he got up and resumed pacing.

At two in the morning, he tried calling her again, but it went straight to voicemail. He left a message. "Kenzie, call me when you get back, no matter what time. Thanks."

Did that sound too desperate?

She was probably partying up a storm with her new friend, Simone. Chances were, she hadn't even looked at her phone. So why did he have this fiery knot in the pit of his belly? He was probably overreacting, but it was the same feeling he'd had the night Bianca was killed.

He tried at three o'clock and again at four. Still straight to voicemail. The knot was a solid mass now. Something was wrong, he knew it.

Unable to do nothing, he got into his car and drove to her house. It was in darkness. He rang the buzzer, but there was no answer. He crept around the back, hoping none of the neighbors would see him and mistake him for a burglar. He peeked through the windows, but it was completely deserted. Kenzie hadn't come home.

Heart thumping a dread-filled beat, he turned around and drove toward the port, unsure what he was going to do when he got there. He didn't even know which marina Ingleman's yacht was moored at.

The sky was turning from black to indigo and the stars were starting to fade. In the end, he called the Coast Guard.

"It's called the *Safe Haven*," he told them, after some exhaustive Googling.

"Give us twenty minutes," the tired-sounding duty officer replied. "We'll get right on it."

Reid thanked them and hung up. He got to an intersection and pulled over, unsure which way to go. There were several marinas in the bay area. Ingleman's boat could be at any of them.

To distract himself, he checked the app that fed back the footage from the hidden camera he'd placed outside the drug kingpin, Alberto Torres's warehouse. It was in the port area, not far away. To his surprise, there was movement.

What? He'd been waiting weeks for something to happen, and now it appeared it was.

Two black SUVs were parked outside the warehouse, along with Torres's car. A bodyguard stood outside, surveilling the area, and that was a very unfriendly M16 assault rifle in his hands.

He should probably get down there.

He'd been watching Torres since the Cuban businessman had started up operations again. So far, Torres had kept under the radar. He'd changed his name and now ran a legitimate business, but Reid knew he was still the head of operations in Miami for the Morales cartel—and by the looks of things, they were active again.

Except a drug bust wasn't good enough for Torres. Reid wanted to get him for murder, he just hadn't figured out how to do that yet. At times, he felt like all he did was sit around and wait for something to happen. Now it was.

He glanced at the time on his dash. Almost five-thirty. The port wasn't far away, he could get there in under fifteen minutes. The occupants of the SUVs were still inside the warehouse.

His phone was ominously silent. There was nothing he could do about Kenzie until he knew where Ingleman's yacht was located. Making a decision, he turned left and headed toward the warehouse.

Reid crawled to a stop a block away and taking his gun and his phone with him, approached the warehouse on foot. He kept to the shadows, grateful he was wearing dark clothing. The morning air was fresh and tangy, the sun had yet to come up. There was a definite tinge of salt, or perhaps it was fish, in the air.

Here at the port, the day had already begun. Trucks rumbled past loaded with equipment, haulage companies picked up merchandise, and vessels docked in the bay.

Outside the warehouse, the guard kept his hand on his rifle, while his head rotated from left to right like a roving satellite dish. Reid was careful not to make a sound.

He approached the back of the warehouse where he knew Torres's office was located and crouched down outside the window. Voices were coming from inside. He couldn't make out what they were saying, but he heard the consistent murmur of a conversation.

Risking a peek, he peered through the dirty glass.

Four men, including Torres, stood in a circle, talking. They were casually dressed in jeans and shirts. This was a clandestine meeting. The light was on which meant he could see them better than they could see him—if they could see him at all. The sky was lightening, but it was still hazy, and shapes merged into shadows. He was safe for now.

He didn't recognize any of the men. They weren't from the cartel, or if they were, they weren't members he knew, and he'd studied them for years. He thought he knew all the major players.

Customers then? American buyers. He took out his phone and snapped a photograph through the grimy window. It wasn't clear, and he couldn't use a flash, but it might be enough to get an ID if they were on file.

The meeting was ending. Nods all around, muted laughter, handshakes and then the men left the office. Reid slunk back to his truck. The only way to find out who these guys were, was to follow them.

He checked his phone. *Still* no word from the coast guard. He tried Kenzie's number again, but like before, got her voicemail. Either her phone was off, or the battery had died.

Where are you, Kenz?

He watched as the men emerged from the warehouse and got into their respective SUVs. He took a few photographs with his phone, just in case, although the vehicles were probably rented. Reid had parked next to a prefab-style office block a few buildings down and with his lights off, they wouldn't know he was there.

The cavalcade of black SUVs filed out of the warehouse parking lot. Reid ducked as they drove past. He was debating following them when his phone buzzed. It was the Coast Guard.

Thank God.

He answered straight away. "Hello?"

"Detective Garrett? Pete Williams, US Coast Guard. We've got the information you requested."

"Yes?"

"The *Safe Haven* is moored at the Miami Beach Marina. According to the dockmaster, she went out last night, but returned at two a.m. She hasn't moved since."

He inhaled sharply.

Shit.

The yacht had been back for four hours. So where was Kenzie?

He watched as the line of SUVs disappeared up the road. If he didn't move now, he'd lose them. Still, he sat there, phone to his ear.

"Okay, thanks. I'll be in touch if I need assistance."

"Roger that."

He hung up, put the car in gear and screeched off toward the Marina. Kenzie ought to have been back by now. Something was wrong.

The familiar feelings of fear and panic spread over him. It was Bianca all over again.

That last text message:

They know.

Then the fear. The fear that came from knowing something bad had happened, and he couldn't get to her in time. Couldn't save her.

His hands began to sweat. He focused on the road, pushing the image of Bianca lying on the bloody floor from his mind. Kenzie wasn't an undercover agent, and Ingleman wasn't Alberto Torres. He was a respected businessman.

He was a loan sharking, racketeering scumbag. That was arguably worse!

Hang in there, Kenz. I'm coming.

He put the siren on the roof and flew along the causeway towards the marina. There weren't many vehicles on the road, but those that were got out of his way. The sky was a pale blue now, the sun rising unseen in the east.

Bloody Ingleman. If he'd hurt Kenzie, he'd kill him.

Reid swallowed over the lump in his throat. He only hoped he wasn't too late.

33

THE SAFE HAVEN bobbed idly on the bottle-green water, straining gently against her moorings.

"She came in on schedule at oh-two-hundred hours this morning," the dockmaster told him. "The guests disembarked, and the crew cleaned up." He grinned. "Looked like a good party."

Reid didn't grin back. "When did the last person leave?"

"The crew left around four o'clock. It took some time to clean her up."

"I need to get on board. I've got a missing person who was last seen on that yacht last night."

His eyes widened. "I'm afraid I can't let you on board without the owner's permission."

Like hell you can't.

Reid strode down the pier towards the yacht.

"Excuse me, sir. You can't do that. This is a private marina. I'll have to notify the authorities."

"I am the authorities," he growled.

He pulled himself onto the stern. The ropes holding it in place groaned under the extra pressure. Reid looked around. The only thing on the wide afterdeck was a jet ski covered by a tarpaulin. He felt the base of it; it was dry.

Reid walked around the main deck, looking in through the windows. The interior was empty and very clean. There were no empty glasses, no plates of half-eaten canapes, no sign of anyone having been there at all, let alone a whole party. He climbed up the stairs to the upper deck, which was mostly open air save for a dark grey canopy. Under it, a six-seater table stood surrounded by leather chairs. There was a bar area, and several high tables to lounge against whilst admiring the view.

No sign of Kenzie.

The dread mounting, he went back downstairs and tried the door leading to the interior of the vessel. It was locked. No surprises there.

He thumped on it and yelled, "Kenzie!"

No reply.

He tried again, rapping on all the windows. Perhaps she couldn't hear him... Perhaps she was unconscious... Perhaps... Oh, God. He couldn't go there.

The only response was the lapping of the dark water against the boat's hull.

The dockmaster stood on the pier, a worried frown on his face. "There is nobody left on board."

Reid hesitated. He wanted to go inside and look around, but he didn't have a warrant. He didn't have a reason to go in either, since the place was deserted.

Then a glittering item on the deck caught his eye.

He bent down to pick it up. A diamante earring. It was Kenzie's! He recognized it from that day at his place, on the deck when she'd told him they were a gift from her mother.

She *had* been here.

Then he noticed a second tarpaulin folded up and lodged behind the jetski. Something else had been standing here. A small motor launch, maybe? A rubber dinghy?

"I'm going in," he told the horrified dockmaster and threw his shoulder against the door. It didn't take much before it flew open. Inside smelled like detergent and bleach.

His stomach churned, but he forced himself to go inside.

Please let her be alive.

He didn't think he could handle seeing her dead or maimed body below deck. Not again. Not like Bianca.

Heart racing, he marched from room to room. The lounge, the helm, then below deck to the bulkheads and the galley. Kenzie wasn't there.

He exhaled. *Thank God.*

Then he noticed a door leading off the galley. What was that for?

He pulled it open to find a room no bigger than a large cupboard, used for storing supplies. He sniffed the air. Was he imagining things?

He inhaled again. There was no mistaking it. That was Kenzie's perfume.

She'd been in here.

He studied the space, large enough for one person. Crouching down, he saw a plastic tie lying beneath a shelf, the kind used to bind wrists and ankles. Kenzie must have been held captive in this room.

He ran back on deck. "I'm sealing off this boat. It's now a crime scene."

"What?" The dockmaster gaped. "But why?"

"Someone was kidnapped here." He pulled out his phone and dialed Sweetwater police station. The officer on duty picked up, his voice sleepy. When he heard who it was, he snapped to attention.

Reid told him to send forensics and some uniformed police officers to the *Safe Haven*. He needed scientific proof that she'd been here.

"Yes, sir!"

"Who's the captain of this vessel?" Reid asked the dockmaster, who was still mouthing like a guppy.

"Captain Reynolds."

"I need you to get hold of him, now. Tell him to come down here

ASAP with the rest of the crew who worked last night. I need to question them. All of them."

"Um, okay." He hurried back to his office to make the call.

An hour later, an annoyed Captain Reynolds and his bleary-eyed crew arrived at the dockmaster's office. Vargas and several of his team from Sweetwater were there too, as well as the CSI unit who were processing the yacht for Kenzie's DNA.

He interviewed the captain first. The dockmaster had been so kind as to offer the use of his office. Reid sat behind the desk, the captain opposite.

Reynolds was an athletic man in his late forties with dark hair, greying at the temples, and eyes that were crinkled from looking into the sun. "What's this about, Detective?"

"There was a young woman on the *Safe Haven* last night, Kenzie Gilmore. She boarded the boat with the other guests but didn't disembark this morning."

Reynolds frowned. "That's not possible. I would have known if someone had fallen overboard. We didn't contact any other vessels. There was no way for her to get off the yacht."

"Did you stop anywhere?" he asked.

The captain shook his head. "We anchored forty miles out to sea for much of the party. It was a calm evening. No wind. Perfect conditions."

"What about the motor launch?" Reid thought back to the extra tarpaulin. "Where is that?"

The captain scratched his head. "Isn't it on the back of the boat?"

"No, it's gone."

Reynolds shook his head. "I left the yacht at three o'clock this morning after a long night. I'm afraid I didn't notice the launch was missing." His craggy face was lined with concern. "That's the responsibility of the crew."

Reid believed him. If Kenzie had been taken off the yacht during the night, the captain may not have known about it. Reid went to find the First Officer.

"Grant Blake, sir," he said with an Australian twang. He had a full head of thick curls and a broad, smiling face. "I hear you're asking about the launch."

"Yeah, that's right."

"Andrei, he works for Don Ingleman, took a seasick guest back to shore."

Reid's pulse spiked. "What time was that?"

"Not long after we first anchored. Around midnight."

"This guest, did you get a look at her?"

"Yeah, kind of."

Reid pulled out his phone and pulled up the *Herald's* staff page. He held up his phone. "That her?"

"Yeah, man. That's her. She looked wasted."

"Drunk?"

He shrugged. "She was definitely on something; she could barely walk. We lowered the launch and Andrei took her back to the marina. The boss was scared she'd fall overboard."

He turned to Vargas. "Get Ingleman picked up and brought down here."

Just then, a silver Lamborghini pulled up outside the dockmaster's office. Reid watched as the loan shark got out. "Never mind."

"What is the meaning of this?" Ingleman demanded, storming over. He wore sweatpants, running shoes, and a loose T-shirt. It looked like he'd been working out.

"Sir, we're searching for one of your guests, Kenzie Gilmore. She was taken off your yacht last night in the motor launch."

He frowned and scratched his head. "Kenzie? I don't know that name."

"A friend of your girlfriend's," Reid pointed out.

"Oh, you mean Kaylee, the waitress?"

Reid gulped. Of course, she wouldn't have given her real name. "Yes, Kaylee. Sorry, my mistake."

Ingleman's eyes narrowed. "I haven't seen her since my assistant took her home last night."

"Your assistant?"

"Yes, my assistant, Andrei. Kaylee had a bit too much to drink and wasn't feeling well. He took her back in the launch."

"She didn't make it home." Tension gripped his throat and made his voice higher pitched than normal.

"That's not my fault. The last time I saw her was on the *Safe Haven*."

Some safe haven that turned out to be.

Reid was fast losing his temper. "Cut the crap. What have you done with her?"

Ingleman feigned a look of surprise. "I don't know what you mean?"

Reid took a step closer to him, his face inches away from the loan shark's. "You know exactly what I mean. Where is she?"

Ingleman held up a finger. "One second."

Reid was left stomping his feet while Ingleman turned around and made a call. "Andrei, remember that girl you took home last night? Where did you drop her?"

He listened while Reid gritted his teeth.

"Okay, thank you."

He hung up.

"Andrei brought her back here and put her in a taxi. He offered her a lift, but she refused. She said she'd make her own way home. That's all I know."

That *did* sound like Kenzie. Could it have happened as Ingleman said? She'd caught a taxi, but something had happened on the way?

His phone beeped. He glanced down, and his heart nearly stopped. It was a message from Kenzie.

Thank God. Maybe this was all a silly mistake.

He clicked on it, his finger trembling. The message popped up. It was a photograph of Judge Heseltine standing next to Ingleman on the deck of the *Safe Haven*. Proof that they knew each other.

He glanced up and saw the flash of fear in Ingleman's eyes.

Did he know Kenzie had taken the picture? Was that why he'd

kidnapped her? To stop it from getting out. Had he figured out who Kenzie was? Either way, he was lying.

Reid clenched his fists. Damn, he wanted to punch Ingleman's lights out. He took a few deep breaths, forcing himself to stay calm. Losing his temper would only get him into trouble, and that's exactly what Ingleman wanted. It was his word against theirs, and Reid had no way of proving Kenzie didn't take a cab home.

He turned away.

"What are we going to do, boss?" Vargas asked.

Reid took a moment to compose his thoughts. He pulled Vargas aside, out of earshot. "I want you to tail Ingleman. See if he leads us to Kenzie. Also, get a plain-clothed cop to tail Andrei, Ingleman's assistant. He might be the one keeping tabs on her."

If she was still alive.

Fuck, Kenzie. What have you got yourself into?

34

KENZIE BENT OVER AND WRETCHED. Her head felt like it was going to explode. When nothing came out, she fell back against the wooden chair. Her wrists were bruised from the plastic ties cutting into them, and her feet were going numb from being bound in the same position for so long.

When her vision cleared, she surveyed the room. She was in...a garage? The double steel roller door was closed, but there was a sliver of sunlight beneath it. The single window was high up and didn't open. Around the edge of the garage was a mishmash of shelving units, mostly empty except for a couple of abandoned tools. A pile of boxes stood in a corner, near a rusty old bicycle.

Where the hell was she?

Another wave of nausea coursed through her, and she closed her eyes. There was nothing in her stomach to throw up, apart from the champagne she'd drunk hours ago.

Was that how they'd drugged her?

No, it was after the restroom, when she'd sent that message to Reid.

She'd emerged into the gangway, and that man had barred her

way. Then, the prick in her neck. He'd injected her with something. Something that had knocked her out.

At some point during the night, they'd transported her off the yacht. She had a dim recollection of floating, but nothing concrete.

Now she was here.

The place smelled vaguely of motor oil, and there were a couple of grease spots on the floor. A vehicle had been parked here until recently. Twisting her neck, she tried to get a 360-degree look.

Her heart sank. There was no door, just the steel roller that was firmly shut. If only she could get her hands free, she might be able to find something to pry open the roller door. Maybe there was a manual override switch somewhere.

She tested the wooden chair. It wasn't bolted to the ground. That was something, at least. She'd seen in movies how if you rocked the chair back and forth until it fell over, the arms or legs would break, allowing you to get free. Except her wrists were bound on the outside of the arms. If she did that, she was liable to break her wrist.

Still, it might be the only way.

How long had she been here? Judging by the beam of light coming through the small window, it was daytime, but she couldn't decide if it was morning or afternoon. If the drug had knocked her out for eight hours or so, it was probably still morning.

What about Reid?

Had he received her pictures?

Would he realize she was missing and come and look for her?

A sob caught in her throat. What if he didn't? What if her text message hadn't gone through? He'd be annoyed she hadn't answered her phone, purposely ignoring him. Perhaps he hadn't bothered to get in touch again. He might not know she hadn't returned with the yacht.

A surge of panic gripped her, and she began to rock the chair from side to side. It gained momentum. She had to find a way out of here. Gritting her teeth, she flipped it over and cried out when her wrist connected with the concrete. Her whole weight came down on top of it and she felt something give. Pain radiated up her arm.

But the vertical slat of wood supporting the arm had broken and she could now slide her hand out. It was useless, still throbbing with pain, but at least half of her was free.

Kicking her feet, she slid them off the legs of the chair, then with her right arm still attached, struggled to her feet.

She gasped at the pain in her damaged wrist, but she had no choice but to use it to get up off the ground. Dragging the broken chair with her, she rummaged around on the shelves for something to use to free herself completely.

Her fingers closed around a wrench. She was about to bring it down on the other chair arm when there was a loud click, and the garage doors began to rise.

Back at Sweetwater Police Station, Reid and his team were searching for clues as to where Ingleman could have taken Kenzie.

"Check to see what properties he owns," Reid barked. "Anything from a factory or office block to a vacant lot or garden shed."

"His offices are downtown," Diaz, the female officer who'd worked with Kenzie on the diary, said.

Reid shook his head. "Too visible. He won't have her there."

"He owns a second house in Los Angeles," another officer said. "He bought it in 2012."

"It's possible, but I don't think he'd bother to transport her across country. He'd know we'd check up on his properties and it's too risky. Besides, if he plans on silencing her, why move her across the country to do it."

Just saying the words made his gut wrench.

"Do you really think he'll kill her?" Diaz asked.

"If we don't find her in time, yeah. She's onto him. She can destroy him with what she knows. He'll want to silence her."

It was too late to get back the photograph though. He knew now that Ingleman or his sidekick, Andrei, had destroyed Kenzie's cell phone hoping to prevent the message from being sent, but they'd been too late.

It wasn't damning in itself, but it was enough to get the judge investigated.

It was nearing midday when Reid got a call from a number he didn't recognize. Heart thumping, he answered it.

"Kenzie?"

"I take it you don't know where she is either?" came a gravelly voice down the line.

"No, who is this?"

"Keith Rogers, her editor at the Miami Herald. She was due to come into the office this morning. She promised me a follow-up."

"She's gone missing," Reid breathed.

There was a pause.

"What do you mean, gone missing?"

"I mean, she went to a party on Ingleman's yacht last night and didn't come back. I've got an APB out on her and we're looking into Ingleman, but so far nothing."

"Holy shit."

You could say that again.

"Have you spoken to Ingleman?"

"Yeah, he denies taking her. Said his sidekick took her back to shore in the launch. We can't prove otherwise."

Keith fell silent.

"She didn't say anything to you?" Reid asked, hopefully.

"No. I wish she had. I'll check with Clayton. He's been working on Ingleman for weeks. He might know where she could have been taken."

"Really? I'm coming over. I need to talk to him."

"Wait—"

But Reid had already hung up.

35

KENZIE FLATTENED herself against the wall, gripping the wrench with her injured hand.

"I see you're up?" Ingleman smirked. "Good."

A stocky man Kenzie didn't recognize marched in and grabbed her wrist. She cried out, dropping the tool.

Shit. She felt like crying. Now her only weapon was gone.

The man kicked it out of the way and Ingleman stepped into the garage to pick it up. The steel doors rattled shut behind him. It was like a death toll.

"Hello, Kaylee. Or should I call you Kenzie? Investigative journalist for the Miami Herald. It's a pleasure to finally meet the real you."

She scowled at him.

"In case you're wondering how I know, a colleague of yours called. Clayton, was it?"

She gasped. Clayton had given her up. That miserable weasel.

"He was worried about you. He called to ask if I'd seen you. Said you were working on a feature about me." Ingleman sneered at her. "Imagine my surprise to find out you weren't a waitress."

Kenzie shook her head. Clayton had outed her, all because he wanted to keep his job at the *Herald*. What a snake.

"He sounded terribly concerned."

She bet he did.

The sidekick still had her by the arm and wasn't letting go. She kept as still as she could because it hurt less.

"Now, what I want to know, Kenzie, is how you found out about me and the Judge. It was the judge you were after, right?"

She clamped her lips together.

"There's no point in keeping quiet. Andrei here has ways of getting you to talk."

Kenzie swallowed but held her ground.

"Very brave." He nodded at Andrei who tightened the grip on her wrist. She winced, her eyes watering. Christ, that hurt!

"How did you find out about the judge?"

"A tip-off," she rasped. The grip loosened.

Ingleman frowned. "Someone called you?"

"They called the office and left a message. I wasn't there."

He grimaced in frustration. "Man or woman?"

"Woman, I think." Anything she could do to divert attention from Carlisle the better.

Ingleman glanced at Andrei who shrugged.

"You're lying," he snarled, marching up to her. Up close he was terrifying. His eyes were dark holes. No emotion whatsoever.

"I'm not. I swear." Her voice wobbled. She hoped it was believable.

"Why would someone tip you off about that?"

"I—I don't know," she stammered. "Maybe they knew you'd paid him off to dismiss the trial."

He scowled. "So, you were investigating this? That's why you befriended my girlfriend and wrangled your way into my life?"

She didn't reply. She didn't have to. He'd worked it out.

He took a deep breath. "You nearly had me fooled," he admitted, reaching up to stroke her face. She pulled back, but he did it anyway. His icy finger slid against her skin. "Kaylee."

She swallowed. Was this it? Was this when he pulled out a gun and shot her?

"You'll be pleased to know I managed to stop your text from going through," he said.

Her heart sank.

No!

Now Reid wouldn't have the proof to investigate the judge. She'd put her life in danger for nothing.

"We destroyed your phone before it got a signal."

"It doesn't matter." She tried to bluff it out. "Lots of people knew I was on your boat. They'll come looking for me."

"Oh, your detective friend has already questioned me and my crew. Unfortunately, we couldn't tell him what he wanted to know. As far as he's concerned, Andrei dropped you at the marina and you made your own way home."

She closed her eyes. It was over. She was going to die.

"Deal with her," Ingleman snarled, and pushed a button on the remote. The doors lifted. "I've had enough talking."

Andrei reached into his pocket and pulled out a knife.

Reid stormed into the newspaper office. He was so mad he was about to explode. Vargas had called to say he'd lost Ingleman in the downtown Miami traffic, and the plain-clothed cop couldn't locate Andrei.

What the hell?

"I want everything you've got on Ingleman," he snapped, marching into Keith's office. The editor shot out of his desk in an instant.

They hadn't met, but now wasn't the time. "Of course. Follow me." Reid was pleased to see he was also concerned about Kenzie.

"This is Clayton Andrews. He's been researching Ingleman for weeks now. Clayton, this is the detective I told you about. He's going to need access to your files."

Clayton looked up and to Reid's surprise, his eyes were glazed with unshed tears. "I've done something awful," he whispered.

"What?" Reid didn't have time for tantrums, he wanted to find out where Ingleman had taken Kenzie before it was too late.

"I called Ingleman," he said.

Keith's eyes popped. "You did *what?*"

"When?" snapped Reid. "What did you say?"

"I told him Kenzie had disappeared and asked if he'd seen her." He stared miserably at his desk. "I thought if I blew her cover, he'd refuse to talk to her, then I'd get the scoop."

Keith stared at him, speechless.

"When was this?" Reid loomed over the reporter, crowding him with his bulk.

"This morning. Around ten o'clock. I knew she'd managed to get onto his yacht last night. I was hoping he'd be angry enough not to speak to her again."

Reid exhaled. "Ingleman already knew by that stage. She was taken last night around midnight."

"You mean I didn't get her killed?"

"We don't know she's dead yet," snapped Reid.

Jesus.

Keith found his voice. "Clayton, can you think of anywhere Kenzie might be held?"

Clayton opened a thick manilla folder. "Everything I have on him is in here."

Reid grabbed a pile of pages and began flicking through them. "I'm looking for a property that's easy to get to. Probably close to the port. A warehouse or a lockup of some sort."

Clayton thought for a moment, then started rummaging through the remaining pages. "I think there was... I seem to remember..."

Reid bit his lip in frustration. "Yeah?"

"Here it is. He rented a garage last year. It's downtown, near the port." Clayton passed Reid a piece of paper with a rental agreement on it. The ink was faded, and it looked like it had been Xeroxed many times, but that was definitely Ingleman's signature at the bottom.

His heart skipped a beat. "This could be it."

Reid took out his phone and called Vargas as he was running for the door. "Meet me downtown," he yelled, and gave him the address.

Please be there, he prayed as he jumped into his car. He couldn't lose her as well.

36

Kenzie closed her eyes as the blade dug into her throat.

Please let it be quick, she prayed. Hot tears ran down her cheeks. She didn't want to die. Now she'd never find out what had happened to her mother, and she'd never see Reid again. Surprisingly, that hurt more than anything else.

Reid.

He'd already lost one colleague, and now her. He'd blame himself because that's the kind of man he was. Even though it had been she who'd ignored his calls. She, who'd refused to listen to him when he'd told her how dangerous this was.

Yet she'd gone and done it anyway—and look where it had got her.

Sure, she'd got the proof she'd needed, but for what? Her phone was destroyed, the picture never went through. It had all been for nothing.

She gritted her teeth, waiting for the flick of the wrist that would end her life. Once her throat was cut, it would be seconds until she bled out.

"Did you kill Barry Marshall?" she whispered.

"What?" Andrei paused, tilting his head towards her.

"Did you kill the witness at the motel?"

He scoffed. "No, why would I do that?"

"To stop him from testifying."

She felt him shrug. The knife dug a little deeper. "There was no need. The case would have been thrown out anyway. The judge was on our side, remember?"

She did.

"But surely he only dismissed the case because the witness didn't show?"

"Our defense attorney was going to destroy that witness," he sneered. "He was an ex-con."

That could have worked. If the witness was unreliable, the judge could well have dismissed the case. There was no other evidence against Ingleman.

That left the question, who killed the witness?

"Do you like doing this?" She felt his arm stiffen. "Killing people?"

"Shut up. Enough talking. It's time to die."

Oh, Lord.

She muttered a prayer, feeling the blade slice into her neck. This was it. One quick motion and it would all be over. Kenzie Gilmore would cease to exist.

Then she heard a loud click, and her heart skipped a beat. Was it possible? In that fleeting moment, she hardly dared to hope.

Yes!

The garage door began to rise.

Andrei hesitated. She could tell he didn't know what to do. If he killed her now, it would be obvious he'd done it. Her bloody corpse would be found at his feet. There'd be no time to get away. No time to dump her body.

The steel rolled upwards, and Kenzie gasped when she saw the bottom of the police car outside. Andrei flicked his blade shut and stuffed it down the back of his pants.

"Hands in the air!" came a loud shout.

It was Reid. He'd found her.

Andrei lifted both hands into the air, releasing her, and she felt her legs give way. Unable to grab on to anything, she crumpled to the ground.

Heavy boots rushed into the garage and Andrei was arrested and taken into custody. Strong arms reached down and lifted her to her feet.

"Thank God you're alright."

Kenzie gazed into Reid's face, unable to believe he was here. She'd never been happier to see anyone in her entire life. "You found me," she whispered.

He held her close, one arm around her back, the other stroking her hair. "Of course. Did you ever doubt it?"

Overcome with relief, she buried her face in his chest and burst into tears.

"I got the photograph."

"You did?" She breathed a sigh of relief. "Ingleman told me he'd destroyed my phone before it had been sent."

They were in the observation ward at Jackson Memorial Hospital. Kenzie's wrist had been operated on and was now in a plaster cast. She was pale, but in good spirits. He was glad to see her ordeal hadn't affected her too much.

"I got it the next morning, while I was questioning him, funnily enough. I knew then he'd taken you. He was scared. That photograph could get him arrested again."

"Even though the case was dismissed?" Kenzie asked.

"Yeah, Judge Heseltine will probably strike a deal with the prosecutor to avoid jail time. He'll try to make out he was also a victim of Ingleman's heavy-handedness."

"I suppose he was, in a way."

Reid shrugged. "Either way, his career is over. Ingleman will be under investigation again by the Feds."

"He claims he didn't kill the witness," Kenzie told him.

Reid frowned. "Who? Ingleman?"

"No, his sidekick, Andrei. I asked him directly. He said they didn't need to. Not with the judge on their side."

"I wouldn't believe anything that creep told you." His eyes dropped to the scratch on her neck where the blade had dug into her. "He nearly killed you."

She touched it. "I know. It was the scariest moment of my life. I still feel sick when I think about it."

Good thing Andrei was in custody. They'd arrested him for kidnapping and attempted murder, but so far, he hadn't said a word. Reid had been hoping he'd give them Ingleman, but he'd lawyered up and was pleading the fifth.

"You should speak to someone," Reid said. "They have trauma counselors for this type of thing."

Kenzie shook her head. "I'll be okay. I just need a few days to recover."

Always so proud, so independent. "Don't be afraid to ask for help if you need it." The irony of his words hit home. After Bianca had died, he'd left the force and wallowed in self-pity for the next eighteen months. He didn't want Kenzie to go through what he had.

"I won't." She smiled at him. "Thank you for rescuing me. If it wasn't for you—"

He waved her thanks away. "I was just doing my job."

"Yeah, right." Her smile said she knew otherwise. He resisted the urge to take her hand.

"I can't believe that little weasel Clayton blew my cover."

"I think your editor was shocked."

"Yeah, he's fired him." She grinned. "Keith popped in on his way to work this morning. I've got the job—and the exclusive."

Reid shook his head. "You're still going to work after all this."

"Absolutely. I've asked him to bring in my laptop, and I'll be filing my article by the five-p.m. deadline. I can type with one finger."

He snorted. "Ingleman's still a free man. Apart from your testimony, there isn't anything linking him to your kidnapping. We can't prove he blackmailed the judge, unless Heseltine talks, and we can't connect him to the death of Barry Marshall."

She frowned. "Do you think he'll come after me again?"

"I've put a guard outside the ward, and I'll do the same when you go home. I don't want you to be alone for a while."

"Are you going to come and stay on my couch again?" She met his gaze.

"If you want me to," he said softly.

There was a moment where time seemed to stand still, then she took a sharp breath and changed the subject. "If Andrei didn't kill Barry Marshall, who do you think did?"

"I don't know. Detective Vargas was looking into a prison drug gang connection, but it didn't come to anything."

At her confused look, he clarified. "Apparently Barry Marshall ratted on someone when he was in prison. We thought there might be a revenge motive there, but when I spoke to the Miami PD drug squad, they said they hadn't heard anything about it."

"Any luck tracing the gun?"

"We're still trawling through CCTV footage, but I don't like our odds. If Matthew Downing dumped that gun in the dumpster two years ago, anyone could have found it."

"That's a bummer."

"Yeah. I wish there was more we could do, but Sweetwater is a small department with limited resources."

She smiled. "You like it there, don't you?"

"What makes you say that?"

"You seem, I don't know, happier than when you were at the Miami PD. Perhaps you should stay on."

It wasn't something he'd thought about.

"Casillas won't like that."

"It's not up to him, though. Is it?"

That was true.

"Anyway, speaking of work, I have to get back. I want to have another crack at Andrei."

Disappointment flashed across her face, but only momentarily. "Yeah, I've got another x-ray this afternoon, then I'm hoping to be discharged."

"I'll call you later."

She shot him a tentative smile. "Okay, great."

He wanted to say something else, but he wasn't sure what. Like he was glad she was alive, that he couldn't stand the thought of losing her, that he'd been riddled with fear when he thought something might have happened to her.

Then his phone rang, and the moment was lost. He held up a hand in a wave and strode from the ward. "Garrett."

"Boss, it's Willie, I mean Detective Vargas." He was breathy, excited.

"What's up Vargas?"

"I was looking on the system for any weapons recovered over the last two years in the Miami area and I think I found it."

"You found the gun?"

"Maybe. A Glock 26, lightweight compact pistol was handed in to the City of Miami Gardens Police Department by a refuse company worker two years ago. They've got it on record as being logged and put into evidence."

The timing fit. "Do they still have it?"

"No, sir. That's the interesting thing. It was signed out two weeks ago."

He frowned. "By whom?"

"A Detective Suarez, but he was on leave at the time. In Montana. He swears it wasn't him."

Shit.

"Does it match our bullets?"

"I don't know, sir. They didn't do a ballistics check on it."

"Why the hell not? A random gun turns up and they don't check it?"

"I'm not sure, sir. Shall I find out?"

"Yeah and ask them if they have a surveillance camera in their evidence lockers. Any way to identify who signed it out."

"Will do, boss."

Reid got outside the hospital and took a moment to gather his thoughts. They couldn't be certain this was the gun that had killed Barry Marshall, not until they'd had it tested. He had to admit, however, it was suspicious. A gun turns up at the same time, then goes missing a week before the witness is shot dead.

It looked like that scumbag Andrei was telling the truth, it wasn't Ingleman's idea to take out the witness. So, whose was it?

One thing he knew for certain was if the gun had been signed out of the police evidence locker, it was an inside job. Had to be. Nobody else would have had access.

Could the person who shot Barry Marshall be a cop?

37

Reid stopped at the Federal Detention Center where Matthew Downing was being held until his hearing. The imposing gray stone building was situated in downtown Miami and housed over 1500 male and female inmates.

After going through security, Reid was led to a small, "private" interview room. He glanced up at the camera mounted to the ceiling. There was no such thing as privacy in here.

The door opened and he heard a rattle of chains as Matthew was led inside. His eyes widened as he saw Reid sitting there. "What do you want? I've already told you everything I know."

The guard removed his restraints, and Reid gestured for him to sit down.

"I want to ask you about the gun."

"I told you—"

"What type of gun was it?"

Matthew blinked at him. "Um, a Glock, I think."

"You think?"

"I'm not a big gun guy. I bought it from a pawn shop in Homestead two years ago. I don't remember what caliber or anything."

"But you're sure it was a Glock?"

He gave a definitive nod.

"Okay, thanks." He got up.

"That's it?" Matthew looked disappointed.

"That's all I need."

He left Matthew sitting there, alone in the interview room, and nodded to the guard holding the chains outside. "He's all yours."

"There wasn't video surveillance in the locker room," Vargas told him when he got back to the station. "But there was in the corridor outside."

"Oh, yeah?"

"I managed to get a copy of the footage."

Reid thumped him on the back. "Good job!"

Vargas glowed. "I've got it up on my screen."

Reid had called a halt to the CCTV search since he was certain they had the right murder weapon. "Sorry to have wasted your time," he told the team. "Consider it training for future cases."

Many of the Sweetwater PD officers were fresh out of the academy, and this would have been a valuable lesson for them. Scrolling through video footage was one of the most boring but essential parts of the job. It required constant concentration over a long period of time, as well as attention to detail, even though it was a laborious task and most of the footage wasn't relevant. Some of the bigger stations outsourced the job to specially trained CCTV operators and facial recognition experts, but Sweetwater was nowhere near there yet.

"What have you got?" Reid asked Vargas.

He played the video. "This is August 18, six days before the shooting. I've isolated the times when someone comes into the frame. Twenty-one people walk down that corridor."

"Can we get their names?" Reid watched as a man with grey hair in casual attire appeared on the screen. "Hang on. Isn't that—?"

He broke off and stared at Vargas.

"Yes," the young officer said. "It is."

Reid sat across the table from Judge Heseltine and his attorney, a middle-aged man with a permanently neutral expression. Vargas had sent a squad car to bring the judge in for questioning. He wasn't pleased.

"What is this about?" Heseltine demanded. "I haven't been accused of anything."

"Not yet," Reid told him.

The attorney spoke up. "Why is my client here?"

"We would like to speak to him about this." Reid slid a photograph of Heseltine in the corridor at the police precinct in Miami Gardens across the table.

The judge glanced down and went pale. "What is this?"

"It's a picture of you at the Miami Gardens PD on August 18, on your way to the evidence room to get the gun you used to shoot Barry Marshall."

"What?" he spluttered, but it wasn't convincing.

The attorney glanced down. Unfortunately, the image was too clear to be mistaken.

"That is you, isn't it?" Reid dared him to deny it.

He gave a sullen nod.

The lawyer stepped in. "Just because my client was at the precinct on the day you specified, doesn't mean he's done anything wrong."

"No, it doesn't. But the gun was signed out at 3:47pm and you, Mr. Heseltine, were spotted in the corridor at 3:41pm. Nobody else walked down that corridor in the six minutes after that. It stands to reason that you must have signed the gun out of evidence using a false name."

"You'll address my client as Your Honor," the attorney said. "He is still a serving state Judge."

For now.

"Apologies, Your Honor."

"I'd like a moment to confer with my client."

Gritting his teeth, Reid nodded. He left the room to give them some privacy, making sure to turn off the recording on his way out. He didn't want any loopholes in this case, nothing that would give the defense a reason to disregard or throw out the evidence.

While he was waiting, Casillas marched into the squad room. "Garrett, you're out," he said.

Everyone glanced up.

Reid frowned. "What are you talking about?"

"I spoke to your old boss, Captain Reynolds, and you're off the case."

Reid stared at him. Reynolds had thrown him off the case.

"Why?"

"You should never have been on it to begin with," he said, his cheeks flushed with zealous satisfaction. "You were a suspect."

"I was cleared," Reid ground out. Was this guy a complete moron? "You should never have arrested me in the first place."

"That is a matter of opinion," he scoffed.

The rest of the team looked horrified. It was clear they didn't want their old boss back. They'd been doing some real police work for once, instead of writing up superfluous reports and handling minor infringements.

"I want to speak to him," Reid fumed, and stalked outside to call Reynolds.

"I'm sorry, Garrett, but you can't investigate a crime you were arrested for."

"It was a wrongful arrest. I was there to help."

"You were involved with the victim. His blood was on your shirt, for God's sake."

"From the night before he was killed," Reid stressed. "What's this really about, sir?"

"Excuse me?"

"Well, this is a flimsy fucking excuse to get me kicked off the case."

"Watch your language, detective. Casillas is right. You can't be working this case, especially with the inquiry into Detective Ortega still underway."

Reid fought hard to control his temper. "What's Ortega got to do with this?"

"You punched him across the squad room and broke his nose. I've spoken to internal affairs, and Ortega is going to press charges."

"You're kidding!" That lying, sleazy sack of shit.

"I'm afraid not. Stand down, detective, and do it now. Casillas is taking over the investigation."

"I've apprehended a suspect," Reid said. His blood was boiling. This was a conspiracy cooked up between Casillas and Ortega to get him thrown off the case. Revenge. My enemy's enemy, and all that. Bastards, both of them. "I've got him in interrogation now."

"Judge Heseltine?"

"Yes, how did you—?"

"Let him go," Reynolds said.

"What? No. I'm sorry, sir, but he's implicit in the murder of Barry Marshall."

"I've seen your evidence, Garrett. It's sketchy at best. He's a judge, for Christ's sake. He can look at evidence whenever he wants."

Reid was silent for a moment, then asked, "Did he speak to you?"

"Yes, as a matter of fact, he called me not ten minutes ago."

"You mean his attorney called you?"

"Well, yes, but I spoke to Howard."

"You shouldn't have done that, sir. Not during questioning." He clenched the phone so hard he thought it might break.

"I'm glad I did," Reynolds remarked. "Judge Heseltine is an upstanding state Judge, and you don't have the grounds to hold him."

"Surely, I should be the judge of that, sir."

"Not anymore, Garrett. Casillas is in charge now."

38

Kenzie sent her article to Keith and lay back against the pillow.

It was done. She'd just made herself a target.

The piece described how she'd infiltrated Ingleman's circle, the party on the yacht and how she'd been kidnapped and questioned about how she'd found out about the dishonorable Judge Heseltine.

Basically, she'd proven the judge was in Ingleman's pocket. The damning piece of evidence was the photograph she'd got back from Reid—of Heseltine and Ingleman on the yacht.

The world deserved to know what a scumbag Ingleman was, and the judge ought to be held accountable for what he'd done. It was no more than the truth.

Deal with her. I've had enough talking.

The only problem was, now Ingleman had another reason to come after her.

Revenge.

. . .

The doctor came in and told her she was free to go. Great. What she wanted now was a hot shower and to watch something mindless on TV.

But first, she had to call Reid. The guard at her door didn't know whether to go home with her or back to the precinct.

She called his phone, but it diverted to voicemail. He must be tied up. She tried the station. It rang for a while before an officer picked up.

"Sweetwater Police Department. Can I help you?"

"Detective Garrett, please."

The voice lowered. "I'm afraid Detective Garrett no longer works here."

"Excuse me?" Kenzie couldn't believe what she'd heard.

"Is this Miss Gilmore?" the speaker asked.

"Yes, who is this?"

"Willie Vargas, ma'am." There was the sound of footsteps, and she wondered if he was going somewhere out of earshot. "Detective Garrett was taken off the case," he told her. "Lieutenant Casillas spoke to Captain Reynolds at Miami PD and got him thrown off."

"But...but that makes no sense," Kenzie stammered. "I don't understand."

Why would Vic throw Reid off the case?

"Something to do with him being a suspect. Oh, and the assault charge."

"What assault charge?"

"I don't know, ma'am. Apparently, there's an assault charge being laid against Detective Garrett."

Kenzie took this in. She bet she knew who that was.

Ortega.

"When did he leave?" she asked.

"A couple of hours ago, ma'am. We had Judge Heseltine in custody too. Detective Garrett was questioning him in relation to the shooting."

Oh, boy. This was bad.

"I've got to go," she said. She had to speak to Vic and find out what was really going on. "Thank you for telling me, Willie. Appreciate it."

"We'll miss him around here, ma'am." There was no mistaking the regret in his voice.

"Captain Reynolds is in a meeting," his secretary called out as Kenzie stormed past.

She threw open Vic's office door. He glanced up.

"Kenzie, can this wait? I'm in a meeting."

"I'm afraid it can't." She walked into the room, so he knew she wasn't going to be put off.

The captain addressed the men sitting opposite his desk. "I'm sorry, let's reschedule."

They got up and left, glancing curiously at Kenzie as they did so.

"Why did you kick Reid off the case? He was about to make an arrest."

"Kenzie, I heard about what happened. My God, are you alright?" He stared at her wrist in the sling.

"Ingleman did this." She stared at him accusingly. "And the judge was going to talk when you interrupted the interrogation and forced Reid to let him go. How could you do that?"

"Kenzie, please..."

"Now Ingleman is still out there. He's going to come after me, you do realize that?"

Reynolds leaned back in his chair. "Aren't you being a tad dramatic?"

She hated it when he patronized her.

"No, Vic. I'm not. I've just written an article outlining *everything* that happened. It's going to be in tomorrow's paper. If you won't see justice done, I will."

Vic's face darkened. "I wouldn't advise that, Kenzie."

"Why not? It's the truth."

"Ingleman is a dangerous man."

She scoffed. "Don't I know it? And thanks to you, he's probably going to get away."

"Garrett can't be working that case," he said. "He was involved in the start of it, and there's now an assault charge laid against him."

"By Ortega?"

"I'm not at liberty to say."

"For God's sake, Vic. Xavier lied to me. He told me that undercover officer was out. I would never have written that article otherwise. That's what got her killed. *He* got her killed."

"And he's been suspended, as you know."

"That's why Reid punched him. He deserved it."

"Garrett knocked him across the station, broke his nose. He's laying charges. I can't blame him. Garrett is a detective, he should have known better regardless of what Ortega had done."

This couldn't be happening.

"Why are you protecting him?" she asked, walking right up to his desk.

"I'm not protecting anyone."

"Yes, you are. You're protecting Ingleman. By letting the judge go, you're ensuring there's no evidence against him, and by taking Reid off the case, you're ensuring that there won't be any more evidence forthcoming. Casillas is an idiot. He won't solve this case."

"Kenzie, be careful what you're saying."

"Why? Is it the truth? Are you protecting him?"

Vic got to his feet. He was a big man and towered over Kenzie. "I think it's time you left, Kenzie."

It was his attempt to intimidate her. "I see. Well, thanks for clearing that up."

And she left him staring after her as she marched out of his office.

. . .

She found Ortega at home, digging up a flower bed. "How's suspension?" she asked. They hadn't spoken since that day at the restaurant when she'd told him not to contact her again.

"Fine. I've decided to plant an herb garden."

"That bad, eh?"

He shrugged. "I like the extra time. It's like a long vacation."

"Have you been anywhere?"

"No, can't. I've got this damn investigation going on."

She put her hands on her hips. "Why are you laying an assault charge against Reid?"

He scowled. "Who told you that?"

"Vic Reynolds."

He picked up his shovel. "He broke my nose. It's still not right." He touched it gingerly. It looked fine to her.

"Was it your idea? Or did someone suggest it?"

"It was my idea. He punched me, Kenz. He can't get away with that." But he'd hesitated a fraction too long.

"Who put you up to it?"

"I don't know what you mean."

"Come on, Xav. I know you too well. This wasn't your idea. You're not that petty. Someone put you up to this, who was it?"

He sighed. "Some guy came to see me a couple of days ago. He told me it wasn't right what Garrett had done. He had a beef against him too, and said if we both laid a complaint, it would have more impact."

"Casillas? Was that his name?"

"Yeah, that was it."

Kenzie shook her head. "He's a corrupt cop and an imbecile. You should never have listened to him."

"He made sense." Ortega pursed his lips. "Why should I be the only one on suspension?"

"Because you're the one in the wrong! Reid didn't do anything—except break your nose. But you deserved that. You have to withdraw the charge."

"I don't know, Kenz."

"Xav, you're not that guy. You don't rat on fellow cops, and you own up to your mistakes. That's the man I was friends with."

He was silent for a moment.

"Casillas is not a good guy," she told him. "Don't back him up. You'll get yourself into even more trouble."

Ortega threw the shovel back into the recently churned earth. "Okay, Kenz. You win. I'll drop the charges. Happy now?"

She stepped forward and hugged him. "Thank you. It's the right thing to do."

39

REID WENT AS FAST as he dared. The airboat flew over the water, skimming the sawgrass and sliding out every time he changed direction. The jet engine roared in his ears, drowning out everything else. Pity it couldn't drown his thoughts.

Fucking Casillas. He had no idea what he'd done. His petty quest for vengeance had resulted in both the judge and Ingleman getting away.

To make matters worse, he was now facing an assault charge.

He ground his jaw and kept going. A flock of birds took flight when they saw him coming and lifted off into the clear blue sky. It was a glorious evening, but everything felt rotten to him.

They'd been so close. The judge was going to strike a deal. He knew it. That's why he'd wanted to speak to his attorney. He'd been about to blow the whistle on Ingleman and the whole nasty racketeering side-business, not to mention Barry Marshall's murder. So Ingleman hadn't pulled the trigger, but Heseltine wouldn't have done it if he hadn't felt threatened.

He kept going, into the mangrove forest where he decreased the speed. The trees stretched above him, their branches intertwining, forming a canopy over the waterway. In the shadows down below, the mangrove roots clawed at the murky water.

He cruised along it for some time, heading deeper into the swamp before he cut the engine entirely. The momentum kept the airboat going for a while, the water gently lapping at the hull.

A splash to the left made him turn around, just in time to see the tail of a large alligator dive into the water. He stared at the spot where it had gone in for a while but saw only bubbles rising to the surface.

The danger was always lurking below, just out of sight.

He sat there, mulling things over until he'd calmed down enough to consider his options. He couldn't go back to Sweetwater, Casillas had made sure of that. Pérez would have taken him back, but not now with this assault charge hanging over his head. He'd have to fight that and clear his name. Otherwise, his career in the force was over.

He sighed. Kenzie was right. He had been enjoying it there. He liked mentoring the young officers and seeing them develop. Vargas, Diaz, they all had potential. Hopefully it had given them a taste of real detective work, and they wouldn't be derailed by old lazy guts.

It was getting dark, time to head home.

He turned around and drove back to his cabin, not quite as manic as before. The setting sun was a fiery ball to the west turning the surface of the water a molten orange hue. He sliced through it until he saw the floating walkway leading from his deck.

A lone figure stood looking out over the water.

Kenzie.

With the sun behind her, she looked like a goddess, her blonde hair aflame.

He pulled in and threw her the rope. "Wrap that around the pole for me?"

She did as instructed, then wiped her hands on her jeans. "Good ride?"

He grunted. "I'm guessing you heard what happened?"

"Yeah, freaking Casillas."

He checked the mooring, then strode past her up onto the deck. "Want a beer?"

"Sure."

He got two cold ones out of the fridge, opened them, and handed one to her. They took them back outside. It was too nice an evening not to enjoy it.

"I had to let off some steam."

"I talked to Vic."

He turned to her. "You did? What did he say?"

"He's protecting Ingleman, I'm sure of it."

Reid gave a terse nod. He'd had the same thought when he'd gone to see the police captain. "Why? Do you think Ingleman has something on him?"

"I don't know. Vic is a sucker for the rules. I can't see anyone getting to him, even Ingleman."

"Why then? Why kick me off the case just when I'm making headway? It doesn't make sense."

"Could it be related to the judge somehow?" Kenzie mused. "Maybe they colluded to send a bad guy to prison or cut a few corners."

Reid shrugged. "I don't know, Kenz, but something's going on."

He took a sip of his beer. "I see you left your security detail at the hospital."

"Yeah, sorry. I wasn't sure what to do with him, so I told him to go back to the station."

He gave an ironic grin. "Yeah, I can't insist on it now that I'm not a detective anymore."

"Reid, I'm so sorry," she said. "If it wasn't for me, you'd never have got involved in the first place."

"That's not true," he said. "I was involved the moment I separated those two guys in the bar fight. What's happened has nothing to do with you."

He clenched his hand. It was the one he'd used to punch Ortega in the nose.

"Did you hear about the assault charge?" he asked.

"Vic told me that's why you were thrown off the case, along with being a suspect."

"Feeble excuse," he growled.

"I talked to Ortega," she began.

He jerked his head up. "You what? Why?"

"I was mad at him," she admitted. "He was being a dickhead laying a charge against you."

Reid couldn't help but smile at her choice of words. He couldn't have put it better himself. "What did the dickhead have to say?"

"I convinced him to drop the charges."

"You did?" He stared at her. "Really?"

"Yeah, I told him to man up to his mistakes and not to be a rat. He didn't like that."

Reid chuckled. It felt good to laugh. Some of the tension in his neck and shoulders dissipated.

"Thank you, Kenzie. Seriously, you didn't have to do that."

"I did, and he shouldn't have laid those charges to start with. Casillas got to him, did you know that?"

"I figured as much."

"Anyway, at least you're in the clear on that front." She gazed up at him, full of self-righteous anger on his behalf.

He embraced her, he couldn't help it, she was so indignant. He put his arms around her and gave her a big hug, careful not to squeeze her injured wrist. She stiffened, then he felt her relax and her good arm snaked around his back. She gave him a little squeeze.

"Thank you," he said, releasing her. She was flushed and embarrassed, but for once, he didn't care. She'd done him a massive favor. "I mean that. You've literally saved my job."

"It's only right."

He took a long draw on his beer. It tasted better than it had before. He could still be a detective, thanks to her.

"What are you going to do now?" she asked, her cheeks calming down.

"I'm going to fight fire with fire."

"Oh, yeah?" She raised an eyebrow. "What does that mean?"

"It means I'm going to get Casillas fired. I'm going to go straight to the Chief and file a complaint. Two can play this game, and I've been in the business a lot longer than he has."

Kenzie smiled. "Your team at Sweetwater will be happy. I spoke to Willie who told me how sad they were to lose you."

He grinned. "They're a good team. Young, but dedicated."

"Perhaps you can go back there after you kick the lieutenant out."

He met her gaze. "Perhaps. In the meantime, do you want me to come and stay at your place tonight?"

She bit her lip. "You really think he'll come after me?"

"I don't think we can take the chance."

She hesitated. "You're probably right. Okay, if you're sure you don't mind."

"I never mind."

40

KENZIE FELT MUCH BETTER HAVING Reid's strong, manly presence around the house. Every time she thought of Ingleman's dark gaze she shivered.

She watched him double-check the lock on the front door. "All secure. If anyone breaks in, I'll know about it."

"Thanks, Reid."

"You're welcome. Now, what are we going to do about dinner?"

She held up her injured wrist. "I'm handicapped. We'll have to order out. I'm afraid there isn't much in the house."

"Do you have eggs? Cheese?"

"Yeah, I think I do."

"Okay then, I'll make an omelet. Unless you'd prefer take-out?"

"Omelet's great."

He got to work in the kitchen. Kenzie started to follow him when her phone rang. She didn't recognize the number.

"Hello?"

"Hi, is this Kenzie?"

"Yes."

"Kenzie, this is Bethany. Bethany Greene."

Kenzie gasped. "Bethany! It's so good to hear from you. You got my message?"

"Yes, sorry it's taken so long to get back to you. I was on a work trip. I just got back and heard your message on my machine. How are you doing?"

"I'm good." If you didn't count the kidnapping, the broken wrist, and the target on her back. "Listen, I need to ask you about something, would it be okay if I came to see you?"

"Oh, well yes, of course. Are you alright?"

It was weird talking to her school friend after all these years. She sounded the same, only more mature, and Kenzie pictured her with long brown hair, a side part, and a toothy grin.

"I'm fine, it's about... well, never mind. I'll tell you when I see you. Would tomorrow be okay?"

"Yes, have you got a pen? I'll give you my address."

Kenzie wrote it down, thanked Bethany, and said she was looking forward to seeing her. Then she went to talk to Reid.

"Well, I've got nothing better to do," he replied, after she'd told him what had happened. "It'll be good to get back to your mother's investigation. We kind of left that hanging, didn't we?"

"This case took over," Kenzie groaned. "At least now my job is safe, and I can relax a bit."

"Tomorrow your article hits the newsstands."

She sobered. "Then it's probably a good thing I won't be here. Bethany lives in Palm Beach."

"It's only an hour's drive, but yeah, it's best if you're out of town for the day."

"Do you think they'll catch Ingleman?" A flicker of anxiety made her gut clench.

"I don't know," he admitted, carefully flipping the omelet. "I wish I could say yes, but he's had fair warning. If he's smart, he'll have left Miami by now. I doubt he'll stay and fight this."

"Even with Heseltine being let off?"

"There's still your testimony. You can do a lot of damage in court."

She gave a firm nod. "I hope I get the chance."

He turned to her, frying pan in one hand, spatula in the other. "I'll make sure of it, Kenz. Nothing's going to happen to you while I'm here."

God, that sounded good.

But he wouldn't be here all the time. He couldn't protect her 24/7. Still, that was good enough for now.

The next morning they set off for Palm Beach. Reid drove, while she flicked through her mother's case file. "You know, Bethany left right after she went missing. Uncle James took her home. She probably won't be of much use."

"Still, we'd better check. Sometimes it's the leads that you least expect that turn out to mean something."

The omelets last night weren't half bad. Kenzie was impressed with his cooking skills. Reid was surprisingly domesticated for a single, loner cop. Perhaps he'd had to be. Then she remembered he had a mother and a sister in Pennsylvania.

They'd sat side by side on the couch and watched a movie, but Kenzie found she couldn't relax. She kept glancing at the window, expecting to hear glass crash, or a gun being fired. In the end, she excused herself and went to bed. Part of her knew she was overwrought from her experience, and part of her just wanted to forget about it.

The night had passed uneventfully, and she felt much better this morning. Cheerful even, which was bizarre considering she may have a hit out on her.

"That's it," Kenzie pointed to a cute cream house with a short drive and a bushy garden filled with flowers. Bethany must like to garden.

The door opened as they pulled in and a woman rushed out.

"Kenzie, oh my goodness. I can't believe you're here after all this time."

"I know, I'm sorry to intrude."

"No, don't be silly. It's lovely to see you." She glanced at Reid. "Is this your husband?"

"Oh, um, no. This is my friend, Detective Reid Garrett. Reid, this is Bethany."

They shook hands, although Bethany shot her a curious look. It must seem odd, her being here after twenty years with a police detective.

"I'm sure you're wondering what on earth this is all about," Kenzie began.

Bethany laughed. "I am intrigued. Come in, and let's have some lemonade, or would you prefer something else? Coffee?"

"Coffee would be good," they both said in unison.

Kenzie flushed.

"I'll help you." She followed Bethany to the kitchen.

"Are you married?" Kenzie asked.

"No, but I'm engaged." She flashed her engagement ring. "He's a lawyer, like me, but he practices family law, while I do contract law."

"Wow, a lawyer! That's great." Bethany had always been smart.

"What do you do? Are you with the police?"

Almost.

"No, I'm an investigative journalist. I work for the Miami Herald."

Bethany raised her eyebrows. "That's amazing. What an exciting job. Is that why you're here? Something to do with an article?"

"No, actually I wanted to talk to you about the day my mother disappeared."

Bethany didn't immediately reply. She poured the coffee, then handed one to Kenzie. "I'm sorry about what happened," she said. "I wanted to keep in touch but my parents... and then by the time I went to college it seemed too late to call you."

"It's okay." Kenzie smiled. "I understand. I thought that's what had happened. It was the same with a lot of people."

Everyone, really.

"Did you ever find out what happened to her?" she asked.

They carried the coffee back to the living room. Reid was sitting on the sofa, his long legs stretched out in front of him. "Thanks," he said, as Bethany handed him a mug. "Smells good."

"No, sadly I didn't. That's why we're here. Reid is helping me look into her disappearance. We've spoken to everybody else who was at the market that day, except you."

"Oh, well I don't know how much help I'll be. I barely remember anything."

Kenzie shot Reid a deflated look.

"Could you tell us what you do remember?" he asked.

Bethany sat down, her back very upright. "I remember walking around with you and your parents," she began, looking into the distance. "There was another man with you, a family friend."

"Yes, James. He walked you home."

"That's right. We went to talk to the boys at the grotto." She smiled. "I had the biggest crush on Tom. We actually dated for a while after that."

"Oh, I didn't know." She'd been too distraught to notice.

"Of course you didn't. I'm sorry, Kenzie."

Kenzie waved her apology away. "Please, carry on."

"Well, after they left, we went back to your dad, but by that point, your mom had gone. Nobody knew where she was. You guys stayed to look for her and your dad's friend walked me home. That's all I remember."

Kenzie's heart sank. It was as she'd expected.

"I remember that nice police detective, your father's partner, wasn't it? He came around later and asked me a couple of questions."

"Vic Reynolds?" It was the first Kenzie had heard of this. She couldn't recall reading about it in the report.

"Yes, that's him. My mom knew his wife quite well. They were in the same book club or something."

"Really?" Kenzie felt her attention waning. They'd come all this way for nothing.

Bethany leaned forward. "I remember after he left, my mom told my dad that his wife suspected he was having an affair."

Kenzie frowned. "Vic Reynolds having an affair? Are you sure?"

She gave a little shrug. "Apparently it was true, because they split up soon after that."

"How do you know this?" Reid asked.

"My mom lived with me up until last year. She passed away. Cancer."

"I'm so sorry," Kenzie said automatically.

"Thanks. Anyway, mom and Yvonne were quite close, even after the divorce. I remember her telling my father how tough it was on her. Your dad's partner suddenly packed up and left. He refused to have anything more to do with her. I think she may even have had some sort of breakdown."

Kenzie tried to process this with what she remembered, but she couldn't. She knew Vic had got divorced, but the timing was blurry. "Did they split up soon after my mother disappeared?" she asked. That could be why she didn't remember much.

"Right after, yes. My parents used to say what a disastrous year it was. First your mother disappearing like that, then Vic leaving Yvonne. It seemed like everything was falling apart for a while. I suppose I felt it too since I was forbidden from seeing you again."

She could feel Reid's eyes on her.

"Did your parents know who Vic was having an affair with?" asked Reid.

Kenzie's heart thumped in her chest. She'd been wanting to ask the same question but couldn't find the words. Perhaps it was because she didn't want to know.

"No, I'm sorry. If they did, they didn't tell me."

Kenzie exhaled.

They talked about random school friends for a while after that, then Kenzie said they had to go. "Thank you so much for talking to me, Bethany. I really appreciate it."

"You're welcome. It was lovely seeing you again. Take care, Kenzie."

"You too."

41

Kenzie was quiet on the way back to Miami.

"You don't know it's her," Reid said, after they'd driven for twenty minutes in complete silence. He could tell it was bothering her, what Bethany had said.

"I had no idea Vic was having an affair." She stared out of the window. "Or that he and Yvonne split up that same year. It's a coincidence, right?"

"Most likely." There was always a chance that Kenzie's mother had been having an affair with her husband's partner. It happened. After all, they would have spent a lot of time together.

"My father and Vic were close," she said. "Surely my father would have said something if she'd been cheating on him."

"Unless he didn't know."

Kenzie's voice wobbled. "It's possible, though. Isn't it? I mean think about it. They were best friends. Partners. We were always at their house and vice versa. They didn't have kids, but I remember going around there for barbecues all the time." She put a hand over her mouth. "Oh, God. What if that's why my father wouldn't talk about her? He found out."

Reid wished he could make this easier for her. The only way he knew how to do that was by getting to the truth. "What was your father's relationship like with Vic after your mother disappeared?"

"Fine. I think. He took some time off work, obviously. Then one day he just announced he was going back."

"Did they go back to being partners?"

Kenzie crunched up her forehead. "No, they didn't. Vic had a new partner by then. My father took almost a year off."

"Did you still see him?"

"Come to think of it, we didn't, no. But we didn't see anybody for a long while. My father never even dated again. He died when he was fifty-seven."

"That's young, I'm sorry."

"Thanks. I think it's the grief that did it. He was never the same after my mother disappeared."

Reid couldn't imagine it. It's the not knowing that would get to him. How did you reconcile that? At least he knew what had happened to Bianca. It was there for him to see in all its vivid detail. The blood on the office floor. Horrific, but undeniable.

For Kenzie's father, there was no closure. The poor guy would have driven himself mad imagining different scenarios, while never knowing the truth.

"Perhaps my father found out and that's when he went back to work. He figured she'd left him. Left them both."

"Why would she leave them both?"

Kenzie gasped. "You don't think Vic killed her?"

Reid slowed down. "Let's not jump to conclusions, Kenzie. We don't know for sure any of this happened."

But she was on a roll, her imagination tumbling out of control.

"What if she ended it, and they fought, and he killed her. It would have been a mistake but... Oh, God."

He pulled over. "Kenzie, listen to me. Don't do this to yourself. We can theorize all we want, but it's not going to help us. If we want to know what really happened, we'll have to talk to Vic. It's the only way."

"I think I burned that bridge when I yelled at him for firing you."

He laughed. It eased the tension. "I'm not his favorite person either, but we have to talk to him. Let's stop here for lunch, then take a slow drive back. We'll go and visit him this evening, at home. He's more likely to talk then."

They parked next to a beachside café that advertised the best burgers in town. "Let's check out if that's true," Reid said, getting out.

They weren't bad, not that Kenzie would have noticed. She hardly touched hers. She did have a glass of wine, though, which was very out of character for her. Especially at one-thirty in the afternoon. Still, she'd had a shock and was processing. He understood that.

"Do you want to talk about it?" he asked, toward the end of the meal. "We could go for a walk on the beach. It might help if we discuss it."

She nodded, so they took their shoes off and strolled along the sand. It was warm, but not too hot, and the ocean breeze made the midday heat more bearable.

"I can't stop thinking about it," she admitted. "I know we have no proof, but as soon as Bethany said it, it made sense. It was like all the unexplained pieces fell into place. My father's strange behavior, the sudden change in sentiment, not talking about her. It's like he *knew*."

"Maybe he did. There are other possibilities, though."

"Like what? You're not thinking that my father—?" Her eyes were huge.

"No. He was with you at the market, right? He couldn't have been involved."

"Yes, he was." She relaxed. "But so was Vic." She turned to Reid. "You don't think he killed her then came back to look for her, like nothing had happened?"

It would have allayed suspicion.

"How soon did he come?"

"Right away. My father rang him not long after she disappeared."

"Then it's unlikely. He wouldn't have had the time to kill her and hide her body."

She shook her head. "I can't bear to think of her like that."

"I know, but you want the truth, right?"

She gave a weak nod, then a stronger one. "Yes, that's all I want. To know what happened."

"We could also talk to Yvonne," Reid said, the thought suddenly occurring to him. "She knew about her husband's affair because she told Bethany's mother."

"That's right." Then Kenzie's face fell. "But I have no idea where she is. I'll have to do some digging."

They turned around and headed back. "If we don't have any success with Captain Reynolds, we'll hunt down his wife. In the meantime, try not to drive yourself crazy thinking about it."

She snorted. "Fat chance of that happening."

They reached Miami shortly before three o'clock. Reynolds finished work around five, so they went back to Kenzie's and she logged onto the internet to search for Yvonne Reynolds. "Just in case she lives close by and we can pop in to see her tonight."

Reid called the Chief and made an appointment for the next day. Then he called Pérez and filled him in on what had happened.

"I had heard something along those lines," his old boss told him. "I'm sorry it didn't work out, but you'll be pleased to know Ortega has withdrawn the charges against you."

He breathed a relieved sigh. Even though Kenzie had told him as much, he wasn't sure Ortega would go through with it. Seems he'd taken Kenzie's little pep talk to heart.

After speaking to the lieutenant, he called Vargas to find out how things were going at the station.

"Awful, boss," the deputy said. "Casillas let the judge go. He and his lawyer walked out of here with a big fat grin on their faces."

"That's okay," Reid told him, even though it wasn't. "I'm working on a way to get Casillas out. Do I have your support?"

"Of course, boss." Vargas sounded more chipper. "You have all our support. The rest of the team want you back."

"Great, thanks. That's good to know."

He hung up feeling better about his situation. If he needed character references or the team's support, it was there. This was a hostile takeover and Casillas would be sorry he'd ever messed with him.

42

Kenzie took a deep breath and pressed the buzzer.

"I hope he's home," she murmured. They'd thought it would be best if they confronted Vic Reynolds together. There was strength in numbers.

"His car's here," Reid said.

A short moment later, the door opened, and Vic stood there, a frown on his face. It was safe to say he was not pleased to see them.

"Kenzie. Garrett. What are you two doing here? If it's about your position at Sweetwater, Garrett, I'm afraid I've said all I'm going to on that matter."

"Actually, it's about my mother," Kenzie said.

He glared at her in annoyance. "Angie?"

"Yes. How long were you two having an affair?"

They'd decided on a direct approach, giving Vic no room to wriggle out of it.

A long moment passed where they all stared at each other. Kenzie's gaze didn't waver. Then the police captain's shoulders slumped, and he held the door open. "You'd better come in."

They followed him into his stylish living room. Kenzie had been here once or twice before and remembered it had always been neat and uncluttered. Tonight was no exception. He'd been watching sports on television, and now he picked up the remote and muted the sound.

"How long have you known?"

"About the affair? Less than a minute, but thanks for clearing that up."

He snorted and looked at her as if he were seeing her for the first time. "Very clever. I may have underestimated you, Kenzie."

Ya think?

Reid sat silently, watching the interchange. She appreciated him letting her handle it. He'd step in if the need arose.

"How long had it been going on before you... before she disappeared?" Before you killed her, she wanted to say, but that was a wild accusation. It wouldn't be wise to go around accusing the Police Captain. It would be better to get him to admit it himself or trick him into admitting it.

He sighed. "A while. It happened slowly. It wasn't a sudden thing. We fell in love. You know how close your pop and I were, we were always at each other's houses."

"I had no idea you were together."

He smiled sadly. "No one did. We kept it very quiet."

"Your wife knew."

Vic froze. "How do you know that?"

"She told my friend's mother at book club. That's how I found out. She didn't say who you were sleeping with, but it wasn't hard to make the leap."

"I loved your mother," he muttered. "She was such a beautiful, carefree creature, so much spirit. She was stifled with your father. We were going to move in together when she—" he broke off.

"When she disappeared?"

He nodded.

"The baby was yours, wasn't it?" Kenzie fought to keep her voice steady. She'd made the connection in the car on the way back from

Palm Beach. "She was pregnant when she disappeared. Everybody thought it was my father's, but it was yours."

"I mourned her too. Everyone rallied around your father and you, but I was suffering too."

That gave her pause.

"You mean you didn't have anything to do with her death?"

"God no. I told you, I loved her. I wanted to be with her, to raise our child together, but then Bud got shot."

Oh, yeah. She remembered now. Her father had been hit by a fleeing suspect who'd robbed a liquor store. It had only been a flesh wound, but he'd had a couple of stitches. "What did that have to do with it?"

"Angie realized she loved him. When he got shot, it scared her. She told me she couldn't leave him, that she was going to pretend the baby was his, like I didn't have any say in the matter."

"Did you fight?"

"We argued, yes. I wanted her to be with me, and I didn't want another man, even my partner, raising my child."

He didn't look like an intimidating police captain anymore. He sat slumped over, his hands in his lap, his shoulders stooped. All the fight had gone out of him.

"What happened?" she croaked. "Did it get out of hand? Did you hit her? Shoot her with your service pistol?"

Vic stared at her as if she were crazy. "No, Kenzie. None of those things. I would never hurt Angie."

"So how did she die?"

"I don't know," he whispered.

"What do you mean you don't know?" Reid said, speaking for the first time.

Vic put his head in his hands. "When she left, she left me too. She left all of us."

Kenzie glanced at Reid, then back at Vic. "Are you saying you had no part in her disappearance?"

He glanced up. "That's what I'm telling you. I don't know what happened to her. I wish I did. I searched with Bud and the others all night. There was no sign of her. It was like she'd vanished into thin air. Eventually, we gave up."

———————

"Do you think he's telling the truth?" Kenzie asked once they'd left Vic Reynold's house.

"I honestly don't know. He seems to be, but then some people are very good liars." He'd met a lot of them in his time. "What do you want to do now?"

She bit her lip. "I'd love to track down his ex-wife, but I have no idea where she lives. There are too many Yvonne Reynolds around, and she may have remarried and changed her name."

"I have an idea."

Reid called Vargas on his cell phone. "Hey, are you still at the station?"

"No, but I live around the corner. I can go in if there's something you need, boss."

"Would you mind? I'm trying to trace a woman called Yvonne Reynolds. And yes, before you ask, it is the Captain's ex-wife."

There was a slight pause.

"Give me twenty minutes," he said, before hanging up. Reid liked that he hadn't asked questions.

"Vargas is on the case," he said. "Twenty minutes."

Willie was true to his word. Almost exactly twenty minutes later he called with an address. "She's moved around a lot, but she's currently living in a retirement home in Orlando."

"That's a three-hour drive," Reid said, looking at Kenzie. "Do you want to go now?"

"We'd get there at ten-thirty." She glanced at the time on her phone. "That's a bit late to visit her at the retirement home."

He could tell she was disappointed. "I had hoped she was closer." She swept her good hand through her hair.

"Why don't we drive there first thing tomorrow?" Reid said.

"What about your meeting with the Chief?"

"I'll reschedule."

"No, you can't do that. I'll go. It's not far."

"What about your wrist?"

"If I take it out of the sling, I can drive. It's supported by the cast, and it shouldn't be a problem."

Reid hesitated. He wanted to be there for her, but he also wanted to get his career back on track, and he knew she'd do most of the talking anyway. He would just be there for moral support. Mrs. Reynolds in the retirement home was unlikely to get violent.

"Okay, fine. But promise to keep me posted."

"I promise."

43

KENZIE SET off straight after breakfast.

Reid had stayed over again, but this time they'd stopped at the store and bought groceries on the way home. Kenzie had attempted to make a lasagna using only one hand. After laughing at her for a full ten minutes, Reid had stepped in, and together they'd managed to put all the layers together. It was tasty, too.

She was vaguely alarmed at how much she liked him being there. Sharing the chores in the kitchen, watching TV together, having someone to share her stories with. It was more than just reassuring, and she'd miss him when this was over and Ingleman was behind bars.

The drive was uneventful, and she made good time. She wondered what state she'd find Mrs. Reynolds in. Bethany had said she'd had a nervous breakdown. Had it affected her or was she still in command of all her faculties?

Kenzie turned into the road where the retirement home was and slowed down.

"What the—?"

There were several emergency vehicles parked outside, lights flashing. She pulled over and ran toward the entrance.

"Please ma'am, you'll have to get back," said a fireman, extending his arm. "It's not safe."

"What happened?" One side of the elegant home was a scorched ruin.

"There was a fire last night. Burned down one of the wings. It looks like arson."

"Arson?"

"Yeah, who'd want to hurt these people?" He shook his head. "We've had two casualties and one death."

Her pulse raced. "Who died?" Please let it not be Yvonne.

"I'm afraid I don't know," he replied. "You'll have to ask one of the staff."

Kenzie looked around. On the lawn, opposite the smoldering remains, she saw a group of nurses in pale blue uniforms comforting worried and agitated residents. She ran over to them.

"Excuse me," she said to a lady with a name badge on her shirt. It said Moira. "Moira, could you tell where Yvonne Reynolds is? I'm an old friend of the family."

"Oh, dear. Yvonne was taken to hospital a short while ago. She inhaled a lot of smoke."

"She's alive?"

"Yes. She was lucky. We managed to get her out before it took hold."

Thank God.

"Which hospital is she in?"

"Advent Health. It's on East Rollins."

"Thank you." Kenzie raced back to her car.

The hospital was an enormous, curved, glass and concrete block that towered above the surrounding buildings. It was much bigger than anything they had in Miami.

"What room is Yvonne Reynolds in?" she asked the slightly frazzled receptionist. "I'm an old friend of the family."

The woman looked her up and down. "One moment, please."

Kenzie waited while she pulled up the patient list on her computer. "Did she come in earlier today after the fire?"

"That's right." Kenzie held her breath.

"She's in room 504, general observation. It's on the fifth floor. Take the elevator down the hall to your left."

"Thanks." Kenzie strode down the hall, dodging patients in wheelchairs and weary staff. The elevator took forever and when it came, it was full. With an exasperated sigh, Kenzie took the stairs. By the time she got to the fifth floor she was panting.

Thankfully, room 504 was one of the first she came to. Peering through the glass panel in the door, Kenzie saw there were only two patients, both in their late fifties or early sixties. Gingerly, she pushed open the door.

One of the women opened her eyes. "Sarah, is that you?"

"No, it's Kenzie." She walked into the room. "Yvonne?"

"That's Yvonne." The woman pointed to the other bed. "I'm Frances. Where's Sarah?"

"I'm afraid I don't know where Sarah is," she replied, going over to Yvonne. Kenzie was shocked by her appearance. She'd aged almost beyond recognition. Her face was lined, and her hair had turned completely white. It was hard to believe this was the woman she used to know. Vic's wife.

Yvonne appeared to be asleep, her chest rising and falling in a gentle rhythm. There was an oxygen mask lying beside her where it must have fallen when she'd dozed off.

Kenzie perched at the end of the bed and touched the woman's leg. "Mrs. Reynolds? Yvonne? It's Kenzie Gilmore, Bud Gilmore's daughter."

There was no response.

"Angie Gilmore's daughter." At her mother's name, Yvonne opened her eyes.

"Angie Gilmore?" She tried to sit up, started coughing, and fell back down again. A nurse came in and scowled at Kenzie. "Who are you?"

"A close friend of the family," Kenzie said. "My mother was her dearest friend."

The nurse put the oxygen mask over Yvonne's mouth and monitored her until she stopped coughing. "Okay, but only five minutes. I don't want her to get too excited. It makes her cough."

"Understood."

Kenzie waited until the nurse left, then she said, "I know about the affair, Yvonne. I know my mother was sleeping with your husband."

The pale blue eyes turned frosty above the oxygen mask.

"That woman ruined my life." She pulled back the mask just far enough so Kenzie could hear. The gas hissed out, forming a fine mist in front of her face.

"Do you know what happened to her?" There was still so much hatred. The years had done nothing to diminish it.

"I knew she was going to have his baby." She inhaled deeply for a few more seconds, then lifted the mask again. "He was going to leave me. For *her*."

"I'm sorry," Kenzie said. "I had no idea."

A grunt.

"She died, and he left me anyway."

Kenzie thought she'd misheard. "Excuse me?"

"I said he left me anyway. It was all for nothing."

Kenzie's heart leaped into her throat. "What do you mean, she died?" But the woman was coughing again. "Yvonne, what was all for nothing?"

She waited until the spasms subsided, and then Yvonne rasped, "I need my pills. Can you get them for me?"

Kenzie glanced around.

"My purse, it's on the chair."

Kenzie got up to get the purse. She opened it and looked inside for the pills. Instead, she pulled out a small, framed photograph.

"That's all I rescued from the fire." Yvonne sniffed. "My brother and me. Half-brother, actually, but we were very close."

Kenzie stared at the photograph, unable to believe what she was seeing. The image blurred, then came back into focus. This was so out of context, so unexpected, that she didn't believe what she was seeing.

"What's your brother's name?" she choked out.

"Donnie. Isn't he handsome?"

Don Ingleman.

He was Yvonne's half-brother.

Kenzie sank down onto the bed. How could it be? How had she missed this?

"My pills?" Yvonne held out a wrinkled hand.

"Oh, yes. Sorry." Distracted, she took them out and handed them over. "Is your maiden name Ingleman?" Was it a coincidence? She knew what Reid would say. No such thing.

"No, we had different fathers. Donnie's a decent man. He knew it was all Victor's fault."

Kenzie went cold. "What was Victor's fault?"

But Yvonne was reaching for a glass of water on the bedside table. Kenzie gave it to her impatiently. "What was Victor's fault, Yvonne?"

She swallowed the pills, ever so slowly. Then reached for the oxygen again. Kenzie stopped her. "Yvonne. Did Victor do something to Angie?"

"Donnie said he'd make him pay for what he'd done." She reached out and clutched Kenzie's sleeve. "Did he? Did he make him pay?"

Kenzie took her hand. "Yvonne, what did Victor do? Did he kill my mother?"

Yvonne laughed hysterically, then started coughing again. The nurse came in. "I have to insist you leave now," she said.

"No, please." Kenzie begged her. Not now, not when she was so close. "She needs me."

"I'm sorry, but you have to go."

Kenzie leaned over Yvonne and whispered in her ear. "He killed her, didn't he? He murdered her because she threatened to leave him."

A slight shake of the head, then Yvonne pushed the nurse's hand away. Vapor curled up over her lips. "It was me. I killed her."

44

KENZIE WAS USHERED out of the ward. She stumbled down the corridor and out of the hospital in a daze. Voices floated above her, muted and distorted. A man bumped into her, but she hardly noticed.

It was me. I killed her.

Yvonne had admitted it, and the nurse had overheard. "Who did you say you were again?" But Kenzie had left.

Unable to drive, she sat on a bench in the garden and tried to process what she'd learned. Vic had known, he must have. He'd been telling the truth when he'd said it wasn't him, but he'd neglected to mention it was his wife.

Questions swirled around her mind, but she didn't have the answers.

Not yet.

Had Yvonne met her mother at the Christmas market? Was that why Angie had left so suddenly? The Reynolds only lived a few blocks from where her mother was last seen, outside Mr. Wentworth's window. It hadn't been a car that had picked her up. She'd gone to Yvonne's house.

All the time they'd been searching, and her mother had been a couple of blocks away. She gasped as the reality hit home, then started sobbing. She couldn't help it. Her mother was gone. All these years of not knowing, of imagining she was alive somewhere, living a different life, when all the time she was dead.

And Victor Reynolds knew.

She gripped the bench with her uninjured hand, her nails digging into the wood. He'd pretended to care about her. He'd visited her in hospital after her accident, he'd stood by her side at her father's funeral, and all the while *he knew*.

Had he been there at the time? Had he helped dispose of her mother's body?

She gulped in air, tears streaming down her face. He would know where she was buried.

Kenzie cried until there were no more tears left to fall. Eventually, almost an hour later, she got up off the bench.

She had to talk to Vic. She needed to finish this.

Reid left Chief Gates's office with a smile on his face. That had gone well. He'd stated his case for wrongful arrest, followed by unlawful dismissal, and pointed out Casillas's many flaws, including his dismal arrest record, poor case closure rate, and the lack of motivation at the precinct. He'd given Detectives Vargas and Diaz as references, as well as Lieutenant Pérez.

Gates had promised to look into it. Corruption and laziness had no place in his police force. Reid was sure when the Chief met Casillas, he'd like him even less.

Earlier that year, Reid had helped Gates's golfing buddy, the billionaire Rhys Evans, find out what had happened to his daughter. It was one of the reasons the Chief had been willing to overlook Reid's lapse in judgement when he'd punched Ortega in the face, but Reid knew he couldn't push it. This was an informal meeting, but he had his union rep and an attorney ready, should he need them.

"It would be a shame to lose you," Gates had said at the end of their discussion. "You're a credit to the force. I only wish we had more detectives like you around."

He wasn't sure about the "credit to the force" bit, but he appreciated the sentiment.

Reid checked his phone as he walked back to his pickup. Kenzie had texted.

Meet me at the Miami PD at 4 p.m.

Strange. No clue why. Or who they were going to meet.

The obvious choice would be Vic Reynolds, but they'd already seen him. Had his ex-wife offered something new?

As he got to his car, a sleek, black sedan pulled up. Before the window had even opened, he knew it was the Feds.

"Detective Garrett?"

He nodded.

"Can I have a word?"

He got into the car. It was freezing cold; the AC had been turned up to full blast. "I was wondering when you'd get to me."

The agent didn't smile. There was a partition between the driver and the back seat, so they could talk in private. "I believe you were the man responsible for arresting Andrei Malkovich, Don Ingleman's right-hand man?"

"Correct. He abducted and was attempting to murder journalist, Kenzie Gilmore, under Ingleman's orders."

"You know this for a fact?"

"Ingleman was there. Kenzie, I mean Miss Gilmore spoke to him while she was being held captive." He repeated what Kenzie had told him.

The agent didn't nod or write anything down, he simply listened.

"We've spoken to Miss Gilmore," he said. "She's agreed to testify."

Reid wasn't surprised. Kenzie wasn't one to back down if it meant justice would be served, and she didn't intimidate easily. His chest swelled with pride. Just for a moment, the feeling scared him.

"Do you have any idea where Ingleman might be?"

"No, I'm sorry I don't. Have you tried his house in L.A.?"

A brief nod.

"The journalist Clayton Andrews is the person who knows him best. He researched him for three weeks. If anyone can find him, it'll be him."

"Clayton Andrews?"

"Yes, ex-Miami Herald reporter."

"Okay, thanks. We'll get on to him."

Reid paused. "You know, I might know of a way to catch Ingleman."

The agent narrowed his eyes. "What's that?"

It was risky, and he'd have to talk to Kenzie, but he was sure she'd go for it. She wanted to end this as much as anybody, if not more. It was her life on the line.

Reid told him his plan.

After grabbing a light lunch, Reid drove to the port to replace the batteries in his hidden surveillance camera. At Alberto Torres's warehouse, it was business as usual. Today, the roller doors were up, and he could see inside. The cars were gone. Whatever deal Torres had been working on had gone ahead without a hitch.

He hadn't been there to stop him.

Reid sat on the roof of the empty office diagonally across the road and watched the men hose down the trucks and store the loading equipment. There'd be other opportunities. In fact, it was probably better that this shipment had been delivered successfully. It would lure Torres and the Morales cartel into a false sense of security. They'd think they were safe, when all the while, *he* was watching.

He thought back to that photograph he'd found in Torres's study. The one of Bianca and the drug lord holding hands. He hadn't told anyone about that, not even Kenzie. Had Bianca really fallen for her mark, or had it all been an act?

The smile on her face had seemed genuine. Her eyes had been sparkling, more so than they ever had when she'd looked at him. But if that was the case, why had Torres shot her? How could he have pulled the trigger on someone he loved?

That meant Torres was a worse monster than he'd originally thought. And like all monsters, he had to be taken down.

45

Kenzie drove straight from Orlando to the Miami PD. By the time she got there, she'd calmed down somewhat. Her eyes were still red and swollen, but she had her emotions under control—for the most part.

Her mother was dead.

That was a fact, and she couldn't bring her back. Now she just wanted to know what had happened to her. Had she suffered? Was it a quick death? A gunshot wound or something else? Anything to help her stop wondering.

Reid walked up to her. "Jesus, are you okay?"

She managed a weak smile. "That bad?"

"You look awful. What happened?"

She took a shaky breath and told him what Yvonne had said. His expression was one of complete surprise. "She admitted it?"

"Yes, right there in the hospital ward. The nurse heard her."

Reid ran a hand through his hair. "We'll have to bring her in."

She touched his arm. "I don't have all the details yet. I want to talk to Vic and find out why he lied. I want to know what happened. Then you can bring her in."

He grimaced. "It's not like I'm a serving police detective at the moment anyway."

"Ready?"

"Yep. Let's go."

They walked into the Miami PD building and took the elevator up to the fifth floor where the captain's office was located.

"I need to see him," she told the secretary, barely breaking her stride. When the woman started to get up, Reid held up a hand and shook his head. She sat back down again.

Kenzie opened the door and walked straight into his office.

Vic got up out of his chair. "Kenzie, what is the meaning of this? You can't barge in whenever you feel like it."

Reid positioned himself with his back to the door in case the captain decided to make a run for it.

She confronted her father's old partner. "You knew."

"Kenzie—"

"All this time, you knew!" Her voice rose a notch, but she kept her temper in check. Freaking out wouldn't get her the answers she required. No, needed. "When we were searching for her that night, she was at your house. You could have put an end to this, but you didn't say anything. You let us think she'd disappeared, that she'd run off. How could you?"

Vic put his hands on his hips. "Kenzie, calm down. What do you think I knew?"

No way.

No way was he going to try to bluff his way out of this one.

"Yvonne told me." She glared at him. "You didn't manage to silence her."

Reid shot her a curious look. "Kenzie?"

She snorted, but kept her eyes on Vic. "The fire. That was your idea, wasn't it?" She shook her head. "You must have driven to Orlando last night. Is that when you set fire to the retirement home? I thought it was odd that only her wing was damaged."

Vic didn't say anything, but his eyes told her she was right. He was cornered.

"You know someone died in that fire?"

"I don't know what you mean."

"Oh, cut the crap." She was beyond being polite. "I managed to speak to your ex-wife this morning. Ingleman's her brother. She told him what happened, didn't she? And he used it to blackmail you."

Behind her, she heard Reid inhale sharply.

"That's why you've been trying to protect him. That's why you derailed the investigation and let the judge go. He knows the part you played in my mother's murder."

Reid took a step forward. "Is this true? Is Ingleman blackmailing you?"

Vic clapped his hands. Slow and deliberate. "Well done, Kenzie. You've worked it all out."

She kept quiet, waiting for him to go on.

"That stupid woman ruined my life. She killed the only woman I've ever loved, then went and blabbed about it to her scumbag brother. He'd been looking for something to hold over me for years. Unfortunately, he found it." He crinkled his nose in disgust. "I'm glad he's on the run. I hope you catch him and put him away for life."

"What happened, Vic?" Kenzie asked. "What happened that night?"

He sighed and sank into his chair. "Okay, Kenzie. It's time you knew." He took a moment to compose himself. "Yvonne found out about our affair and as you can imagine, she was livid. But when Angie and Bud told us they were expecting, she completely lost it. I'd never seen her like that before. She looked demented. I should have known then she'd do something crazy, but I never in a million years imagined..."

"What did she do, Vic?" Kenzie's voice was a strangled whisper.

"That night, she went to the Christmas market and confronted your mother. She said they needed to talk. Angie agreed, she didn't like the animosity that had grown between them, and she'd decided to stay with Bud by that stage. Angie went back to our house with Yvonne, we lived a few blocks away."

"That's when Mr. Wentworth saw her in the street."

"Yes, it must have been." He closed his eyes, remembering. "When I got home from work, I found Angie's body on the living room floor. Yvonne had stabbed her multiple times with one of the kitchen knives."

Kenzie's hand flew to her mouth.

"I tried to help her, but it was too late. She was already dead. Yvonne was staring at her like a zombie. It was the scariest thing I've ever seen. I looked into my wife's eyes and knew she was completely crazy."

Kenzie was at a loss for words. She stared at Vic, frozen.

"What did you do?" asked Reid.

"I panicked. I wrapped Angie's body in the rug and put her in the trunk of my car. That's when I got the frantic call from Bud saying she'd gone missing."

Kenzie gasped. "You drove to the market to help us search and the whole time her dead body was in the trunk of your car?"

He gave her a plaintive look. "I didn't know what else to do. I couldn't leave her at home, Yvonne was having some sort of mental breakdown, and I didn't want anyone to find her."

"You were thinking of yourself," Reid said icily.

Vic turned to him. "Can you imagine what would have happened if I'd called it in? My own wife killing my pregnant lover in a fit of rage. My career would be over. Angie was gone, it was the only thing I had left."

Kenzie let out a muffled moan. "Oh, God."

"After the search, I drove down to Islamorada, to the cabin we used to rent sometimes, and I buried her there. It was our special place."

Kenzie didn't realize she was crying until she felt the hot tears running down her cheeks. "I want to see her."

"We'll bring her back." Reid put a reassuring hand on her shoulder.

"I go and see her regularly," Vic said, as if that made a difference.

Kenzie shot him a look of pure hatred. "You disgust me. I can't believe you lied to us, to everyone, all these years. You pretend to be so righteous, upholding the law, when you're the biggest liar of them all."

"I did what I thought was best at the time." His broad shoulders slumped. "It was an impossible situation. Angie was dead and nothing I could do would change that. I moved out the very next day. I never spoke to Yvonne again."

"I'm going to call Pérez." Reid took out his phone.

For a moment, Kenzie thought Vic might try to flee, but instead he gave a small nod. "It's time." He looked around his office, his gaze lingering on a photograph of him being made captain.

What a hypocrite.

Kenzie couldn't look at him anymore. "I want the location of my mother's body."

He reached forward and scribbled an address on a Post-it Note. "I truly am sorry, Kenzie. I hope you believe me."

Her voice was cold. "I know you didn't kill her, Vic, and you may even have loved her, but I will never forgive you for keeping this from me for all these years."

"Your father never knew," he murmured. "I think he realized she'd been having an affair, but he didn't know it was with me. About a year after her death, he'd found a letter I'd written her, a love note. It wasn't signed. At least I spared him that."

"He died not knowing," she said. "That's worse than anything you could have told him."

There was a knock on the door and Lieutenant Pérez came in. He nodded at Reid, then looked at Vic. "Captain Reynolds, I'm arresting you for perverting the course of justice. You have the right to remain silent and refuse to answer questions. Anything you say may be used against you in a court of law."

He didn't know about the arson attempt on the retirement home yet.

Kenzie watched as Vic was led from the room. Pérez hadn't cuffed him out of respect, but with Reid and the lieutenant beside him, he wasn't going anywhere.

She sank into an office chair and closed her eyes.

It was over.

46

THE UNMARKED FBI vehicle drove her to an out of the way motel in Fort Lauderdale. Agent Smith, as he was called, came in with her and checked the room. "It's best if you stay here until the trial."

She nodded and closed the door.

It was a basic, double room with a bathroom. The bed creaked when she sat down on it, and the bulb in the lamp flickered when she turned it on. There was an adjoining room, but it was locked.

Great. So, this was her home for the next few days.

The dramatic showdown with Vic had drained her, so while she didn't want to be stuck in here, she was also glad of the rest. Keith had given her a few days leave, and she was going to use it to recharge her batteries. That was the cover story, anyway.

Taking out her phone, she texted Reid.

I'm in position.

She got a thumbs up in reply.

The plan to entrap Ingleman had been mapped out to the last detail, but would he go for it? With the judge having got off, Kenzie was his biggest threat. If she was out of the way, there'd be nobody to testify to the kidnapping or attempted murder.

Andrei still hadn't talked, and probably never would. Nothing the American judicial system could inflict on him was as bad as the prison camps in his native country, and according to Reid, he'd survived those.

Vic Reynolds had used the burner number he'd been given to text Ingleman the details of where the Feds were holding Kenzie. Like Barry Marshall, she was unguarded, the risk not deemed high enough for around-the-clock security.

The Feds had jumped at the chance to catch their suspect. They'd been gunning for Ingleman from the moment Barry Marshall had gone to the police, and after the trial had been dismissed, they'd thought they'd lost him. Now they were being given another shot. This time they could add kidnapping and attempted murder to his rap sheet.

It had been Reid's idea. At first, Kenzie had been skeptical, but she knew it was the quickest way to get this over with. She didn't mind being used as bait. Reid would protect her.

And... she got to write about it.

Keith was beyond excited at the prospect of a frontpage scoop on how the *Herald* had contributed to the apprehension of the infamous Don Ingleman.

To kill time, Kenzie took out her laptop and began working on the article. Reid had told her that Ingleman wouldn't come until after dark.

Four hours later Kenzie had finished her article, apart from the ending which remained to be seen. Fingers crossed it all turned out okay.

We're here, don't worry, Reid had texted her. It was strange to think of him and all those Feds holed up in the next room. They had lookouts on the roof and both approach roads. The moment Ingleman made a move, they'd know.

Finally, it was time for bed. Kenzie switched the light off and the room fell into darkness.

Ten o'clock... Eleven o'clock... She was getting twitchy. Where was he?

Midnight.

Kenzie yawned and closed her eyes, just for a moment.

Her phone buzzed.

He's here.

Her pulse went into overdrive. How was he going to kill her? A gun? Or something more silent like a knife? Perhaps he'd try to make it look like an accident? A fire? Oh, God. If he set the place on fire, would they still catch him?

She kept very still, waiting for the sound of footsteps on the walkway outside. The creak of the door as it opened. It was so very dark, she wished she could turn on the light or at least use the light on her phone.

Her killer was in the room before she even knew it. The click of the door had been so quiet, she hadn't heard it.

The gun went off. A loud pop.

She jumped, startled.

Then three more times. *Pop. Pop. Pop.*

He was making sure she was dead.

Then the connecting door burst open and a voice yelled, "FBI. Drop the gun and get down on your knees. You're under arrest!"

She heard a scuffle and more shouting. Had they caught him? Was it over? Then Reid pulled open the bathroom door. "You can come out now, Kenzie. We've got him."

Thank God.

She emerged in time to see Ingleman being led away in handcuffs. The bed had four bullet holes in it, but no blood. Dummies didn't bleed.

"You did great." He smiled at her. "I hope you weren't too bored."

"No, I managed to write most of my article." She looked up at him. "I always knew it would work out. Good job, Detective Garrett. And thanks for giving me the ending I wanted. Keith will be delighted."

He grinned. "That's a win for Sweetwater PD." Vargas and Diaz stood outside on the landing looking mighty pleased with themselves.

"The first of many, I'm sure."

He put his arm around her shoulders. "Come on, let's get you home."

The roads were quiet, and the drive took less than half an hour.

"It's over now," Reid said, as he walked her to her door. "Ingleman can't hurt you again."

"What about the judge?" She was still annoyed he'd gotten off.

"His reputation is ruined, thanks to your article. I believe he's taking early retirement."

"I guess that's good enough. At least he's no longer involved with the law."

They stopped outside. Reid turned to face her. "We did good, Kenz. We solved Barry Marshall's murder, got Ingleman put away and solved the mystery of your mother's disappearance."

She took his hand. "Thank you for helping me get closure. I couldn't have done it without you, without that report."

"You would have found a way." He gave her hand a gentle squeeze. "I have no doubt about that. You're one of the best investigators I know."

That was high praise, coming from him. Kenzie looked up at his unshaven, smiling face and was overcome with an emotion so strong, it took her breath away. Maybe it was the adrenaline of apprehending Ingleman or the release that came with knowing she wasn't in danger anymore, but whatever it was, it made her do something crazy, something she told herself she'd never do.

She kissed him.

If you enjoyed Deadheat, you'll love Heatwave. Follow the link below to purchase now!

www.amazon.com/dp/Bo9MPN5176

Sign up for Biba Pearce's newsletter here to stay up to date on new Kenzie Gilmore and other exciting series releases!
https://links.withoutwarrant.ink/Pearce1

HEATWAVE

Chapter 1

The humidity clung to her like a damp cloth. Cloying, suffocating. The palm trees drooped, their fronds limp, even more so than the people who staggered around like zombies, hollow-eyed and wilting. The pavement shimmered like a mirage, and she could feel the heat radiating through her thin sandals with the strength of an underground furnace.

Kenzie darted into the air-conditioned mall and heaved a sigh of relief. Swiping a damp strand of hair off her face, she stood for a moment, absorbing the welcome coolness.

Miami was in the grips of a brutal heatwave, and Fred, the environmental editor at the *Herald*, had warned it wasn't about to end any time soon. *Swampy Summer* they were calling it, and they weren't wrong. The stifling humidity made it feel like you were swimming through the day, drenched in sweat. Kenzie's skin glistened with perspiration and her thick, blonde hair only added to the misery, so she'd scraped it into a ponytail. Glancing at her reflection in a shop window, she grimaced. The smattering of makeup she'd applied that morning had melted off her face hours ago.

The heat was on at work, too. Ever since Clayton had been fired, she'd been the senior investigative reporter on the crime beat. The promotion had come with a frantic schedule, a new assistant she hadn't gelled with yet, and deadlines that made her eyes water. The fact this heat had led to a spate of violent crimes across Miami, didn't help. Tempers flared, literally, in the heat of the moment, and patience wore thin as the relentless temperatures pushed those ready to snap over the edge.

Assaults had doubled, gang violence was on the rise, and there was a spike in homicides. And she was expected to cover it all. Be everywhere. To top it all, the AC in the car had gone on the fritz. It probably wasn't designed to be on full blast for hours on end.

So now she was sheltering in the mall.

An iced coffee made her feel marginally better. She checked her phone. Still no messages from Reid. Understandable though, given the current crime wave. Sweetwater Police Department, where he was based, was situated southwest of the city and included part of the Glades—the accessible part, that is. Those folks were a law unto themselves at the best of times. He had his work cut out for him.

Reid.

A frisson of excitement shot down her spine. She still couldn't believe she'd kissed him like that. It had been impulsive, reckless, and too damn good. Mind-blowingly good, if she was honest. At first, he'd been surprised, then he'd reciprocated, kissing her until they were both gasping for breath.

But it was the look in his eye when they broke away that had startled her the most. Intense, filled with desire and unspoken questions.

And she'd panicked.

At that moment, when she'd felt his breath on her lips, his hand in her hair, it could have gone either way. Her apartment was right there. Just steps from her front door. Yet she'd backed off, stammering an apology.

It was the excitement of the night. The sting operation. The relief it was over and she was safe.

Giving her a long look, he said quietly, "It's okay. I understand." And he'd gone.

Left her alone with her feelings, her confusion, her desire.

"Excuse me," came a feminine voice beside her. "Are you Kenzie Gilmore?"

Jolted out of her reminiscence, Kenzie glanced up. A teenager stood in front of her, a backpack slung over one shoulder. She wore a pretty summer dress with daisies on it, and a silver chain with an H-shaped pendant around her neck. She looked surprisingly cool given the temperature outside and the general frazzled state of everyone else.

"Yes, I am." Kenzie smiled.

She shifted in her strappy sandals like she wasn't quite comfortable standing there and straightened her dress. "I'm sorry to disturb you. It's just... Well, I need to talk to you."

Kenzie frowned. The girl was nervous. "Sure, have we met?"

"No." She shook her head, then pointed to the vacant chair opposite Kenzie. "Do you mind if I sit down?"

"Of course not."

Kenzie was intrigued. What was this about? The girl was perfectly groomed; manicured nails, styled hair curling softly around her face, a light layer of mascara emphasizing wide deer-like eyes, and just the right amount of lip-gloss.

The backpack was a designer label, she noted, as the girl slid it off her slender shoulder and placed it at her feet, under the table.

"I'm Hannah Radcliffe," she began, voice trembling. "I read your articles in the newspaper. I'm going to do media studies when I go to college. I want to be an investigative journalist, just like you."

Ah, a fan. Sweet. Kenzie broke into a grin. "That's great. Is that what you wanted to talk to me about? Do you need some advice?"

"Actually, no." She wrung her hands under the table. "Not advice, I need your help. My boyfriend was murdered last week and the police aren't doing anything about it. I want you to look into it for me. I want you to find out who killed him."

Kenzie stared at her. Was she serious? But the brown doe eyes fixed on Kenzie were unwavering. Holding her breath, she waited for an answer.

"Um..." Kenzie tried to get her thoughts in order. "Hannah, I'm sorry about your boyfriend, but I'm not sure how I can help. You should take your concerns to the police."

Hannah snorted, a prim, ladylike sound. "The police think he was killed in a drug-related incident. That's what they said." She leaned forward across the table. "Matt didn't do drugs. He hated all that."

Kenzie's heart went out to the young girl. "I'm afraid I don't know the details of the case and there's no way I could get access to the files." She spread her hands out. "You really are better off taking this up with the detective in charge of the investigation."

Hannah's head bowed like a wilting flower, her shoulders caved in on themselves. "I can't." It was a strangled whisper.

"Why not? I'm sure they'd listen to you."

"Because nobody knew we were together. Matt was, well, he was on probation."

At Kenzie's arched eyebrows, she stammered, "F—For stealing a car. It was some time ago, and he was drunk. It was a stupid thing to do, and he regretted it. I swear, he's not a bad person." Her eyes filled with tears. "He was kind and gentle, and I loved him." Blinking, they fell anyway, slipping down her face. "Matt didn't deserve this. He didn't deserve to be stabbed in the street and labelled a criminal and a drug dealer."

"I'm so sorry for your loss." Kenzie reached over and squeezed her hand. The girl was clearly grieving, an emotion she understood well. "Don't you think you should tell your parents? If not them, then someone else? A school counselor, a police officer?"

She needed support. Going through something like this alone was not good for her mental health. That she knew firsthand, too.

Endless questions, no answers. Nobody to talk to. It ate away at you, affecting all areas of your life.

"My parents would kill me," she sniffed. "Matt's not the type of boy they wanted me to date. He wasn't wealthy or well-bred. Didn't have a membership in a country club."

Yeah, she knew the type. Matt had been a juvenile offender, probably from the wrong side of the tracks. All types of wrong for their little princess.

Kenzie felt herself wavering.

No. Don't do it. You have enough on your plate.

"Where was he killed?" she heard herself ask.

Hannah wiped the tears away with her French mani nail-polished finger and managed to get herself under control. "South Coconut Grove," she mumbled. "He was on his way home from school."

Kenzie sucked in a breath. How awful. "Stabbed, you say?"

"Yes, in the stomach. I don't know how many times. They didn't tell us much."

"Us?"

"His friends at school. We have—had—some of the same classes."

"Is that how you met?"

She gave a tiny nod. Helpless. Like there was no point to the memories anymore, now he was gone.

"What was Matt's full name?"

Her gaze brightened. "Are you going to help me?"

"There's not much I can do," Kenzie repeated. "But I will ask some questions and see if I can find out what happened." The girl deserved that much. It would save her from wondering.

Endless wondering. No answers.

"Thank you." Hannah broke into a smile. "You don't know how much this means to me. I need to know what happened and find out who was responsible."

"His name?" Kenzie slid a small notepad and a pen across the table. Like all reporters, she kept one in her purse in case she had to jot something down.

The girl wrote Matteo Davis in neat block letters. All capitalized like he was important. Important to her.

"Is there anything else?" Kenzie asked, curiosity getting the better of her. "Was he acting weird in the lead up to his death? Anything like that?"

"Well, now that you mention it, he was worried about something. He told me it was a school thing but didn't say what."

"A school thing? Like a problem with one of the other kids?"

"No," she frowned, her face crinkling. "I don't think so. Maybe something to do with his probation. I suggested he talk to Principal Hogarth about it."

"And did he?"

She stifled a sob. "I don't know."

"Okay, thanks." Kenzie made a note on her pad.

Hannah scribbled her phone number beneath Matteo's name. "That's me. Call me anytime. Day or night." Standing, Hannah said, "Thank you so much, Kenzie. Is it alright if I call you by your first name?"

Kenzie nodded. "Please do."

Hannah shook her hand. "It's been a pleasure meeting you. Thanks again." And she dashed off into the hoard of shoppers, all of whom had the same idea Kenzie'd had, to get out of the stifling heat.

MATTEO DAVIS.

Kenzie stared at the name written on her pad until her eyes went blurry. Then she blinked and glanced away. One phone call, that's all it would take. Reid would be able to help her find out how the boy had died.

Then, hopefully, Hannah could get some closure.

HEATWAVE

Chapter 2

Reid stood on the rocky ledge at Snapper Creek and watched as the emergency services pulled the dead girl from the mangrove fringe. She was tangled up, her hair swept forward over her face, pale arms floppy like a rag doll's, head lolling to one side. She wore a white dress, dulled and stained by the water. It clung to her limp figure making her appear even paler.

Swallowing hard, he brushed the perspiration from his brow with the back of his hand. Another dead teenager. The third this month.

Two police divers stood waist-deep in the murky water and passed her lifeless body to two other men in a motorboat. The side of the canal where she'd been found was pretty much inaccessible, a mass of tropical vegetation, entwined root systems and swampland, which was why they'd launched from the other side.

Turning around, he whistled to the waiting ambulance to get ready. She was coming across.

Behind him was the sprawling residential area of Kendall West, but the two-lane road and maintained lawn that sloped down to the canal meant no one could see the waterway unless they were right at the edge.

"What state is she in?" Reid asked one officer in the boat.

He just shook his head.

Reid took out his phone and snapped a few photographs as they took her out of the boat and laid her on a stretcher. He winced. She was young. A teenager. Couldn't be older than seventeen or eighteen.

The body was intact. No obvious wounds or bite marks. No decomp. The wild animals hadn't had a chance to get to her yet. She hadn't been in the canal very long. Two or three days at the most.

A suited-up CSI professional leaned in. He felt for a pulse. Protocol demanded it, but he was just ticking a box. There was no way she was alive. Then he inspected her face, her eyelids, her mouth, and worked his way down her body. It was a brief overview, a preliminary study. The more thorough medical examination would happen a few days later, in the morgue.

"Cause of death?" Reid asked.

"Hard to say," he mumbled. "No visible injuries to speak of. Slight frothing at the mouth, vomit stains on her dress. No track marks in her arms or other signs of drug use, but looking at her, I'd say she died of a drug overdose." He shrugged. "You'll have to wait for the autopsy for a more concrete diagnosis."

Reid nodded. Out of respect, he watched as she was zipped up and lifted into the waiting ambulance. Only when the emergency vehicle took off down the street, sirens ominously silent, did he walk back to his pickup.

"Looks like another drug-related death," he told his team when he got back to Sweetwater Police Department. Since he'd taken over from the inept Casillas, the general morale and work ethic had improved tenfold.

"The working day starts at nine sharp," he'd told them on his first official day as lieutenant. "I expect you to be here by eight forty-five. There are people depending on us to do our jobs properly and to the best of our ability. No more rolling in at ten o'clock. We need to win back the community's trust."

He'd got several firm nods, a couple of half-assed ones, and a few murmurs. It was a change from his predecessor's lax policies and lazy work attitude. No more freeloading. They were here to solve cases, and this neighborhood had its fair share.

He hadn't fired anyone yet, but it was early days. There were one or two officers loyal to Casillas, who were badmouthing him behind his back. The hushed tones. The conversations that halted when he walked past. It was pretty obvious, but he was waiting to see whether they'd toe the line or be a problem.

Detective Dempsey was in his late fifties, overweight, divorced, and close to retirement. Like Casillas, he wanted to do the bare minimum until he could leave with a full police pension. Whether he deserved it or not was another matter. Reid hadn't seen him pulling his weight much since he'd arrived.

Detective Monroe was similar in age, but unlike Dempsey, he'd been a good cop in his day. Starting out at Miami PD, he'd garnered a reputation as a hard worker and someone who got stuff done. When he hit fifty and packed on a few pounds, he'd been transferred to Sweetwater to handle the paperwork. Demoralizing for such a seasoned detective. Reid could understand why his morale was low. In this game, unless you rose through the ranks, there was nowhere else to go.

It was hoped his years of experience would benefit the younger officers coming out of the academy, but Reid had yet to see that happen. Either Monroe didn't know how to be a supervisor, or he didn't care. The jury was still out on that one.

Detective "Willie" Vargas had turned out to be a smart, motivated young man, and Reid was relying on him more and more as his lead detective. Officer Diaz, the only female police officer in the squad, was also proving to be an asset to the team. It wouldn't be long before she got her detective's badge.

They weren't a big police department, only twelve officers. Five detectives including himself, and seven uniformed police officers in the next room. They all worked the day shift and rotated the nights. The majority were young graduates in their early twenties, with Reid more than a decade older at thirty-five and Monroe and Dempsey at the other end of the scale.

Glancing at them now, he squeezed into the small briefing room, Vargas and Diaz at the front, Dempsey and Monroe at the back. The older two wore tired expressions, like they'd seen it all before, but the rest were leaning forward, eyes glued to the white board behind him. Under Casillas's rule they hadn't done much real investigating, and the novelty of a dead body pulled out of the canal hadn't worn off.

"The victim's name is Sasha Holden." Standing at the front, he faced them. "She was sixteen years old." Diaz cringed.

Sweet sixteen. How different her year should have been.

The photographs he'd taken at the crime scene were pinned on the board. The victim lay on her back in the water, dark hair splayed around her, arms outstretched like she was floating in a swimming pool on a sunny day, gazing at the sky.

Ophelia sprung to mind. He didn't know a lot about art, but his sister had a copy hanging in her house in Philadelphia. She and her husband had taken a trip to Europe back in the days before they'd had kids, and she'd fallen in love with the painting in a gallery in London.

It was the same striking visual, but instead of meadow flowers, Sasha had leaves and bits of mangrove hanging off her.

"Most likely she died after taking an illegal substance," he explained. "But we won't know for sure until we get the coroner's report."

"Pink cocaine?" inquired Vargas.

Reid shrugged. "Could be."

The designer drug, a potent mix of cocaine, acid and God-knows-what else had been turning up on the streets of Miami for weeks now. This concoction was proving to be lethal. Killer coke, they'd nicknamed it. Three deaths, all teens. None of them hardened drug addicts.

"Do we know where she got it?" Diaz asked.

Reid looked at her. "That's what we need to find out. Talk to her friends at school. Find out where they partied. Trace her movements on the night she died, which is probably going to be the weekend. I'm guessing Saturday night judging by the state of her, and when she was reported missing. See what you can dig up."

"Yes, boss." Vargas had started calling him boss when he'd first taken the job as lieutenant, and despite Reid telling him otherwise, it had stuck. Now everyone was doing it. Everyone except Monroe and Dempsey, who were sulking at the back.

Reid looked over at them. "Monroe, Dempsey, will you look into local dealers? Find out who's selling what and where. Reach out to your contacts. Word on the street is that this is a new designer drug. We need to find out who's bringing it in." Grunting, they shuffled back to their desks.

Reid glanced at the other officers waiting for their instructions. "Everybody else, hit the streets. Talk to the residents. Find out where the kids are buying this stuff. Vargas, you and I will talk to her parents." They'd be waiting for news about their daughter. They'd reported her missing on Sunday when they realized she hadn't come home.

Vargas swallowed. He hadn't done a next of kin notification before. Reid wished there was something encouraging he could say to reassure him, but there wasn't. It never got any easier.

Sasha Holden's parents lived in Olympia Heights, several blocks east of where her body was found. They were understandably shocked at the news.

"A—Are you sure it's her?" her father stammered, ashen under his tanned complexion. He was above average height with square shoulders and an upright posture. Except, right now he was stooped over like someone had sucker-punched him in the gut.

There was always doubt. A desperate hope that this was all some terrible mistake.

"She had her student ID card in her back pocket," Reid said.

Sasha's mother collapsed into an armchair. "No," she whispered. "It can't be true."

Reid gave them time to assimilate. It always took a while. The brain had to register what it had been told. That this wasn't a nightmare they were going to wake up from. It was real.

Once the initial shock had worn off, he asked, "Would one of you..." He looked at the father, "be able to come and identify her?"

Mr. Holden nodded. "Of course." He reached for his wife's hand. "It may not be her."

But his wife was sobbing. Grieving tears streamed down her face.

She knew.

She knew her daughter was dead.

"I'm really sorry to have to do this," Reid said. "But we need to ask you a couple of questions."

"Surely you should wait until we've officially identified her?" Mr. Holden snapped, then he raked a hand through his hair. "I'm sorry. Sure, go ahead."

Reid nodded. It was hard for anyone to hear. He forgave lapses in manners and angry retorts in these kinds of situations. The shock was enough to render anyone speechless, let alone answer questions. Sasha's father was doing better than most.

"When last did you see your daughter?"

He heaved a sigh, his chest rising, then caving in as he buckled and sat down heavily on the couch. "Saturday night. She went out with friends."

"Was that a usual occurrence?"

"Yeah, fairly usual. They didn't go out every weekend, but they were celebrating completing their SATs. This was Sasha's last year of school." His voice caught, and he squeezed his eyes shut.

It proved too much for Mrs. Holden who stumbled from the

room, her sobs echoing down the passage. Vargas looked at Reid who shook his head. Let her go. She needed time to process.

Mr. Holden stared at the carpet under his feet, his arms folded across his chest like he was hugging himself.

"I'm sorry to ask, but did your daughter ever take drugs, Mr. Holden?"

His eyes blazed, momentarily, before the light faded again. "No, of course not. She wasn't wild. Our Sasha was a good girl. She wanted to go to college. Florida State..."

Reid didn't tell him it didn't take a wild teenager to try drugs, especially for the first time. An end of term celebration. Too much alcohol. In the party spirit. It wasn't impossible to imagine she might try the new designer drug everyone was doing.

"Do you know where she went?"

He shook his head. "No, we trusted her. I don't know how she ended up in Kendall West... They usually went out locally."

The body could have floated down, but it was unlikely. The currents weren't that strong. More likely one of her friends panicked and dumped her body.

"Do any of her friends drive a car?" Rob asked.

Mr. Holden thought for a moment, then shook his head. "I don't think any of her friends did, but they were at that age where they were dating older boys. One of them could have had a car."

"Okay, thank you, Mr. Holden. I'm sorry for your loss."

"Shall I come with you now, you know, to look at the...her..." He couldn't say the word. Because if he did, he'd be admitting she was really dead. That it was actually her.

"No, I'll send a dispatch car to pick you up. She's not at the police department, she's downtown." In the morgue, although he didn't say that.

Sasha's father nodded.

Reid said goodbye and strode out. Vargas, a little shaken up, beside him. In the car, Reid turned to his lead detective. His voice trembled with anger, even though he tried hard to keep it even. "I want to find the fuckers who are selling this shit, and I want it taken off the street before I have to tell another set of parents their kid is not coming home."

Follow the link below to purchase now!

www.amazon.com/dp/B09MPN5176

ALSO BY BIBA PEARCE

The Kenzie Gilmore Series

Afterburn

Deadheat

Heatwave

Burnout

Detective Rob Miller Mysteries

The Thames Path Killer

The West London Murders

The Bisley Wood Murders

The Box Hill Killer

Want to stay up to date and to read the latest news from Biba Pearce? Sign up here:

https://links.withoutwarrant.ink/Pearce1

ALSO BY WITHOUT WARRANT

More Thriller Series from Without Warrant Authors

Dana Gray Mysteries

Girl left Behind

Girl on the Hill

Girl in the Grave

ABOUT THE AUTHOR

Biba Pearce is a British crime writer and author of the Kenzie Gilmore series and the DCI Rob Miller series.

Biba grew up in post-apartheid Southern Africa. As a child, she lived on the wild eastern coast and explored the sub-tropical forests and surfed in shark-infested waters.

Now a full-time writer, Biba lives in leafy Surrey and when she isn't writing, can be found walking through the countryside or kayaking on the river Thames.

Visit her at bibapearce.com and join her mailing list to be notified about new releases, updates and special subscriber-only deals.

Printed in Great Britain
by Amazon

79951884R00180